FIVE YEARS BEFORE WHITECHAPEL - THE BEGINNING

DAWN
OF THE
RIPPER

BOOK ONE

MATT ROSS

For Debi

ABOUT THE AUTHOR

Matt Ross grew up in Brighton and has always loved books about the dark or macabre. He would spend most of his younger life reading until the small hours of the morning. He now writes full-time, and lives in Mid Sussex with his wife, two sons, and their Cocker Spaniel, Stanley.

The world has ne'er known,
such cruelty before, on some savage shore
Tho' for a time
This monster may flee Burnt at the stake this fiend out to be.

Author unknown. c1888.

PROLOGUE

SOUTH OF ENGLAND 1870

The manor house was as beautiful inside as it was out, a perfect example of wealthy Victorian architecture. It had suited the surgeon and his wife for the years they had lived there. It was to have been their forever home, but after recent events, he was likely to consider moving from the area, if not the country. Dr Arthur Lawson arrived at the house as requested and was shown into the lounge where the surgeon and his wife were waiting.

'Thank you for coming, Arthur,' the surgeon said, standing up from the sofa. 'I've asked you to attend as the lead specialist in this field to give my wife and I your professional opinion. Now that you have examined the patient, we can discuss the best course of action to be taken given the circumstances.' The surgeon watched Arthur, who, like himself, was a consultant at a number of London hospitals. However, Arthur had decided some years ago to move away from orthodox medicine and focus his skills on matters of the mind.

'I must first thank you both for having faith in this new area of science and allowing me to treat your son. I hoped that permitting me to undertake new and groundbreaking experiments would be a helpful insight into what ails him.'

The surgeon looked over to his wife, who remained seated, looking tired and withdrawn. Arthur was concerned for them as parents but more so for their twelve-year-old son.

'So, Arthur, what is your prognosis? What is your recommendation? You know money is no object, so what do you propose we do?'

'I have had several sessions with your boy over the course of his treatment at the hospital. As you know, his torture of cats and dogs was the beginning of the illness. The dissection of them and removal of organs for what purpose we have yet to discover worries me greatly. However, as I understand from you, your son has a keen interest in your work as a surgeon and the human anatomy. Since his stay at the hospital, he has been reading many books on the subject, which, at first, I thought productive and, given his age, promising. But lately, I'm afraid I have to admit this might have been naive of me. I have carried out tests, and all of them have yielded the same results. He is extremely intelligent but very manipulative. He sees the cracks in others and their weakness and will use them for his own ends. There is no remorse, no sense of right and wrong in his thinking. Your son is incapable of feeling on any level. Simply put, the boy does not function as a normal human does–'

'–But I don't understand,' the mother interrupted. 'He has had the very best upbringing. He has had the foremost education and has never wanted for anything in life. When we pass, he will inherit everything, the money and the house to use as he wishes; he could do so much in life. I…have never given him anything but encouragement and affection. He's always been different from other boys, didn't make any friends, preferred to be by himself. But he was…is loved.' Her husband passed her a handkerchief, seeing how upset she had become. She snatched it from him.

She glared back at him. 'This is your fault, bringing those street women into our home. He knew, you know. Your son

2

knew he saw you with one of them; he told me. Your own son, for Christ's sake. You disgust me.' She crumpled in tears.

The surgeon looked shocked, turning to Arthur. 'I'm sorry…My wife is upset and doesn't know what she's saying. You can't possibly think that I…'

Arthur raised his hand in defence. 'Please now don't concern yourself, your private affairs are yours and yours alone. They have no bearing on this, of that I can assure you.'

'I…I mean, my wife and I only want what is best for our son; we care very much for him.'

'You say that, and I believe you, but all this aside, however great parents you think you have been, make no mistake, he would cut both your throats in a heartbeat and feel nothing at all. The incident with the local carpenter's daughter that made you contact me…' Arthur looked over to the surgeon. 'The cuts to her face and abdomen with one of your surgical knives were life-changing, it was a miracle that she survived. She will never be the same, physically and mentally scarred for life, she has lost the use of one eye completely. Her mental state is such that I doubt she will ever leave the family home again because of the vicious and unprovoked attack by your son. I know you have paid the family generous compensation, which will ease the difficult road of recovery they will have to endure. But what distresses me is his uncontrolled rage, this dark storm inside him that comes from nowhere. When I questioned him about it, he said nothing in his defence.'

'Did he give no account or provocation for his attack on the girl?'

'None. He sat silently with a wide smile, just staring at me.'

Arthur had been informed sometime after the attack that the family were good people respected in the community, and he felt awful about the girl. But he knew this demonstrated how dangerous the boy was and what he was already capable of.

'Is there any cure?' the surgeon asked Arthur.

'Well, there is always hope. But it will be my recommendation that your son be transferred from the hospital where he is now to a secure mental institution for the foreseeable future. I will endeavour to do my best, and there are always new methods and medicines to try. I have to say however, I have never seen such a case such as this. There is no life in his eyes; there is a part of him that I cannot reach…or he will not let me. A secure unit is the best place for him…For everyone.'

The surgeon looked again to his wife. Both were sick with guilt and sadness for what they were hearing.

'He's still ours. I carried him for nine months and gave birth to him. He's just a child.' The mother's words were lost through her tears as she started to weep uncontrollably. 'When it's our time, and we are no longer here, he will have no one. I…I can't bear the thought.'

'Arthur, please, I must press you again on this. Will he ever be free of this terrible affliction? Maybe grow out of it?' The surgeon wanted to sound hopeful for his wife's sake more than his.

'If I am called upon to give counsel toward his state of mind, I do not see that possibility for a very long time. In my work, I have concluded that there are very distinctive types of people who commit such atrocities. Those who become evil through the association and the influence of others or through social conditions. Then, some are born evil. Your son, in my professional opinion, is of the latter. I have been a medical man of many years and a devout Christian, but I have to say being in a room with him is a chilling experience and deeply disturbing. I have no doubt he is and would be capable of the most heinous crimes if ever released into the community. He should stay locked away and, like Pandora's box, never be opened.

ONE

BRIGHTON 1883

Mary Quinn walked at pace through The North Laine, weaving in and out of the fog that had wrapped itself around the town like black treacle, smudging buildings and people. She covered her shoulders and bright, rust-coloured hair with a shawl, looking behind her – something wasn't right. She paused, changing direction several times, but the footsteps still followed. These weren't the staggering, clumsy steps of a drunk trying their luck; these were more menacing and determined. She was used to the ways of men, her mother's many boyfriends. The smell of sweat, stale breath, drunk from cheap booze pinning her down under their grotesque bodies, with no one to hear her screams and no one who cared.

Other women at The Crown, where she worked, had warned her not to walk home alone and never to use the alleyways that crisscrossed the area to save time, as bad things happened. But they were old, and she was just eighteen and had speed on her side. The rent was late, she had to get back and settle it tonight. The landlord was not one you wanted to keep waiting and would set the dogs on her or throw her out onto the streets if she didn't pay her way. *Can't have you taking the piss, or others will think I've gone soft and that won't do.*

So, she took the shortcut; she had to. *I'll be ok…I'll be quick.*

The alleyway, like many in this part of town, was lined on either side by a wall that had fallen into disrepair, leaving broken bricks strewn on the cobbled ground. Behind were a few abandoned properties, a refuge for the many homeless. It was a dangerous area; piles of rotting waste and excrement infested with vermin everywhere, and the stench was so strong that it made her eyes burn. Disease and violence were commonplace, and with no boundaries between the properties, people moved freely day and night. There were two gas lamps like sentries, one at the entrance and the other at the exit. Black poles with glass crowns, paint blistered and peeled back, revealing the decaying metal beneath. Both provided the glimmer of a yellow flame that seemed to flicker on and off in unison like the wings of a dying bird.

She entered, moving carefully along, glancing back, hearing the same footsteps reach the entrance. It was hard to see anything as she lifted her skirt and petticoat to her knees to move faster. She felt confined, trapped, and claustrophobic, putting one hand onto the wall as a guide, feeling her way along as a blind person would. The brick felt wet, clammy, and rough against her skin. Someone was behind her; she could feel it in her bones; she had to get out. *Just keep moving, girl.* The smell grew worse, reminding her of a gutted animal she had once encountered on the street. She felt bile rising to the back of her throat, she wanted to vomit. She kept glancing back. *Just leave me alone.*

Reaching halfway, she stopped. She heard a noise like glass breaking, maybe from one of the derelict houses. Mary had a strong impulse to run, but something brushed past her ankle. Peering down, she saw large objects weaving around her feet. Rats with yellowed teeth squealing, darting in and out, gnawing on waste. She hated them, they made her skin crawl, their pink eyes staring at her, feasting. She kicked one, watching it scurry away. Somewhere, a door slammed shut, making her jump, followed by a gruff voice swearing, then bottles being thrown, bouncing off the ground and smashing. The palms of her hands were sore and cut, bleeding from the rough surface of the bricks. She was alone, scared, and vulnerable as tears filled her young eyes.

Footsteps again were not far behind, her heart started to race, her breathing became quick and deep, her mouth dry. *Can't hardly see me hand*, but the stench and the thought of being trapped in this confined space made her panic. She stumbled, tripping over, her knees crashing down on the hard stone. *Crack.* She let out an agonising cry, filling the night air. She held her hand to her mouth, muffling the pain, turning her head from side to side, praying the person following hadn't heard. She waited, silence.

A break in the wall gave some exposed masonry to pull herself up, but the injury made it hard; both hands heaved her body up, gritting her teeth, stifling the pain. She looked towards one of the buildings, the yellow glow of a makeshift fire the only sign of life from a window, and for a moment, she thought she saw a figure standing, watching. The exit was close; she could see the lamp, its tell-tale flicker only a few feet away. *She would crawl if she had to.* Her knees throbbing as she scrambled to her feet, she wanted to yell, wanted her friends. *Why didn't I listen to them?* But the footsteps had stopped. *Oh, thank Mother Mary and Jesus.* Making the sign of the cross on her body. *Maybe he's given up. I'm safe.*

Two hands suddenly wrapped around her throat from behind, the grip tightened like a vice, squeezing harder and harder; she couldn't speak or swallow. Her lungs burned, ribs expanded, cracking; gasping for air she desperately tried to escape, trying to pull away. The attacker's strength so great that she was lifted off the ground. Every fibre and nerve in her body wanted to burst. Her feet kicked and twitched in the air like the dance of the hanged. Then without warning, she was dropped like a sack of coal, a crippling pain shot through her knees that had split open to the bone.

Coughing and retching violently, her mouth filled with blood. Her hands went to her throat; it felt sore, raw, and crushed. She saw him circle slowly, savouring the moment, then pulled her up by her hair, snapping her head back against the hard brick with such force that she heard it fracture. She could sense him excited, he had the scent of her fear, his breathing erratic. A black leather glove reached out and touched her lips, stroked her cheek carefully, slowly, almost with compassion, then paused momentarily; she watched as his head leaned over to one side inquisitively.

'Please, Sir, I beg you, please, I won't tell no-one, please …please.' Blood and snot muted her words, crying. 'I'll do anything...Please.' She felt the warmth of her urine against her skin.

He stepped back, raising his arms; his hands were clenched, and the serrated blade glinted for a split second, then descended into her chest repeatedly. Ripping into her and opening her up like a carcass. Her body fell backwards almost in slow motion and slumped to the ground like a broken doll, arms by her side, her legs splayed out in front of her, her head resting on her blood-covered chest.

Her torn body was dragged out into the alleyway and thrown up against a rat-infested mound of garbage for the world to see. The killer finished his work, then vanished into the cold night, and Hell followed.

TWO

Elsbeth Hargreaves closed the door to her drawing room as the six participants took their positions around the table. There was a low hum of whispered voices, awkward first encounters, some exchanging pleasantries while others stayed silent. Elsbeth knew everyone had their own story but had one thing in common. They were haunted by the loss of someone, unable to move on, governed by grief.

She knew not every encounter with the other side was a joyous or comforting experience. Sometimes, it was darker and not always what the clients expected. Elsbeth had seen spirits manifest through sound, moving objects, and, in rare cases, apparitions. She walked softly around the room as the clients prepared for the evening events. A young married couple, an older husband and wife in their late sixties, and two single women probably in their late thirties. She let the group settle in, drawing shut the long, heavy crimson curtains at each end of the room to keep the unwelcome spirits out. She turned the gas lamps down and lit some candles, feeling that the soft light was more inviting for the departed. It was now a snug, safe place from the unrelenting weather outside. Winter had come early this year, torrential rain and a howling gale bent trees at the back of the house, stretching bark as if it were skin.

The room had two formal settees, a number of bookshelves lining the walls, a writing bureau with newspapers at the back of the room, and a black slate fireplace to one side. In the centre of the room was a circular table where they all sat, above which hung an ornate crystal chandelier with hundreds of cut-glass pieces reflecting the fire's glow. Three large mirrors adorned the room, all covered with a black cloth, which caught the attention of one of her guests.

'Tell me, why do you cover the mirrors in such a fashion?' one of the single women inquired.

'I do it so the spirit's reflection will not get trapped if they visit tonight. Everything must be prepared for the departed as well as the living.'

The woman smiled and nodded her head in response. Elsbeth knew it was a delicate balance, and conditions had to be right, the room, the atmosphere, everything needed to be made welcoming and safe. The deceased needed encouragement and were not always eager to reveal themselves, particularly those who had been taken quickly, by accident or murder.

She joined the others at the table, knowing little about them besides their names; she preferred it that way. She placed her hands lightly on a clear glass tumbler on a rectangular pine board positioned in the centre of the table. The alphabet was printed in black ink and arranged in two curved rows. The first row was from A-M, then the second row from N-Z. Below the letters, a single line of numbers in a straight line ranging from one to zero were also printed in black. The room fell silent as Elsbeth took a deep breath.

'As you know, we are here tonight to see if we can connect with someone who no longer walks this earth. None of you have told me anything about who you seek, and as I have said in my correspondence, there is no assurance that any spirits will cross over, I am merely a portal through which they can communicate. We may get one or many, we may get none. I can do little to persuade them if they choose not to work with us tonight. It is their decision, not ours. With this in mind, I ask you to all turn to the one next to you and take their hand. Whatever happens, please remember not to break away; stay joined. We shall now begin.'

Elsbeth lowered her head. The room was expectant, only the wind and rain outside broke the peace. Her breathing slowed and became deeper and deeper, rasping as she entered a trance-like meditation, focusing on the glass tumbler beneath her hands. 'We are here tonight to request any departed soul who wants to make contact, make your presence known. You have nothing to worry about, you are safe in this space.'

The glass remained still. Elsbeth looked around the table to ensure nobody had broken hands. She noticed the young couple looked nervous, the wife more so, her husband gripping her hand tight to reassure her. The older couple also seemed anxious; their eyes fixed on the glass. The two single women seemed more excited, Elsbeth thought.

'We ask you to reveal yourself to us.' Elsbeth suddenly felt the glass move, slowly to begin with, then faster across the board to the right-hand edge, not landing on any letter or number. Elsbeth felt the interest rise in the room as the young wife gasped in amazement, looking over to her husband.

'Oh my God, John, did you see that it moved? The glass, it moved.'

'This is normal, don't worry. Someone is trying to get our attention,' Elsbeth informed the group with a warm, reassuring smile.

'Can you tell us who you are, please? Just move the glass to the letters. Can you do that for us?' Elsbeth waited; she knew that sometimes the spirits could be shy or uncooperative, as often they hadn't adjusted to death.

The glass began to move once more, each letter in order.

I-M S-O S-C-A-R-E-D.

'Is the person you wish to reach out to sitting at the table?' Elsbeth continued.

The glass moved across the board to the row of numbers. The numbers two and nine were selected. Then returned again to the same two numbers.

'Does the number twenty-nine mean anything to anyone here tonight?' Elsbeth asked the group.

The young woman sitting on her left suddenly let out a cry, again gazing at her husband. 'Oh, John, it's her, our Elle, it must be! Don't you see the connection to the number?'

John looked at his wife, his face ashen.

'It must be her, John. She's trying to show us. It's the day she died. The twenty-ninth.' The mother then spoke to Elsbeth with a mixture of anguish and hope. 'You told them to give us a sign, and nobody else has any connection to that number; it must be our daughter,' she said, desperately.

'She may be frightened; this is normal, be patient, she is preparing,' Elsbeth reassured her. 'Remember, this is hard for them, and it takes a huge effort, especially for a young soul. Tell her you love her. Tell her she is safe.' Elsbeth checked the others around the table, who appeared intrigued but slightly uncomfortable.

'Elle is that you, my darling, it's mummy; I love you so much, we both do. We miss you, my darling. God, I…We just need to know you're alright. Daddy's here. It's all right, you're safe. Please, Elle, come back to us.' Elsbeth watched as the young mother's tears streamed down her face, her voice breaking, she could see how much she wanted, needed it to be her daughter, the pain and the memory of losing her child were clear to see for all.

'Elle, I'm here to guide you; you can speak through me.

Move the glass to help us understand what you want to say.'
Elsbeth looked down at the board. The glass moved quickly,
the words coming faster.

I C-A-N-T M-O-V-E. P-A-I-N. P-L-E-A-S-E.

H-E-L-P. C-U-T-T-I-N-G. M-E.

Elsbeth quizzed the couple. 'Cutting me?' Does this mean
anything?'

'No, no…I don't understand. Elle drowned in a river near
to our home when she was eight years old. She was playing
with her friend. It was an accident, she wasn't cut,' the father
answered, bewildered.

'You're her parents. I want you to reach out to her again;
you must gain her trust,' Elsbeth instructed. 'Sometimes, spirits can become confused, messages become muddled. I know
this is difficult, but please be patient.'

The mother wiped her tears away, asking once more, 'Elle,
please, it's mummy; I… We really want to speak with you.' She
broke down, crying uncontrollably, the emotion all too much
to bear; her husband grasped her hand tighter.

The temperature in the room suddenly went ice cold, a rush
of air sped down the chimney with such force that it extinguished the fire. The wooden sash windows at both ends of
the room rattled in their frames faster and faster, like someone
had hold of them, trying to break in. The flames on the candles
flickered violently as a sweet aroma of lilies filled the room,
Elsbeth knew was a flower associated with death. A gasp went
around the table, and the mood amongst the guests instantly
changed to alarm.

'Stay together, stay joined,' Elsbeth repeated, seeing the

look on their faces. 'This is a strong presence; they may be trapped between this world and the next.'

The tumbler moved with force across the board as the table started to rock violently from side to side. The guests began to look at one another, not knowing what to think or do, their hands gripped tighter onto one another. A thumping banging sound, like two fists on the door to the room, was heard by everyone, followed by the echo of a small child weeping. The chandelier above started to swing from side to side, faster and faster the glass clinking against each other as the door opened and slammed with such force that it jammed shut, sealing them in like a tomb. A petrified scream of a woman came from nowhere, bouncing off the walls, deafening them all. Then, within an instant, the room fell quiet and still.

'This is an abomination, ungodly. This must cease, I implore you. We want to leave; it was a mistake coming; we want no further part of it,' the older couple shouted nervously, breaking hands and standing up from the table. The two single women, deeply anxious, leaned against each other for comfort, also making known their concerns.

'We had no idea it was going to be like this. We just thought it would be a bit of fun, we never thought anything would happen. That scream. My God…it…It felt so real, as if they were in such agony. It was awful.'

'I am sorry,' Elsbeth replied. 'Contacting the dead should never be taken lightly. Spirits can be frustrated, scared, and react differently, just as the living do. Please, we must continue to find out who is trying to come over,' she explained to the younger couple while gesturing for the older couple to take their seats.

The young mother pleaded with them also. 'We must try; if it's my Elle, we…I can't leave her. I won't leave her again, please?' The older couple looked at each other, feeling sorry for her, feeling the loss of their own son, and against their better judgement, reluctantly sat back down. Elsbeth asked the room to form the circle again and waited. Then, almost immediately, the glass traced its way across the board.

Twenty-Nine. The same number repeated.

'Is this you, Elle?' Elsbeth asked.

N-O.

The glass moved back over and over again to the same letters, leaving marks on the board, each time getting faster and faster.

N-O N-O N-O.

'I don't understand. I thought it was…' the young mother blurted out.

'Please, I know this is difficult, but I have to concentrate. Who is this?' Elsbeth asked.

The glass stopped. There was a pause that seemed to go on for ages, you could hear a pin drop. Then it started to move, but this time in the direction of new letters. One by one, they spelled out a name.

M-A-R-Y.

Then, back again to the number Twenty-Nine.

'Does anyone here have a connection to a Mary who has passed over, please?' Elsbeth addressed the others. Each guest, confused and worried, said no.

The room suddenly smelt disgusting. The pungent stench of rotting waste made them nauseous.

'Who is this, Mary? Why is she here?' The two younger women asked Elsbeth.

'Why are you here, Mary, what do you want to tell us?' Elsbeth spoke as clearly as she could. The sound of glass smashing from a back window followed the wind howling in, pushing the curtains aside, swirling around the room, extinguishing the candles, and putting the room in near-total darkness. Objects were picked up and hurled against the walls, vases, pictures, books flew across the room; settees moved, scraping across the floor, all the guests, now petrified, paralysed with fear. Elsbeth watched her eyes transfixed as the figure of a girl slowly appeared from the far corner of the room. Her arms were out in front of her, her hair matted with blood, and her clothes patterned by deep slashes that covered her body. The others followed Elsbeth's gaze, horrified at what they were seeing.

'Speak to me, Mary? Tell me, what happened to you?' Elsbeth asked, trying to control her voice from trembling.

'Look what he did to me.' Tears streamed from the eyes of a girl who had not yet lived life, taken too early. Mary, shaking from the absolute terror she had gone through, fell to her knees, sobbing. 'I begged him to stop, to leave me alone, but he kept hurting me, I tried to run, but …I couldn't move. He…will kill again,' Mary's voice became faint as something seemed to pull her back to the other side.

A newspaper flew across the room, pages flapping landed on the table. A loud crack in the ceiling, followed by white plaster raining down, made them all look up. The chandelier creaked and moaned, tearing free from its fixing in freefall. Elsbeth and the others covered their faces and eyes; in a split second, they threw themselves clear as it crashed down on the table. Glass-like spears flew in every direction. Elsbeth turned her head to where Mary had been, but she had gone, swallowed by the dark. The wind stopped, the room fell quiet again, nobody moved or said a word.

The group helped each other back up, brushing off the debris from their clothes and hair. Elsbeth noticed the newspaper had been impaled to the table by the metal frame of the chandelier. It had the grainy image of a woman who had been found dead in the North Laine area of Brighton. The report said she had been mutilated and subjected to such a brutal and savage attack; nobody had seen anything like it. Elsbeth felt a cold chill run over her like someone had walked over her grave as she looked down at the words printed at the bottom of the article.

The dead girl was known locally as Mary Quinn thought to be 18 years old, she had been stabbed twenty-nine times.

THREE

It had been two weeks since the séance and the appearance of Mary Quinn. Elsbeth adjusted her dark hair in the dining room mirror, making alterations one way then the other until it worked. She was a striking woman of slender frame with the kiss of a European complexion, high cheekbones, and deep green eyes. She would have the attention of male admirers wherever she went, but fiercely independent, she didn't need or want a man controlling her life. She had long known that society was not approving or accepting of single, unconventional women, particularly ones that spoke to the dead. She couldn't care less about the opinions of others who were only too eager to offer unwanted counsel.

She moved over to the table where she conducted her séances and readings, the deep marks left in the wood still evident from that night. She picked up and shuffled a deck of old and worn tarot cards with dog-eared corners, and set them down next to the local paper, which was still selling issues on the back of the murder of Mary Quinn. Her thoughts were plagued by what she had experienced that evening and the look of despair and pain on Mary's face. An apparition was rare enough, but to be conscious of exactly how much suffering the poor soul had endured was traumatic for all who attended.

She had felt something else in the room that night which she kept to herself. A rage, an evil, and sense of foreboding, but she wanted justice for Mary and for her spirit to rest, to find peace.

Elsbeth had tried to assist the police several times with other investigations. Often gaining valuable and accurate information through her psychic ability but had always been ignored. Uniformed officers and detectives had little regard for her and would snigger and joke as she petitioned them. They considered her to have no place in the world of crime detection and to be no more than a fairground attraction. The hypocrisy sickened Elsbeth, as some of her clients were senior policemen and members of the judicial system, so it was acceptable if it benefited them privately, but publicly, they mocked her.

It was clear that Mary Quinn was not ever going to be a priority for the police; to them, she was just another prostitute. The coroner's preliminary report had leaked to the press, but it was tainted with snobbery and ill-judged guesswork. It noted that the wounds had been delivered by an extremely sharp blade with a serrated edge, possibly not dissimilar to one used by a doctor or surgeon. However, it stressed that they should dismiss any concerns that the perpetrator could ever be a person of such high professional standing. But almost sure to be an individual of low intelligence who had come by such an instrument by illicit means. It concluded that this was most likely to be a domestic attack fuelled by overindulgence in alcohol, by a jealous boyfriend or just plain thuggery.

Elsbeth put the cards down, reading the leaked report, shaking her head in disbelief until she saw her name and words about the case appear towards the bottom.

"*Local Spiritualist Elsbeth Hargreaves offers dumbfounded police her services.'*

In my opinion, the police are not taking this seriously. My reputation speaks for itself, and I know what Mary Quinn went through, I saw and heard it directly from her. This was not the work of some random drunk or an argument with a boyfriend. This was the work of a monster. I would think our police should take all the help they are offered, unless, of course, they see the butchering of a single woman on our streets somehow insignificant and not worthy of their time. I would like it to be known that I will not charge anything and will continue to send any information I have to the relevant authorities to assist them in their investigation. This is not about ego. It's about catching a killer who is still out there. The police need to think less about protecting their reputation and more about protecting the women of this town.'"

She remembered the anger in her words at the time of speaking to the paper; she still carried the same doubts about the methods being employed to apprehend the killer. She picked up the set of cards again and held them close to her chest for a moment. Nobody really knew where the Tarot had come from, their origins shrouded in mystery, lost in the mists of time. But reading the cards had become very popular at after-dinner parties, and many beautifully illustrated sets were available, some more ornate than others but all containing seventy-eight cards split into two main sets. Cards of Greater Secrets and Cards of Lesser Secrets, also referred to as the Major and Minor Arcana. Groups of people would gather around after supper and ask questions of the host, who would attempt to make a reading, usually related to love, marriage or money. But for Elsbeth, the cards were not a game but a tool, only to be used by someone with deep knowledge and insight to interpret their meanings. They were for guidance to help better understand a situation, to provide clarity and direction, and to act as a vehicle of discovery, not for fun or personal gain.

There were many methods Elsbeth employed, laying the cards or spreads, as she called them, such as The Horseshoe, Celtic Cross, or the Tree of Life. All had different meanings, some complicated, others simpler, and only a highly skilled reader like Elsbeth would know which would be appropriate. Elsbeth laid all seventy-eight cards out in a line across the table face down, then randomly selected four cards and put them to one side. She moved the remainder of the deck away and slid the chosen cards in front of her in a row, keeping them all faced down and the last card slightly separate from the other three.

Elsbeth kept Mary Quinn's face in her mind as she turned three of the cards over to reveal their message. They were The Hermit, the Two of Cups, and the Emperor. The Hermit suggested that a person of wisdom and decision would soon enter her life. The Two of Cups meant there would be balance but also moments of tension, and the Emperor meant a figure of authority, maybe a policeman. Elsbeth sat and thought for a while about the cards that she had drawn and what they meant for her. Then, she asked the most important question out loud for the fourth and last card. 'Who killed Mary Quinn?' She breathed deeply, pausing for a moment, then turned the card slowly over. She felt sick to her stomach; her skin went cold as ice as she looked down at the image, a winged person, half man, half beast, sitting upon a throne. She had been given her answer—the Devil.

FOUR

Rosie Meeks was asked to lock up the shop as her employers had been called away on an urgent matter. A true cockney, born within the sound of Bow Bells, Rosie had moved to Brighton and found employment at a well-known bakery in The North Laine, earning the owners' trust for the past five years. It was a small shop with 'Bakers of Brighton' painted in slightly flaking red lettering with a gold surround on the front window. The proprietors lived above it in a small two-room apartment, and each morning, would descend in the early hours to create their baking alchemy at the back of the shop. The recipe for their award-winning pies was a closely guarded secret, apparently going back generations, or at least that's what they told everyone; not even Rosie was privy to the ingredients.

A small, naturally jovial woman, Rosie loved serving customers. 'Be nothin left but crumbs by the end of the day,' she would always say. Some were visitors, just passing trade, while the locals would come in at least two or three times a week. After putting on her workwear, comprising a white linen hat and apron over a black dress, she laid everything in order out on the counter, ready for sale. She had decided to take a rabbit pie home tonight, a perk of the job, to have for supper by the fire with her eight-year-old son James. They made a game where James would guess what filling was inside. It made her laugh as James would come out with all sorts of strange ideas, such as an elephant or whale. 'You're going to end up looking like a whale, you keep stuffin' all of them pies into such a tiny tummy,' she would joke, touching noses. Afterwards, she would tuck him into bed and read a story until he fell asleep.

Rosie walked around the counter towards the front of the store to open up for the day, her shoes clip-clopping on the wooden floor which creaked with a provenance that came with the age of the building. A small bell above the door rang as she opened it to a queue of regular customers that had already formed down Gardner Street. 'Morning, ladies and gents,' she announced in her London accent. A mature lady who came every week waited at the front of the queue, holding a large wicker basket with blue chequered cloth in the base, and nodded in reply. Someone caught her eye; a well-dressed stranger in a dark cloak standing at the back. There was something about him; she couldn't think what it was, a feeling, a sense, but it unnerved her; he seemed to be staring, not just at her, but right through her. But before long her attention was taken back to the voice of someone she did know.

'Oi, Rosie, hope you kept me buns warm. Or I can come round later when ya locking up, eh? We can warm 'em together if you've a mind,' came a loud, coarse voice followed by laughter mixed with coughing from somewhere in the middle of the queue.

Rosie recognised it as Jack Robertson, one of her regulars who had been coming to the bakery for the last five years. Jack was a cheeky man of similar age who worked at Brighton Station in one of the engineering sheds. His comments were the same every day, but she enjoyed the friendship and light-hearted banter they had between them and would often slip him an additional bun to keep his strength up.

'I don't think so, Jack; my boy might well take offence and sling your scrawny body out and give you a good hiding.'

'Your boy is a young'un, only knee high to a grasshopper from what I heard.'

'Still big enough to take the likes of you on, Jack.'

There was a jeer from the crowd, followed by raucous laughter.

'Anyways, after I get me grub, I'm straight off to catch a train to Leeds in half an hour, have some urgent business to attend to, so you won't be seeing me for a while.'

'Thank God for small mercies,' replied Rosie, followed by more laughter from the customers.

She pretended to curtsey before the crowd as they filed through into the shop. Everyone was served, and it was a typical day, with only crumbs left as usual. She turned the sign to "Closed" on the door, grabbed a broad brush from the back, swept the floor, and cleaned the countertops ready for the next day. She liked tidying up as fast as possible so she could get home and spend time with her son. They didn't have much, one room and shared a bed, but they had each other. Getting back to steal a cuddle from him meant everything to her, she loved him deeply. He would often climb onto the window seat, waiting for her to return from work. She had shown him how to breathe on the glass and then press his small hand onto it, creating a handprint for her. *There, you see a part of you to tell mummy how much you love her.*

While at the back of the shop, she heard the bell from the door ring, not just once but a few times in succession. *That's strange; I'm sure I locked the door.* She finished cleaning up and put the broom back in the cupboard. She closed the door and started to walk back into the shop, calling as she did.

'Hello, is anyone there? I'm sorry we're closed; you'll have to come back in the morning.' As she reached the front, there was no one to be seen. The door was ajar, opening and closing in the wind, catching the bell as it went. She thought it odd; she never left the door open after closing and was certain she had secured it. She went over to it and pushed it hard shut while turning the key clockwise twice until she heard it lock. *There, that'll do it.* She returned to the counter, casually glancing back at the door. She picked up her rabbit pie and turned the lamp off in the room, leaving only the light from the streetlamps to bathe a soft yellow lustre into the premises. She looked around one last time, checking everything before making her way to the back door, where she would exit the building. Walking past the staircase that led to the owners' living quarters, she thought she heard something being moved or dragged across the floor above. She stopped listening intently, but nothing, just silence. Then, there it was again, this time even louder. *But it couldn't be her employers. They had been gone all day and wouldn't be back until tomorrow morning.* She waited and fretted, thinking about what to do next.

She had been left in charge, it was her responsibility, and there shouldn't be anyone left inside once she had gone. Maybe someone had snuck in the front when it was open. *Probably, kids saw an opportunity to sneak in without me seeing–* as she placed one foot on the bottom rung of the stairs. It groaned as she put her weight onto it. She decided to say something to warn anyone who might be hiding that someone was still about.

'Look, you don't want no trouble, just come down, and you can be on ya way.' Waiting for a response, she moved further up, the light leaving her as each step creaked slightly more than the one before.

'Come on, let's be havin' you, we can forget about it, no one will know.' Still no response. 'I got me own boy to get back to, he'll be worried if I ain't back on time, you wouldn't want that, would ya.'

Halfway up now, her gut told her to go back down, get out,

and get help. *It's probably nothing, just me hearing things, me being on me own* she kept telling herself. But she was becoming sacred, alone, her back against the wall, sliding her way up to the landing, getting closer to the last step. She couldn't afford to lose her job. If there was someone up there and she did nothing, she would be out of work with no wage, she would be on the streets. She had to make sure. Slowly, as dark crept around her, she reached the landing; the door to the room was shut. She tip-toed towards it. Her hand reached out, took hold of the small round brass handle, and turned it slowly; it stuck. She held her breath, then turned it again; this time, it clicked, and the door opened slightly; a low light broke through the crack.

'I'm coming in.' Her voice a mix of fear and trepidation, she leaned her head gradually round, then stepped into the room, leaving the door open just in case. The area was divided by a brass pole across the centre with a curtain that was partially open so she could see the sleeping quarters behind. It had a bed, a small china wash basin on a pedestal, and a leather armchair. The main living area where she stood had a settee in front of an open fire that had not been cleaned and a large threadbare rug that covered most of the floor.

There were one or two pictures on one wall and a single sash window with its curtains tied to one side with a rectangular pine table and two chairs at either end. A lamp which was on was suspended from the ceiling by four chains surrounded by white opaque glass. Rosie thought it odd as the owners would never leave lamps burning if they were not there. She moved slowly around the room, trying to see what could have caused the noise. She noticed the table by the window had been pulled away out further into the room. *Maybe this was the dragging noise. But no one's ere, so how's that happen…?* She moved towards the table, tracing the top slightly with her left index finger and around to the window. She leaned against it, looking out, and saw a young couple kissing in a shop doorway opposite; it made her smile. It made her think back to when she was in love, when the world seemed full of promise and life was simpler.

The light in the room suddenly dimmed, something crossing in transit; she felt the warm breath of someone on the nape of her neck, and she turned to the silhouette of a man standing before her. A gloved hand reached out and grabbed her by the throat; she tried to pull away, desperate to escape. She couldn't breathe, couldn't scream. She tried with all her strength to fight back to loosen his grip, trying to force his hands away from her, but the grip was too strong. She was thrown back against the window, her face pushed up against the glass. The young couple were still there – she prayed they might see her. *Please, God, look up.* A hand moved to cover her mouth and nose; she gasped, choking. She felt dizzy, slipping away her body went limp. She slumped against the frame, her breathing misting the window.

She tried to speak, her windpipe crushed, a whisper coming out: 'Please, no, please, please, I have a son, he's only eight he needs me…Please don't.' She twisted with pain as she felt something thrust into her back two or three times, then into her kidney; the blade moved slowly one way and then the other, cutting deep. Rosie, paralysed with pain, petrified, images of her little boy waiting alone, watching for her, worried where she was swamped her mind. In the last seconds of her life, she reached up with all her might and pressed her bloodied hand against the glass, leaving her handprint so he would know how much mummy loved him.

FIVE

SCOTLAND YARD, LONDON.

Frederick Abberline had been summoned to a meeting with his boss and head of CID, James Monro. It was a long way from his humble beginning as a watchmaker in Dorset to become an Inspector at CID H Division at Scotland Yard. He had risen through the ranks, from constable to sergeant and then to Inspector within just a few years. His superiors had seen his potential, admiring his determination, hard work, and resolute attention to detail, and he got results. But he could be direct with others and often preferred his own company, making him a loner. His world was built on logic, facts, and evidence, and he didn't like things that didn't fit or make sense, they troubled him. Monro, a harsh Scotsman, was not a supporter of Abberline and didn't approve of his meteoric success. In comparison, it had taken Monro a long time to gain advancement in the force. A short-tempered man disillusioned by the politics of rank, and the hawkish interference of police commissioner Sir Charles Warren —an ex-military man who was impatient and highly demanding of those working under him.

Abberline arrived on time – in fact, early – but had been kept waiting for more than thirty minutes. It was Monro's deliberate ploy to make sure Abberline didn't forget his place, and that it would be a cold day in hell before he sat in his chair. Abberline, always smartly dressed, adjusted his tie and suit jacket, pushed his glasses back on his nose, checked his shoes for any scuffs or marks before sitting on one of the wooden chairs provided. It was a process, one of many he lived his life by, little details that gave structure. He sat staring at the large clock on the wall opposite, marked with Roman numerals, which was precisely one minute and 20 seconds slower than his pocket watch. It aggravated him, and he wanted to correct it, but the glass front was locked, and he didn't have a key. He moved his chair to align it with the others, making minor incremental adjustments until it was exactly right.

'Enter,' came a short and abrupt voice from behind the glass of Monro's office.

Abberline was slim, six foot, clean-shaven with a full head of blond hair – a complete opposite to his boss Monro, a small bald man of five foot three, with a pot belly and a large handlebar moustache. Monro sat behind a substantial desk covered with paper files and reports and waved impatiently for Abberline to be seated. The chair was noticeably lower than the table, giving Monro a height advantage, literally looking down on visitors, which Abberline put down to *small man* syndrome. Abberline found it challenging to ignore the unorganised mess of paperwork strewn across the desk of his superior; he wanted to tidy it up and give order to the chaos. He became hot under the collar, pulling the starched white material slightly away from his skin; his compulsion taking over, he moved one of the folders hanging precariously off the side back onto the desk. Monro, clearly annoyed, leant forward, his eyes narrowed, glistening with irritation.

'Have you seen this?' Monro barked at Abberline, pushing a copy of The Brighton Herald towards him, knocking the saved folder off the table. 'This business in Brighton, a young woman murdered, made a bloody mess of her by all accounts, and nobody in custody. The local rag with nothing better to do has whipped this up into a storm with the public, saying the police are incompetent and asking if the streets are safe, yet somehow, they printed extracts from the coroner's report. But to make matters worse, a local woman, Elsbeth Hargreaves, has stuck her nose in and claimed to have had important information on the incident that was ignored. This makes a mockery out of the CID, which, by default, makes us all look like idiots. See what she said–' Monro prodding his finger at the article harder and harder, nearly tearing the paper. 'Now it's landed on my desk, and I want it contained, understood. I don't need this; Commissioner Warren doesn't need this. Or his friend, the Home Secretary, who, like you, is also trying to fast-track his career, doesn't need it. And now I understand another murder has occurred, making this all the more urgent that an arrest is made soon.'

'Does Brighton CID have any leads, sir? Anything?' Abberline chose not to take the bait about his rise through the ranks, still with one eye on the folder on the floor, its contents jumbled.

'That's for you to find out, you're going down there. I want this matter resolved quickly and somebody arrested, charged, and swinging for it, do you hear me?' Monro raged.

Abberline noticed the blue vein on Monro's forehead pulsate and enlarge as he became more aggravated.

'I want somebody's head for this, and if it's not forth-coming, it's going to be yours that will be served up to the Commissioner. Do you understand me, Inspector Abberline?'

'Very clear, sir. But what is my remit? Brighton won't like Scotland Yard coming down and getting involved in what they will identify as very much a local matter, sir?'

'You will have to cut a finger on this, Abberline, and take what comes. The matter has been decided, and you will be taking over and running the investigation against my better judgment, I may add. Brighton is to follow your lead. It comes from the top, and don't expect any favours; it's not London down there, no *friends* in high places to protect you.'

'What about the cases I am working on, sir?'

'Reassigned. I'll be honest with you, Abberline. I don't much care for your type. There's something strange about you. But others seem to put their faith in you, so you had better not let them down or me, or you'll be back in Dorset fixing clocks. Now I have work to do.' Annoyed, his attention was drawn back to sorting through the mound of documents in front of him.

'Yes, sir.' Abberline rose from his chair. The compulsion to pick up the folder and its contents from the floor was too strong. He quickly bent down and placed it neatly back on Monro's desk as before, slightly adjusting it. Monro paused for a second, looked up, saying nothing, his expression saying it all.

'I'll be on my way then, sir, and of course, I will keep you updated with events.'

'See Detective Rawlings down there, he's expecting you. He will give you all they have, which isn't much. And Abberline, make sure you talk to the Hargreaves woman and get her on board. Don't make her a problem. Find out what she knows, I don't want to see any more press statements from her.'

'Yes, sir, of course.' Abberline took the copy of the Brighton Herald off Monro's desk, reading through the details of the horrific murder and the subsequent interview with the woman and the byline *Local Spiritualist Elsbeth Hargreaves*. The word spiritualist caught his attention, making him feel uncomfortable. He pushed his glasses back onto his nose, concerned he was entering a world that didn't conform, didn't fit.

SIX

Abberline sat in his compartment next to the window and waited for the train to depart to Brighton from London Bridge, the glass reflecting a man with much on his mind. He had little to go on and much to do to find who was responsible. Whoever had committed these heinous acts was clearly insane, given the horrific injuries inflicted on both women. Still, they were careful enough to avoid capture, and that meant they were dealing with someone who also thought about their actions and the consequences that would follow. There was intelligence behind this. From what information he had read, he could see no apparent link between the victims, so they had to be random, and that bothered him because it made his job harder. Murder was usually committed by someone the victim knew, and the reason why it happened was more straightforward to see, such as money, revenge or just an argument gone too far. To have a stranger commit such vicious crimes made it all the more difficult and a crucial bit of information was missing – the motive.

Abberline hated small talk, he didn't know what to say and would try to avoid it. He looked out onto the busy railway yard, hoping the train would leave on time, making it less likely that another person would join him, invading his space.

Since the line had opened in 1841, there had been many improvements over the years, and now it only took two hours to reach the coast, which meant Abberline could get back to London the same day if needed. Brighton was becoming a more popular place for people in the capital to live and visit, but with that came increased crime. He watched with intrigue as other trains entered and left the station – huge iron beasts on wheels, growling as they moved. Clouds of white steam smudged with black soot billowed out into the air and, for a time, obscured his view of the platforms as people and porters rushed about with their trolleys, piled up with luggage.

He was lucky to have secured second-class seating, and for now, he was still the only one in the compartment. First Class was only for the wealthy, and his expense account certainly did not provide for such extravagance. His carriage came with its own door and the comfort of upholstered seats in brown and stone-coloured paintwork. It was a far more pleasurable way to travel than the overcrowded wooden benches of Third Class. All ages and abilities crammed tight together, often with dogs, chickens, and geese, snarling, barking, and squawking, plus any commercial freight. If Monro had anything to do with it, he would have him travel on the roof to save money. If there was one thing Monro didn't like other than Abberline, it was having to pay expenses.

The case in Brighton was complicated and fast becoming a prominent feature in the local newspaper, which his superiors wanted to quash as soon as possible. They didn't need or want it spreading, creating a media frenzy. The incompetence of the local police force, run by Detective Rawlings, and the brutal slaying of two women was feeding the insatiable hunger of the public. It was a gift on a plate for the press, who took full advantage of criticising the police and its methods in general. It was one of those situations that could be career changing, either positively or negatively, depending on the outcome, and there were many in the Yard who would be very pleased to see the back of Frederick Abberline.

Abberline adjusted himself, looking down and checking that his shoes still had a shine and that there were no abrasions or marks. He was always neatly turned out, but London was expensive, and on an Inspector's salary, his clothes were never cut from the finest cloth or made by an expensive tailor like his seniors' were. His black suit was always clean and pressed with a white shirt, black tie, and bowler hat, he looked every bit the part. He took his pocket watch from his waistcoat and checked the time. The train was running late by a minute, and that irritated him. He liked everything to be correct and to have structure. As a child, he would put all his toys together by size and colour, and if one was slightly out of place, he would have to make sure it was corrected so that order was resumed.

Tuberculosis had taken his first wife Martha, when she was just twenty-five, only two months into their marriage. Sometimes, he would see her smile on someone else's face, and the pain of his loss would return, but eight years later, not expecting to find another partner, he met Emma Beament, the daughter of a merchant. Then, on a summer's day in 1876, they married; he was thirty-three years old and already an Inspector in H-division, Whitechapel. Although children had not blessed their lives, Emma supported his career and understood his ways; she had observed the same peculiarities of obsession in her father. She would tell people that her husband just liked everything done properly, even though, at times, he would irritate her when he was at home checking and rechecking things around the house.

His preoccupation with detail and rational thinking would put him on a collision course with Elsbeth Hargreaves, the renowned psychic he was to meet in Brighton. But these qualities also made him a good detective and far more thorough than his peers, who found him unusual, annoying, and very much a maverick, which made them suspicious. In truth, he found his colleagues clumsy and lazy, who often abused their powers to intimidate and bully offenders into admitting crimes they had little or no evidence of committing. Witness tampering and even cases of corruption higher up the chain of command made him feel isolated in his job, but it was a job he loved and had dedicated his life to it. His china-blue eyes looked out from his compartment window onto the station yard and the metal tracks that took people in all directions and marvelled at the engineering behind it.

His attention was broken as the stationmaster, standing on the platform's edge, blew his whistle and held a green flag aloft, waving it fervently to let the driver know it was time to depart. The train shunted forward, moving slowly like a goliath sliding out of its cave, clouds of vapour rose on either side. An hour into the journey, he was far from the smog-filled streets of London, now making his way through open countryside. Field upon field left bare and desolate of produce, trees stripped of leaves, skeletal branches swaying in the wind, the ground frostbitten and hard from the touch of winter. He watched two gulls from the coast high in the sky side by side, riding the air currents on a journey of their own that seemed to follow his as a dense cloud of steam suddenly passed his window, blocking his view. When it cleared, he peered out again, but they had disappeared into the grey sky. Leaning his head back, he closed his eyes and sighed, his thoughts returning back to the case and the dark days that lay before him.

SEVEN

Detective Rawlings collected Abberline from the front of Brighton Police Station and walked him through to his office at the back.

'Good of you to come down and give us your expert opinion on this.' Before Abberline could speak, Rawlings continued. 'Mind, I'll bet you can't wait to be back in the smoke rather than down here with us yokels, eh?' Rawlings laughed awkwardly, marked by more than a note of sarcasm in his voice.

Abberline could see that Rawlings was unhappy that the investigation had been taken away from him, and handed over without discussion to someone from Scotland Yard who would now tell him how to do his job.

'As you are fully aware, I am here at the solicitation of Chief Inspector Monro not to help you as you say, but to lead the investigation, as I believe was made clear to you prior to my despatch.'

Rawlings, an unrefined but experienced officer, took his seat behind the desk. He was a heavy-set man with greying hair and bushy sideburns, at least ten years older than Abberline and with more years on the force. He found it difficult to contain his displeasure at the disrespectful manner in which he was being addressed, but had little recourse but to accept the situation. His contacts at The Yard had told him Abberline was not liked or trusted by his fellow officers; they found him remote, arrogant, and his behaviour, at times, odd.

Abberline took a folder containing the statements and photographs from a battered leather briefcase. Opening it, he lay the contents on Rawlings's desk, separating the statements from the pictures. 'The first victim, Mary Quinn, approximately eighteen years of age, a local prostitute, was on her way home when the attack took place, according to witnesses.' Abberline pointed to the image of her body found in the alleyway and used by the Brighton Herald. 'Then, recently, the second victim, a single mother, Rosie Meeks. She is believed to be in her early to late thirties, and she was employed at a bakery in a part of the town called The North Laine. Her body was found by the owners returning from a business trip.'

Rawlings nodded in response; his demeanour changed, sickened, as if recalling the dismembered body in the bedroom. 'The owners are too traumatised to speak about it, refusing to return to the place.'

'Seems strange as they have to earn a living,' Abberline mentioned while moving the images to align with each other precisely.

Rawlings appeared taken aback by the directness of the remark and lack of empathy as Abberline continued.

'I have read through the witness statements and coroner's reports; it seems evident there are similarities between the victims. The angle, direction and depth of the wounds make it very likely that the killer is left-handed, which only we know. The ferocity and the conclusion from the coroner is that the same or very similar weapon with a serrated edge was used. But as we can see, the Meeks woman suffered far worse mutilation, and we need to ascertain why. So, at this juncture, we can't definitely say it's the same killer, but it is very likely, given

37

the weapon and the nature of the attacks.' Abberline leaned back on his chair in a thoughtful pose.

'The press leaked parts of this report but not all of it, so let's make sure we keep it that way. I know, Rawlings, you have visited both crime scenes, although I note much later than I would have expected. However, that aside, I will visit the mortuary first as I need to see both bodies. After that, I will inspect the locations where these killings occurred.'

'Of course, sir, we have told the coroner, Mr Cripps, to hold onto them until you came down. Anyway, nobody has come forward as next of kin for either of the victims. It's late now, so I will make arrangements for the morning if that is acceptable and send a cab around to your lodgings first light?' Rawlings made some notes in the to-do page of his pocketbook.

'What concerns me is why these two women? Is there any connection between them, and what could be the motive for such a relentless and barbaric attack? One is a prostitute, the other a working mother.' Abberline considered for a moment, his mind working away, sifting through the possibilities.

'I don't know, sir. I've never seen anything like it in all my years, and I hope to God I never do again. It's like some wild beast got to them, opening them up like that, and what he did to Rosie Meeks, not much left of her to recognise. If it is the same person, must be insane, must have a taste for it, is my thinking, to do them things…Hanging's too good for him.' Rawlings moved his head over to one side, mimicking having a rope around his neck.

'Hmm, indeed, Rawlings, but a prostitute walking the streets alone in the dark is vulnerable, as in Mary Quinn's case. And like it or not, people are less likely to raise an eyebrow at her screams than they would someone in a shop as our second victim was. And yet, her injuries were even more severe.' He picked up a pencil lying on its own on the desk and repositioned it neatly against the others. Abberline continued to think out loud, looking down. 'Maybe he's experimenting, living out a fantasy, with whomever he randomly chooses, the level of violence increasing with his rage.' He looked back up at Rawlings, who was trying not to show how unimpressed he was by Abberline's deduction.

'Anyway, Rawlings, what's important is that we catch the perpetrator and fast.' Abberline leaned forward. 'Elsbeth Hargreaves, what's your side of events on this? She claims she had information about the first victim, Mary Quinn, but you didn't take her seriously.' He sat back, curious as to why Rawlings had disregarded anything she had to say.

'She's one of those people who speak to the dead, sir, and she reckons she had some message from the grave of the Quinn girl. Nobody takes that stuff seriously,' he smirked. 'Not the first time she's been down here spinning her yarn. She holds them séances at her house and charges a pretty penny for them. Ain't right giving people false hopes; the dead should stay dead in my mind, anything else ain't Christian.'

'It seems we have something in common at last, Rawlings. As police officers, we must only deal with logic and evidence, not the ramblings of a sideshow operator. However, my boss Monro does not want any more of these articles, as he feels they distract from the investigation and give the public more reasons to doubt us. He thinks we should work more with her than against, but I'm here, and he's not. So, whatever messages from those that have passed from this life she thinks she has, we have to tread carefully. Hear her out, be seen to take an interest, humour her, make some notes, thank her, and politely tell her we will look into it. Then forget it.'

'Yes, sir,' Rawlings replied.

'I suppose I must meet this deluded woman; you must have her address on file? It will have to be soon. I want to get her out of the way. I wonder if she is about now?'

Rawlings suddenly seemed to have his attention drawn to

something else rather than what Abberline was saying, which irritated him.

'Rawlings? Have you listened to a word I've said? Do you think she will be available?' Abberline snapped at him.

'Er… yes, I'm sure she is. She's right behind you.' Rawlings's speech was slow and quiet, but Abberline noticed a slight grin on his face.

There was an awkward silence as Abberline stared at Rawlings like a rabbit in headlights. Turning slowly around, he saw Elsbeth Hargreaves standing in the doorway of the office.

'Good evening, gentlemen. Nobody was at the front desk, so I made my own way through. As Detective Rawlings is aware, I've been here many times in the past, as I'm sure he has informed you, Inspector. And please do not concern yourself, I have been here long enough to hear how much you value my services. Perhaps you may do me the courtesy of hearing out a deluded woman regarding this killer, or should I go back to the press, who I'm sure would be more than pleased to listen to what I have to say?'

EIGHT

Abberline instructed Rawlings to make himself scarce so he could hold his conversation with Elsbeth in private. Feeling sidelined, Rawlings collected his things and made his way out to the mess room, a general area for staff, giving Elsbeth a cold stare while closing the door with a noticeable amount of force. The office was minimal, with a desk covered in green leather embossed with a faded gold border and a single drawer, some writing paper, pens, several folders in no particular order lying on top. A wooden chair sat behind the desk with two on the other side. A solitary photograph hung from a cracked and yellow-stained wall of Queen Victoria, her miserable demure dulled more from the dust that clung to the glass. Abberline took his seat behind the desk and gestured to Elsbeth to take one for herself. She noticed him oddly rearrange the pens and folders on the desk to be in line with each other. Then, he moved them to the other side to do the same again.

'Miss Hargreaves, your comments in the press have not gone unnoticed, and I have some sympathy for your frustrations. But the investigation, I can assure you, has now taken a more... focused approach. I have been asked by Scotland Yard to take over and proceed at speed and apprehend the individual responsible for these crimes. I can promise you any concerns you may have about the case and its urgency to be resolved will be heard and, of course, taken seriously. Any information you give will be documented and investigated thoroughly.' Abberline paused, looking directly at Elsbeth, who sat listening attentively but unconvinced.

'Your recent appointment to Brighton, Inspector Abberline, is welcome given the underwhelming efforts of the Brighton Police so far to do anything. I have attended this station several times to assist in not just this case but many before. But given that I am a woman of independent means, which appears to be an issue, and worse, a woman who is also a psychic, I have been made to feel like a fairground freak and dismissed without once being interviewed by any of your officers.' Elsbeth's body leaned in, making her point clear to the Inspector. 'So please do not feel offended if I find your assurances worthless.'

'As I have said, I understand your frustrations. But I have to clearly state as a fact that I personally don't know of any police force that currently takes advice from a person who communicates with the dead. We…I deal in facts and logic, which is how this matter will be resolved and resolved soon.' Adjusting his position, he was becoming uncomfortable and sat back in his chair to subconsciously create additional distance between them. He found it preposterous that people believed she could contact the dead and saw it very much as a money-making venture playing on the feelings of the desperate, but he had to keep his opinions to himself.

Elsbeth, still far from satisfied, continued to make her point. 'My skills differ from yours, but make no mistake, they are skills even if you disagree. Not everything in life, Inspector, lives in the light.' She noticed a slight smirk appear across his face but persevered. 'There are many layers of our existence, and our physical body is but just one form of that. I didn't ask to be like this; I was born like it, I had no choice. I am often mocked and ridiculed for having this ability, notably by your officers, but I use this gift to give comfort and help. Grief is a terrible thing; most people prefer to lock it away, thinking it's better that way, but it eats away at the soul, feeding off it like a disease.'

Abberline looked past Elsbeth, his thoughts suspended, lost for a moment.

'The information you said you had, what was it?' His attention returned to Elsbeth.

'Mary Quinn appeared during one of my private séances. She said she was followed and begged the killer to stop, but they kept stabbing her over and over again. She was petrified, and she said that the murderer would kill again, which they have. This is not a domestic or a robbery or some paid sex gone wrong. It is far, far darker than that. Her injuries were abhorrent, and I feel the same hand at work here with the second murder, and I do not think this lunatic is finished yet.'

'Police work is not based on feelings, Miss Hargreaves; we deal in fact. I have no definitive evidence that the two crimes are linked at present. Rawlings has also informed me it wouldn't take long to find out how Mary Quinn died, as news travels fast around this town. And, of course, let's not forget that the details appeared in the newspaper along with some of the coroner's report. So, you hardly need your gifts to ascertain those facts, do you?' Abberline replied. 'And what of your other guests that evening? Did they see the dead Mary Quinn appear in front of them?' Elsbeth fell silent for a moment, used to this kind of derision but still vexed by it.

'My evenings are private affairs, and people expect their identity to be kept secret as they attend for personal matters that do not concern the judgment of others who most likely would not approve or understand. If I were to reveal their names, some of which may be familiar to you, my reputation, along with theirs, which is everything, would be damaged.'

Elsbeth folded her arms across her chest in defence of her situation. 'Trust is *everything*, Inspector.'

'Ah, I see. Well, you can understand my scepticism, Miss Hargreaves. With no one willing to corroborate your story, it's hard for me to consider your testimony.'

'The killer struck with his left hand. That was not printed in the paper or is *common knowledge*, as you like to put it. Check your own account and see for yourself. That detail must have been held back.' Elsbeth watched Abberline as he retrieved the autopsy report from the pile of folders, looking at the page where it listed the wounds and method of delivery, which he was already very familiar with.

'Hmm…It seems that you are correct, but there is half a chance to be right if I were a cynic to arrive at such a conclusion.' His rational brain, unable to accept anyone can just come to *know* such things.

'You will find it's the same in the second murder, Inspector. The killer is left-handed.'

'I have yet to see the coroner, Mr Cripps, about either of the murders, so I can neither confirm nor deny that that is the case. I have a meeting with him at nine in the morning to discuss this and other matters. So, as I said, that has yet to be determined, and even if true, it still doesn't mean it's the same killer.' Abberline, intrigued by her confidence, stood up from his chair, making it clear from his point of view the discussion was at a close.

'I want to be present at the coroner's, to be there when you realise that I am right. There is more to be concerned about here, but it requires you to keep an open mind.'

Abberline ignored the comment of an open mind, preferring tried and tested methods rather than magic.

'I'm sorry, The Dead House is not a place for…the public, Miss Hargreaves.' He paused, selecting his words carefully.

'You mean a woman, Inspector, don't you? I'm a lot tougher than you give me credit for.'

'It's a police matter, that's all I meant, it has nothing to do with your gender.'

Elsbeth rose from her chair; her black lace and silk dress sprung out from beneath her as she held out her right hand to shake his. He put his hand in hers, irritated by her uncompromising and direct manner but at the same time admiring her honesty. He had no desire to duel further with this enigmatic and complicated person who possessed both beauty and intelligence.

'Thank you for your time, Miss Hargreaves. I appreciate your comments, and I apologise for any disrespect shown to you earlier. I will ensure that this does not reoccur if you need to revisit the station.'

She removed her hand from his and smiled politely.

'You need to come to terms, accept there was nothing you could do, Inspector, stop blaming yourself.'

Abberline stopped, caught off balance. 'I'm sorry – I don't understand. What are you talking about? Are you referring to the case?'

'Someone died who was very close to you – a woman. A wife, maybe, it had something to do with her chest. She was young when she passed over. You hold yourself responsible but try to forget. But that's not good for you or her; the departed, like the living, like to be remembered.'

'How…how on earth could you?' Abberline sat back on his chair, taken aback at what he was hearing. But still not convinced – he knew that people who say they can speak to the dead use many methods to fool.

'It's ok, she is safe, she loves you very much. What I'm able to do is not magic, it's real. I don't do this for money, Inspector; I do this to heal and to help the living and the dead to cross over and find peace. She gave you a locket she wore the day you proposed to her so she could always be with you whenever you were apart.'

'Yes.' He paused. 'I still carry it with me. Always.' Abberline looked visibly shocked at her revelation. He spoke quietly as he remembered. 'She died two months into our marriage. Tuberculosis, she coughed blood for ages. It was awful.' He paused for a moment, thinking back to the pain of her suffering evident to see.

But then he snapped, not wanting to go back to that time. 'I don't know how you came to know that or much care, but it is a personal matter, and you would do well to remember that.' He looked back up to see Elsbeth halfway out of the office door; mixed feelings of remorse, guilt and anger at her audacity fought for his attention. A trick, she's a fraud, somebody told her, he thought quickly, recovering from his melancholy pool of thoughts, but something still bothered him. *How did she know about the locket his wife had given him?* He had never told anyone about that, *it was their secret.*

'I will meet you, Inspector Abberline at the mortuary, The Dead House as you call it, tomorrow morning.' Her voice trailed off as she passed Rawlings on the way out, returning his icy stare from earlier.

NINE

November had brought grey skies over the town, as snow swept across the county from the North Sea, freezing winds that bit through bone and feather. The streets with fresh layers of white quickly transformed into a dirty brown, black soup as random patterns of footprints and wheels from horse-drawn carts cut through the surface. Elsbeth kept her head down, pushing forward. It was hard going, and the slippery conditions made the journey even more treacherous. Her nose and cheeks rosy from the winter weather, she clasped the lapels of her coat together in one hand while holding her bonnet with the other.

The mortuary was located at the top of St James Street in Kemptown. A ghetto area of Brighton frequently inhabited by drunks, prostitutes, and sharpers, not safe for anyone of standing. Elsbeth darted into an empty doorway, rummaged in her coat pocket, taking out a crumpled piece of paper, her fingers numb from the cold. She checked the directions she had been given; it was still a way to go. It was clear she looked out of place; aggressive shouts and lurid comments directed towards her, the mistrusting eyes, young and old, followed her from dark corners through thick smoke and burning embers of open fires, desperate, huddled together like ravenous wolves.

Babies crying from illness or hunger could be heard coming from the tenements, blackened with soot on each side of the road, some buildings so fragile they were falling into their neighbour. The gnarled and twisted street, with its broken cobblestones poking up through the snow, and upended carts, just left abandoned, made the going slower. Children with sticks, unaccustomed to seeing well-dressed women in this part of town, ran around her while dogs barked at the commotion. Elsbeth accepted that poverty and deprivation were everywhere and felt sadness and anger at how these people lived. It was common knowledge that disease took hold quickly in these slums, killing many, but little was made to improve their lot. It was a dangerous place, and she was on her own.

'What's such a woman as you doin visiting the likes of us then, eh,' a man's voice, gravelled and hoarse, came from the side of her as she eventually reached the mortuary building. Ignoring him, she looked for some signage. It was a small, insignificant, single-storey red brick building with three windows running down both sides. There was no name plate to give the purpose, just a cream door fitted with a large back door knocker and a small window above that was shut.

'Come up ere on ya own to The Dead House, eh? That's what they call it round ere. You show me what you ave under those pretty little scanties, and I might let you live.'

Shuffling feet, leather on stone, moved in the shadows of a small alleyway to her left. Elsbeth continued to pay little attention to the threats, knocking loudly on the door. She was there just before nine o'clock the time he had said, but Abberline was nowhere to be seen, which annoyed her. *Maybe he was already inside conducting his business with the coroner.* He had shown no interest in the prospect of sharing information, but she was sure he would benefit from her attendance.

An overweight and balding man appeared beside her wearing a tattered jacket and trousers held up with some rope.

His shirt was torn and filthy, which seemed to stick to his skin from the tar that had been smeared on it. An old sailor's trick to keep them waterproof. Elsbeth noticed the bloodied nose and cuts to his forehead. Most likely a street brawl or disagreement of some kind. His skin was grey with sickness, and yellow and black teeth, with most of the top ones missing, giving a menacing smirk across his face. 'I ain't going to hurt you, precious; I just want to make you happy, that's all, me dear. Me, I'm real good at making women happy, you ask anyone round ere.'

'Go away, I have no coin on me. There's a police officer behind this door.' She glared at him, hoping he would get the message.

'Hmmm, police, there ain't none round ere, me dear. Last one, they found him with his throat cut, nasty business. I'll take what's on offer, not fussy me, shout all you want, nobody gives a shit.' He pulled a small knife from his trouser pocket, holding it close to Elsbeth's face. 'I want you, bet you're nice and juicy, eh?' His tongue with sores protruded, licking the air, flinty eyes narrowing with expectation.

Elsbeth shoved him hard backwards; he staggered, snarling like a rabid dog, the excess skin of his stomach folding over the top of his trousers; he started to move towards her. 'I'm going to give you something to remember, or maybe I'll cut the skin off that pretty face.' He became more excited as he got closer. She shouted for help, but no one even turned; she was the enemy here; this was another country. She felt scared and vulnerable for the first time in her life as the hard iron of the door's knocker pressed into her back, and she had nowhere to go.

'Lift that pretty skirt up of yours, or I'll cut ya.' His other arm extended, grabbing her collar, his face close, breath so putrid it made her want to vomit. She could feel him rubbing himself against her, pushing her against the door. Elsbeth turned her head one way, then the other, trying to push him off. *She shouldn't have come. She should have listened to Abberline.* This was no place to be. Without warning, the man was pulled with force backwards: a kick and a punch, then another rained down on him. The man groaned, fell to the floor and then another kick was delivered hard into his side. She heard his ribs crack; he rolled into a ball, screaming in pain, raising a hand in defence.

'Please, I don't mean no harm, just havin a bit of fun.' The beating ceased; he took a moment to unravel himself. Seeing an opportunity, he quickly scurried back on all fours like a monkey to the alleyway. Abberline stood before Elsbeth, not saying a word, as Cripps, the coroner, opened the door to the mortuary. Abberline stepped through, with Elsbeth quickly following.

TEN

Elsbeth entered the hallway of the mortuary where Cripps and Abberline stood waiting. It was silent, cold, and unnerving; the sweet, sickly smell of amber used to clean the bodies for embalming and burial hung in the air. Elsbeth removed her coat, shook the snow off, placed it on a spare peg on the wall, rubbed her hands and stamped her feet to get the circulation going again. She thanked Abberline for his intervention outside, but the atmosphere was not welcoming. Clearly, neither man wanted her there, but out of courtesy, she waited for Cripps to speak. Cripps had been the coroner for Brighton for the past ten years. A tall, bony man with thinning, long grey hair swept across one side, hollow cheeks, and a large, thin, pointing nose protruding from his face. His eyes were small and beady, emotionless, like a shark. He pulled a silver pocket watch from his waistcoat and huffed. Elsbeth didn't like him; she felt something more behind the slimy persona, something cruel and rotten.

'As you can plainly see, I have much to do, so make this quick.' Addressing Abberline only, Cripps's voice was gruff and snappy. 'This bloody weather has had them piling up, and you can see–' pointing to a number of wooden tables with naked bodies lining the corridor down to the main examination area– 'with just myself to work the backlog, I have neither time nor the inclination to assist you.'

Abberline and Elsbeth didn't answer but followed Cripps down the narrow corridor; his words lost in the echoes of their footsteps. The passage was dimly lit by four wall-mounted gas lamps, two on each side, and the white tiles that lined the walls took on a yellow hue. Their shadows elongated as they traversed the corridor in the low light, edging past the dead, some covered with blood-stained sheets, others without any cover on full display, arms falling over the side. Men, women, and children of all ages lay still, their heads turned to face the living, eyes milky white, skin cold and grey from death's silent kiss. It was both sombre and chilling, Elsbeth now understood why it was called The Dead House.

They entered the main examination room, a large rectangular area with windows on either side, the walls covered from top to bottom with the same white tiles. Four wooden tables where the autopsies took place were positioned in rows and bolted to the concrete floor in the centre of the room; each one had a number of holes drilled into the surface to allow drainage. An inch-thick pipe stretched across the ceiling, spurring a section over each table; at the end, each had a shower head attached for cold water to wash away fluids during an examination. Below the tables, a gutter had been excavated, leading to a drain with a cast iron grate cover. Blood from the deceased had flowed down from the tables over the years and into the hollowed-out channel, creating a crimson-red patina.

A large pine cupboard where Cripps kept his leather apron was at one end of the room, with some shelving. A blue and white patterned oval wash basin and jug were to the side for him to wash by. At the other end, a doorway leading to an outside alley, which ran behind the building where bodies were often delivered and despatched for burial. Inside and to the left of the door sat two coffin-shaped preserving chambers attached to a frame on wheels about waist high, strange objects to the uninformed. Each was double-lined and constructed for a specific purpose. The inner coffin was lead-lined and packed with ice, while the outside was made from English oak. A wooden lid was kept in place by brass clamps on the outside that were screwed tight to keep the body frozen at the right temperature. A small glass window at the top of the coffin was created so the face and identity of the deceased could be easily made. Cripps walked over to the units and wheeled each one over towards the examination tables. Elsbeth and Abberline looked on as just the wheels creaking, broke the silence. 'This is your first victim. Mary Quinn, approximately eighteen years of age, died from severe loss of blood from deep slashes and stab wounds to the torso and neck, twenty-nine in total, to be precise.'

Elsbeth and Abberline moved closer, looking through the glass at the face of Mary Quinn. Elsbeth immediately rec-ognised her as the woman who had visited her at the séance. Her face was no longer young, blushing, and full of life, but cold and grey, her lips blue from death.

'I keep them in these double-lined coffins packed with ice to stop the deterioration of the body. I was told to keep these two back until you arrived, as you wanted to see them before I dispatched them. But the ice only lasts so long, so time is of the essence. Don't want them stinking out the place attracting the flies, do we?' Cripps smirked, looking over at Elsbeth.

Cripps unscrewed the clasps on either side and opened up the lid to reveal the inner coffin displaying the naked, mutilated body of Mary Quinn. Her petite frame seemed lost inside the casket, her skin shredded and ripped open by the many wounds. Elsbeth looked away for a second, coughing, feeling nauseous; shocked by the reality of the young girl who lay there, not one part of her untouched by violence. Cripps picked up his notes and flipped through the pages until he got to the details of the autopsy. "A madness of some kind clearly defines and drives the killer, but there is a purpose and as difficult as it is for you to accept or understand,' he paused, 'there is method to this work."

'You say *purpose* and *method* as if you admire this butchery?' Elsbeth spoke with annoyance.

'You misunderstand me, missy,' Cripps retorted. 'I am only pointing out that to someone with an untrained eye, such as yourself, you see nothing other than what lies before you. But to me, a trained professional with many years of experience, I see–' Another pause. 'I see something else. A textbook understanding of the human form, maybe even the beginnings of a style albeit basic and unrefined, but it's there all the same, and it gets more interesting with our second victim.'

Elsbeth looked at Abberline with a sick and angry look but decided to say nothing further until later. She looked on as Cripps began to read from his notes.

"'The first cadaver belongs to Mary Quinn. Her throat was cut from left to right with two definite cuts on the left side, and with the windpipe, gullet, and spinal cord beg cut through, death would have followed relatively swiftly. We have bruising on the throat, which suggests she was almost certainly strangled, and on the lower right jaw from several blows or punches. There were a number of deep stab wounds to both breasts, one nipple being sliced off completely. The abdomen had been cut open with some force from the centre of the bottom ribs along the left side, under the pelvic bone, and left of the stomach. Jagged cuts which match the pattern of the weapon are made up of several incisions across the torso, cutting through all tissue and causing massive blood loss. We also can see several frenzied cuts to the privy parts, of which a proportion of the area has been cut away and removed along with other organs. These I presume missing, as they have not yet been recovered. The knife seemed to have been serrated, thin, and extremely sharp. I also conclude that the killer is most likely left-handed from the delivery of the attack.'"

'You have been most thorough in your examination, Mr Cripps.'

Abberline looked to Elsbeth to see her unsettled by the events. 'If it suits you, you might want to wait outside, Miss Hargreaves.'

'I'm quite all right, Inspector, and no, I do not need to wait outside like the weak woman you think me. I came here today of my own free will, and I have every intention to see this out. I need to see if there is anything they can tell me.'

'My, my, you have a feisty one there, Inspector,' Cripps laughed. 'I've seen her type before, believing that they can talk to the dead, utter rubbish, of course. I had no idea the police had resorted to employing such tactics to do their detective work. Running out of ideas, are we?' Cripps sneered and chuckled as he returned the second casket for inspection. 'You might not be so keen on staying, missy, after seeing what our lad has done to this one.'

Abberline ignored Cripps's remarks and could see Elsbeth was irritated by his condescending attitude, he gestured for Cripps to open up the second chamber so the body of Rosie Meeks could be seen. As Cripps removed the top, it was hard to see anything that resembled a human being. The body of Rosie Meeks had been literally torn to pieces. The sight was so grotesque that even Abberline turned away. 'Dear god in heaven.' He quickly retrieved a handkerchief from his trouser pocket and held it over his nose and mouth. He could feel the sick rising from his stomach. Elsbeth stood motionless, her eyes fixed on the abomination before her, unable to speak or move. What someone had done to this poor woman utterly disgusted and numbed her.

'As with the first victim, this one was also strangled. There were so many wounds, cuts, abrasions, and slashes it was hard to count them all, and again, as with Mary Quinn, he had removed some of her organs. Never seen anything like it, quite remarkable.' Cripps moved his notes, finding the details of the injuries. '"The abdomen removed, the peritoneal cavity was empty, both breasts were cut off, and arms were mutilated with numerous slashes and stab wounds. The neck was sliced down to the spine. The face was lacerated, with cuts across all features, the nose and lips completely removed; the front right thigh was skinned down to the bone; the left thigh was stripped of skin and muscle. The pericardium, the fibrous sac, was cut open, and the heart, small intestine and kidney are missing along with the right lung."'

Abberline and Elsbeth remained speechless as Cripps continued.

'Not much is left of her, as you can see. I would say the killer is left-handed due to the direction of the cuts. Are the two murders connected? Possibly, the wounds are very similar, and I would say that the same serrated knife has been used, of that I'm certain.'

'Would the killer need to have any anatomical or medical knowledge to remove the organs? And why would the killer do that?' Abberline quizzed Cripps.

'The manner of removal was chaotic, to say the least, as we can see. But recognising the organs and knowing where to locate them, yes, they would need to have required some knowledge or interest in anatomy. As I said earlier, there is method at play here. Why they were removed and for what purpose, I could not tell you.' A pause. Looking over to Abberline. 'Perhaps your psychic can enlighten us, eh?' Cripps's high-pitched laugh filled the room.

Elsbeth looked up, not saying a word. Trembling from the carnage in front of her, a tear trickled down her right cheek; she felt claustrophobic as beads of sweat appeared on her brow; she walked quickly out of the room. Cripps looked over to

Abberline, smiling sarcastically. Feeling dizzy, Elsbeth leaned against one of the windows in the corridor to steady herself, catching her breath, bending over and trying hard not to retch. She breathed deeply, calming herself. *My god, what evil could do such a thing to someone?* As she stood back up, something from the corner of her eye caught her attention momentarily, but enough to know she was not alone.

She could hear the voices of Cripps and Abberline in the examination room, so she quickly checked around her, but nothing, just the sound of the flames dancing from the lamps. Shaking her head, she breathed deeply once more and turned to rejoin the others. Suddenly, a loud thud on the window where she had been resting stunned her. She jumped, seeing a hand against the glass pressing down, then gone, leaving just a ghostly outline. Rosie Meeks stood before her; her face grim; she moved towards Elsbeth. 'He's here.' A pause. 'Stop him… Seen him.'

Rosie Meeks' voice was slow, shaking with fear. She raised her right arm, pointing past Elsbeth. Elsbeth stepped back, stopping; she felt a heaviness on her chest, pressing down, pushing her lungs into her ribs. Dark thoughts of the butchered bodies she had just witnessed flooded her mind. She sensed warm air gently breathing against the back of her neck…Someone was right behind her.

ELEVEN

As Elsbeth turned, Abberline stood in front of her. 'Are you alright? I thought I had better come out and check. You looked…well, pale, and God, notwithstanding what we have just witnessed, it's not surprising.'

Elsbeth stared at him, still seeing Meeks in her mind's eye. 'I'm fine, thank you, Inspector; I just…just needed some air. I need to collect my shawl, which I left in the examination room.' Elsbeth walked past Abberline, glancing back down the corridor where she had seen the ghost of Rosie Meeks, and thought about what Rosie had said; something stuck in her mind the words. *Seen him.* She wondered what she had meant by this: did she know her killer, or did she mean something else? Abberline followed behind, back towards the examination room.

Waiting at the door before entering, Elsbeth turned to Abberline to confront him. 'I hope, Inspector, that now Cripps has confirmed that we are looking for a left-handed killer, at the very least, this will give some credence to my disclosure of this fact at the police station before our visit here. How could I have possibly known this in advance?' Elsbeth wanted to get the matter across to prove she was not deluded or inventing stories.

'This is still very much a police matter, Miss Hargreaves, and we are not open to employing the services of a psychic. It was, to be honest, a fifty- fifty chance. As I have said previously, it was perhaps, at best, a lucky guess.'

Elsbeth looked bemused at his response, but it wasn't unsurprising, and she decided this was not the time, nor place, to argue the point as she pushed through the doors into the room and collected her shawl as Cripps was removing his apron and washing blood off his hands in the basin provided.

'Are we done now, Inspector?' Cripps asked.

'Yes, thank you for your time. It has given us some insight into the killer and the dangerous, insane individual we are dealing with.'

'What happens to the bodies of these murdered women, may I ask, Mr Cripps?' Elsbeth inquired.

'They get collected and taken to ground put aside for the poor. Those who can't afford a proper burial.' His tone was so clinical; without any emotion, he could have been talking about the rubbish being taken out.

'You mean somewhere out of sight. Not even any words said over them, I wager?'

Cripps, ignoring the remark, turned to Abberline.

'Our business here is now concluded, Inspector. I must prepare these and others for collection if you don't mind. I have given enough of my time.' Cripps deliberately addressed only Abberline. 'I have prepared some photographs of the bodies and another copy of my autopsy report on both women for your reference.' Cripps handed a folder containing the information to Abberline.

'Thank you, Mr Cripps; we will not keep you any longer.' With that, Abberline motioned to Elsbeth to leave Cripps to his work and make their way out. They walked back down the corridor to the main entrance, where Elsbeth retrieved her coat from the peg.

'I suppose the job of mortician attracts a particular type, but Cripps must have been a gift from God when he applied. A snake of a man, one who clearly thinks that women should not be involved in such matters,' Elsbeth commented as she put on her coat and gloves.

'Is that your psychic ability talking here, Miss Hargreaves?' Abberline quipped as he opened the door out onto the street.

'No, Inspector, it's called observation. Maybe the police could incorporate that into their training methods, which might assist you in solving cases.' Elsbeth walked out, wearing a smile. 'Where to now?'

'For me, the scene of the first crime. The murder of Mary Quinn.'

'If we are going to work together, Inspector, I think it would be best if we drop formality don't you, and you call me Elsbeth.'

'Working together? I ...Don't believe I ...' But before he could say another word, Elsbeth had climbed into the waiting cab. He followed her in, sitting opposite as the driver called out. 'Where to Inspector? Are we dropping the lady off first?' Abberline waited for a moment, staring directly at Elsbeth.

'No. Drive on. Vine Street, in The North Laine, as fast as possible!'

TWELVE

The driver pulled the horse-drawn cab to a halt at the beginning of Vine Street in the heart of The North Laine, the street Mary Quinn would have travelled down from her place of work. Abberline paid the driver and helped Elsbeth alight from the cab. The snow had paused momentarily, settling on the road as a cold wind blew into the town from the sea just a few streets to the south of where they stood. They wrapped their coats tight around themselves as Abberline led the way down to the corner of Gloucester Road.

'I thought we were going to the place where Mary was murdered? Surely this is going in the wrong direction?' Elsbeth shouted at Abberline so he could hear.

He stopped briefly and turned to face her, his eyes squinting in the icy chill.

'We are, but first, I want to talk to the people who worked with her and the last ones to see her alive.' He pointed ahead at a painted sign of a crown, creaking back and forth on rusted hinges.

'Here, The Crown, the place of her employment and where she was last seen that night. We need to find out why she decided to walk back alone. She knew this part of town well enough to know it wasn't safe, especially for a young girl on her own late at night. Normally, the women working in these places would stick together to ensure they got back to wherever they called home.'

The conditions made it hard for Elsbeth to hear everything he was saying, his words getting lost on the wind. She decided to save any conversation for later, nestled her head into her coat, looked down and traced his footsteps in the snow. The pub was built on two levels and located on Gloucester Road. The ground floor housed the drinking area with two windows on each side of the building, while the first floor was used as lodgings for the current proprietors. As Abberline and Elsbeth entered, the overpowering smell of tobacco and beer, accompanied by raucous laughter and drunken singing, greeted them. Thick smoke had yellowed the ceiling and walls, with people crammed in like sardines.

The bar area was packed with mainly working-class men, with a number of women who were not their wives or sweethearts hanging onto their arms or sitting in their laps kissing and singing along to the music played by a man at the piano in a corner. Elsbeth looked out of place, refined and elegant, as suspicious eyes tracked her movement. The bar top was solid oak and ran from one side of the room to the other, heavily stained from spilt beer and gin; rings from tankards scarred the wood. Faucets of ale from the Gloucester Road brewery were fitted along the surface, and mirrored glass panels behind the bar advertised Harry Hall, who had taken ownership of The Crown and many other pubs in the town. It was a typical drinking hole with wooden plank flooring and basic tables supported by empty beer kegs from the brewery. It was one of the most popular pubs in the town, but with over four hundred to choose from, competition was fierce, with at least two pubs on every street in The North Laine alone. Landlords and owners had to develop new ways of attracting customers and keeping the ones they had.

As Abberline approached the bar, requesting to see the manager, a tall man with dirty work clothes saddled up close to Elsbeth, leering at her, his gaze fixed and frozen. She turned, noticing him standing and staring. 'Is there something you wanted to say?' Elsbeth, annoyed, asked. The man said nothing, appearing unbalanced, about to fall over until another drinker pulled him away by the arm.

'Sorry, love, he don't mean nothing, you're just not the sort we get down ere, if you know what I mean; he's a bit worse for the drink, I'll take him off ya hands.' Elsbeth quickly realised he was no better than his friend, sniggering while looking her up and down at the same time.

Abberline had become uneasy at the attention Elsbeth was receiving and wanted to remind her why they were there. 'Please try not to draw more attention than is necessary. It appears your presence has caused somewhat of a stir.'

Before Elsbeth could reply, a lean man of about forty years of age with a large, thick beard and stained apron appeared in front of them from behind the bar.

'Yes, sir …and madam, what's your poison?'

'We're not here to drink. I'm on official duty from Scotland Yard.' Abberline showed his identity card to the barman. 'I'm here to find who is responsible for the recent murders of Mary Quinn and Rosie Meeks. Mary Quinn, I understand, used to work here, and this was the last place she was seen alive on the night she was killed. So, I need to speak to anyone who knew her and can help with the investigation.'

The barman looked over at Elsbeth. 'You're that woman who talks to the dead, aren't you? The one in the paper. I read what you said. Now, suddenly, we have Scotland Yard down here to save us all, eh? Why, well, let's see, oh, yes, it's because our own police in this town don't give a damn about us and couldn't catch a cold if they tried.' A jeer from the bar echoed around the room, which now made Abberline and Elsbeth the main attraction. The barman looked over towards Elsbeth. 'If you can talk to ghosts, why don't our Mary tell who did it.' More laughter rang, followed by swearing and finger-pointing towards the pair.

'You're just a circus freak.' A voice echoed across the room as even the piano man had stopped, standing up to see what the hubbub was all about.

Elsbeth felt the anger and resentment towards them growing as she tried to correct the banter. 'It's not as simple as that. I'm afraid the dead are not always eager to come forth, let alone go over the trauma that ended their life. They often prefer to stay in the shadows, adjusting to their new existence.' Her explanation caused more sounds of confusion and disapproval from the crowd.

'It ain't God-like. Tis the devil's work ask me,' someone shouted.

Elsbeth could see these people were clearly not of a mind to listen.

Abberline banged his fist on the bar top and shouted above the noise. 'Quiet now, please quiet. We are here to try and gain any information to help us find the killer of one of your own. I can assure you that we are not here for any other purpose or, indeed, to question you on any other matter. All we want is to find who took the lives of these two local women and put that person on the end of a rope.'

The commotion subsided for a brief moment.

'We heard this before from you lot; you don't give a damn. Treat us like dogs is what you do,' a man said near to them.

'Then why are we here? Ask yourselves that.' The rabble's discontent worsened as the jeering and muttering increased. 'Look…Look,' Abberline shouted, holding up the photographs of Mary Quinn and Rosie Meeks, turning them around for all to see. 'This is what he did to them. This could have been your wife, sweetheart, your daughter.' A pause. 'Observe what he did. This maniac showed no remorse. Look carefully. Mary, eighteen years old, received stab after stab, and then once he had finished with her, he left her to rot on a pile of rubbish. Rosie Meeks was ripped to pieces and mutilated beyond recognition. She had an eight-year-old son, now all alone in the world. We need to catch this madman soon before he takes another life. So, if you have any information, I implore you to help us.'

The room fell silent, wide eyes of disbelief focused on the images of the butchered women. Gasps and low chatter filled the room. Most looked away, shocked and nauseated by the images.

'He can have my bloody wife with blessings on,' a man remarked, breaking the silence as the room quickly descended back into laughter, joined by the piano and more singing.

The barman leaned in, signalling to Abberline to come closer. 'Don't mind this lot. It's the way they deal with things round here. I wasn't here that night, someone else was running the place. But a few of the girls who worked the place were. Maybe some of them ere now.' A pause. 'Maybe try Polly over there, she's regular.' He nodded towards a woman sitting alone towards the back of the bar. 'Don't expect much; you ain't going to win any popularity contests,' he smirked, cleaning a glass tumbler and placing it on the shelf behind him.

'We will take our chances, thank you.' Abberline turned to Elsbeth. 'We might have someone who can help, follow me.'

THIRTEEN

Abberline and Elsbeth approached the woman who sat with her head face down on folded arms. Abberline went to wake her from what he assumed was a drunken state, when Elsbeth intervened quickly. 'Best I do this, woman to woman, if you want to get anything out of her.'

Abberline said nothing but nodded in approval as Elsbeth sat down opposite and gently touched her arm, moving it slightly.

'Excuse me, Polly. I wonder if I might… If we might, have a word with you?'

'I know who you are, lady. I know what you're doing here. I ain't thick like the rest of them, you know.' Raising her head, she gazed at Abberline, her eyes tired and red from booze. And I ain't drunk, neither I knows what he's thinking,' Polly said, waving her finger at Abberline.

'The barman said you might be able to assist us with information about Mary Quinn, the girl who worked here and was murdered in the alleyway. Any information you have would be helpful.' Elsbeth waited for a response as Abberline took a seat next to her, watching carefully.

'You want information? You pay, I talk. That's how things work 'ere, nothing for nothin. And something from her,' pointing at Elsbeth. 'We know all about you.' Polly shuffled on her seat, asserting herself.

'Can we get you a drink?' Abberline asked.

'You can't buy me off with cheap beer. I told you, money first. You both have plenty. I can see the way she dresses. Fine cloth, that is, cost a pretty penny, no doubt. Pretty face as well, you'd do well with the punters.' Polly grinned, her teeth cracked, gums blackened with disease. She stretched out her hand, feeling the black lace of Elsbeth's dress cuff. Elsbeth moved her arm away from the woman's hand, reached into her purse and placed ten pennies on the table.

'There, enough to keep you warm and in beer for a while.'

Polly slumped in her chair, fiddling with her black curly hair, thinking whether to cooperate or not. 'Mary was young and stupid; she was told not to go alone down them alleyways; none of us do. We warned her, but she didn't listen. Cocky little strumpet. She had men all over her, they couldn't get enough of our Mary.' Polly let out a loud laugh, watching the disgust on Abberline's face. 'Look, she left here before close. I told her to wait, said we'd go together safer that way. She said she had to get across town to see her landlord. Owed him money for rent which she didn't ave. She was going to tell him she would get it but needed more time, she knew she had to pay him, or she'd be feeding the fish off the pier. That's all I know. Next thing we hear, she's been found dead, gutted like a pig.'

'But was she at work here that night?' Elsbeth pressed her.

Polly laughed again. 'Worked, that one. She worked to get blokes out the back to make some coin. That's all she did in here. She called herself a barmaid, I never saw her behind any bar, but I saw 'er on her back a good few times. She was no better than the rest of us.'

'Doesn't sound as if you liked her very much,' Elsbeth inquired as carefully as she could.

'I liked her well enough, she was pretty, so men swarm

round her like bees round honey, plenty for us all. We all got trade on the back of her like. Her dead ain't no good for anyone, is it, eh? Your type wouldn't know what we have to do to survive.' Polly glared at Elsbeth.

'Her landlord, you say, she had to get back to him, owed him money?' Abberline asked, ignoring the last remark, writing notes in his pocketbook.

'Yeah, Seamus Keane, Irish, an evil Fenian bastard and has a temper, hates everyone, carries a hammer around with him, likes to cripple people, especially those that owes him. Shouldn't be hard to find him. He has a scar running down from his left eye to his chin from some fight or somin.' She traced an imaginary scar on her own face. 'He can get you whatever you want, whatever your fancy; Mary was one of them who worked for him. No doubt she earnt him a nice sum. Don't be taking this fine lady down there in her fine clothes,' Polly said, shaking her finger at Abberline across the table. 'Not a place for the likes of her.'

'Do you know where she lived?' Elsbeth joined the conversation.

'Down by the seafront, above the pub run by Keane in Ship Street, that's all I know. Mary put it about everywhere, know what I mean. But be careful. Keane's crazy. He won't care who you are. If he don't like you, you're as good as dead.'

'Did you see anyone following her when she left here that night? Anyone watching her, anyone like us that stood out, didn't fit?' Elsbeth thought it was a good idea to ask; maybe she remembered someone in the pub that night.

'No, nothing, same lot always in here, getting drunk, fighting, whoring as is.'

Abberline had met many people like Polly in London. 'I need your full name and where you're from, for the record, you understand? Don't worry, you're a witness, that's all, you're not going to be arrested.' He wanted to make sure she didn't run.

'You make sure that Detective Rawlings stays away from me,' Polly said. 'He's a wrongen. I ain't talking to him, I don't have nothin to do with him or any of them peelers at Brighton, understand!'

'As I said, I am overseeing this investigation. I assure you no harm will come to you. Now, your name and background, please.'

'Polly Nichols. Well, me birth name is Mary Ann Walker, but call meself Polly, as I likes it better. Nichols is me married name like.'

'You're from the East end of London, Polly? I recognise the accent.' Abberline knew he was right, but Polly didn't answer him, turning to Elsbeth instead.

'Tell you what. If she's so good let ere tell you.'

'We are not here for cheap theatrics, Polly. We are here investigating the murder of two women, one of whom you knew. And we do not have the time. So, answer the question here, or we can go to the station, and I'll let Detective Rawlings do it.' Abberline was not joking and wanted her to know that.

Polly, frightened, answered. 'Yeah, alright, calm down, just fooling with ya. I'm from The East End, Whitechapel. Met a bloke, he promised the world, married the bastard, he knocks me up, then he started having his way with the neighbour's wife, so I left him. Ended up in the workhouse, but they treated me worse than he did. So, I started selling other things, if you get my meaning. I came down here; a friend told me how good it was, rich pickings. Thought I'd get me some sea air. Get that smog out of my lungs. Me friend was right. They pay more here for what's between my legs.' She cackled, coughing and bringing up phlegm at the same time.

Polly's gaze returned to Elsbeth as she held out her palm to be read. 'Am I going to meet me a rich man then, take me away from all this? Read me hand, tell me what lady luck has in store for me. But I ain't paying you nothin.'

'I need an object, something you hold dear to you, anything,' Elsbeth asked, not thinking she would have anything of value.

'Elsbeth, we don't have time for this,' Abberline interrupted, becoming impatient.

'This won't take long, please,' Elsbeth insisted.

Polly undid a plain brass and copper necklace and handed it to Elsbeth. 'That's all I ave left, ain't much but it's mine so don't you go taking it, you hear,' touching Elsbeth's hand longer than was necessary, as she handed over the item.

Elsbeth held the necklace tight in her hands and bowed her head, concentrating on the object. She breathed in and out deeply, then spoke.

'You have children, four, but one passed over some time back. Your husband has something to do with paper. You are thinking of going back home to London, to Whitechapel? Don't. I sense something very bad, terrible, if you do return…I see you–' Elsbeth broke off, distressed by what she had seen.

Polly sat upright, eyes wide, and focused on what Elsbeth was saying. 'How … how could you know that…how you doing this?'

'Am I right?' Elsbeth asked, quickly regaining her composure.

'Yeah, me husband, that cheatin' bastard, he was a printer, so guess you could say he handled paper. I had a boy.' A pause. 'Lost him at twelve months, consumption what did for him, died in my arms he did.'

'Listen to me, Polly, don't go back to Whitechapel. You must listen to me. I saw you… I saw–'

Polly interrupted Elsbeth before she could finish getting up from the table.

'What you talkin about? I'm as safe as houses there, know it like the back of me hand. Anyway, not going back for a bit; money is to be made ere. I think we're done here, Inspector. Don't know how you do it, luv, but you're good.'

With that, she grabbed her necklace from Elsbeth's hand and disappeared into the crowded bar.

Abberline looked at Elsbeth, trying to understand how she could have known those things without ever meeting the woman. 'You were going to say more. You told her not to go back to London, to Whitechapel. There was something else that clearly seemed to distress you; what was it?'

'I saw her dead body, and you standing over it.'

FOURTEEN

The alleyway where Mary Quinn's body was found was dark, wet, and dangerous. Not just because of the discarded rubbish that littered the floor but mainly because of the slum buildings on either side, and the troubled, violent people it was home to. Made worse by the thick sea fog that had rolled in early that morning, it crept through every nook and cranny, freezing and damp, chilling right down to the bone.

'You need to watch your step, Miss Hargreaves. There's broken glass, and human waste everywhere, a rat's paradise masked by the snow and this damned fog.' Abberline lit a small portable lantern, holding it up as he walked through to help guide the way, but the illumination proved to be of little use, dulled by the murky surroundings.

'You *can* call me by my first name, you know, Inspector, as I have told you, and yes, the stench more than gives away the condition of the place.'

'I'm not comfortable with first names. It signifies a relationship, a friendship which we don't have.'

Elsbeth, amused by his directness, understood how others might be offended by it. She stepped carefully around anything that looked suspicious and was liable to cause injury. But it was hard to see anything due to the sheer amount of rubbish. 'Where was her body found?' she asked.

'Near the end, slumped on a pile of debris, half-naked, blood everywhere, much it soaked through to the brick, so it won't be hard to locate."

'What do you expect to find?' Elizabeth asked curiously while shaking something hanging from the heel of her boot.

'I'm not sure. Maybe something, maybe nothing, anything that the local bobbies might have missed.'

'Like the killer.' Elsbeth's humour fell flat on him as he kept walking.

'Actually, this is something we need to do more of, study the crime area to see what clues it can give us. We don't always do this, and I believe it is important that a search of the area is carried out as soon as possible. How can we have any idea of who has committed the crime or, indeed, its motive, otherwise? That is how we will catch this killer, make no mistake, with evidence and facts.'

'Well, if I can be sure of anything, it's that the police certainly wouldn't bother collecting any evidence if the victim is a fallen woman, a prostitute. As clearly, that type of woman is not even worthy of a decent burial.'

Abberline said nothing, continuing his way towards the end of the alleyway. Elsbeth heard footsteps coming from behind her. She stopped briefly, and in unison, they also stopped. She looked back, but there was nothing; she turned and looked ahead, squinting, not wanting to lose sight of Abberline. The footsteps started to follow her once more.

'Abberline, someone's behind me, I'm sure of it,' she yelled ahead, hoping he would stop.

He didn't. He shouted back as he continued ignoring her concerns, 'Come, we have work to do.'

Elsbeth glanced behind again, but she couldn't see anything. The person following, if there was, had gone. She waited a minute to be sure, then moved to catch up with Abberline, checking to the rear of her every now and then. As Abberline reached the spot where Mary Quinn's body had been discovered, he could see the splatter of blood across the wall and the mound of rubbish piled up where the body had been found.

Elsbeth arrived and stood by Abberline's side, looking at the scene before her. 'Dear God, what a place to end up; no one deserves this.' Seeing where the girl was murdered brought home the real terror, the fear this girl had endured – it was awful.

'I agree, but if we can help find out who did this to her, we can make some recompense for what happened.' Abberline lowered his lantern to the floor, moving it side to side, looking for anything to help find out who did this. Elsbeth's gaze turned down towards the alley, the footsteps she heard still bothering her as Abberline bent closer to the ground.

Abberline was talking, but to Elsbeth, it seemed to be more for his benefit than hers.

'This place is secluded; few people would venture down here, especially late at night, so whoever was responsible knew this, knew the area, and took advantage of the privacy it would provide them. She was a woman alone, open to attack, and known in the area as a working prostitute. This may prove to be significant or not, but he chose her for a reason, and I believe it was not random.'

Elsbeth placed her hand out against the wall just above the blood splatter. Almost immediately, a vision came crashing through of Mary Quinn running through a dark alleyway, breathing deeply and heavily. Elsbeth could see Mary looking panicked and scared; she saw her trip and fall as the images went in and out of focus. There was a glint of something metallic, somebody standing over her with a knife. Elsbeth was witnessing the last seconds of Mary Quinn's short life as the blade hammered down. Elsbeth fell back, gasping, feeling an agonising pain in her chest.

Her mind was still busy with sounds and images; she shook

her head from side to side, trying to clear it. Elsbeth looked around, Abberline had gone. A thick fog had descended, and he had vanished, as if it had swallowed him up. Suddenly, from nowhere, out of the mist, a grotesque face formed in front of her. His skin was covered in lesions and scars, and his breath stank of rotten meat and beer, a low, slurred voice pitted with pauses as he tried to string the words together. He moved closer, a small knife in his hands. Elsbeth froze, unable to move, she wanted to scream but couldn't. His face nearly touching hers; watery grey eyes, pale and dimmed, but with fear behind them as they looked into hers.

'I know what he did to that girl, I was ere. I saw him.'

'You say you saw him?' Abberline suddenly reappeared, pulling the man away from Elsbeth by the wrist, twisting it as he did, forcing him to drop the knife.

'I did. I saw him, no mistakin, I just come from over there, where I been kipping like.' The man pointed to one of the derelict houses behind them. 'I saw him, I'm telling you.'

'You saw this person kill the girl?' Abberline now positioned him further away from both of them.

'I did.'

'What did he look like? Was he tall, short, fat, thin, old, young? You must remember something, man, think? Anything will help.' Abberline stepped forward and grabbed him by his collar, making sure he understood how important this was.

'I dunno.' He paused. 'It was dark; I couldn't see much. He was tall, thin, I think.' He paused again. 'Yeah, that's right, skinny. Kept his face hidden, turned away, so I don't know what he looked like. He wore a cloak, black I think, and carried a bag, small like them doctors do.'

Abberline released his hold on the man.

'Anything else, please?' Elsbeth asked, her tone softer.

The man looked down at the ground for a moment, then back up at her. 'He was wearing gloves. And his voice...' The man seemed to slip off into a sort of gaze, a petrified look coming over his expression.

'He spoke to you?' Abberline exclaimed excitedly, knowing this was a crucial piece of information.

'Yeah.' He looked over at Elsbeth.

'He said…He said this was just the beginning.'

Abberline, desperate to know more, questioned the man further. 'Did he have an accent? Think, man, try and remember; this is very important.'

The man looked confused, shaking his head. 'I…I dunno know, can't recall. The drink makes me mind go blank sometimes.'

Elsbeth turned to Abberline with a frightened look in her eyes.

The homeless man started to walk away, raising his voice. 'I done what you wanted, told you wot I know, now, you leave me alone; I never want to see him again. What I saw him do… He was like an animal he was.'

'Wait a minute,' Abberline shouted after him. The man stopped and turned back round.

'From what you've told us, could you recognise him if you saw him or heard that voice again? If you do, leave word for me at Brighton Police Station; I'll make sure there'll be something in it for you. We need to find who did this to this girl, soon.'

The man looked at both Abberline and Elsbeth for a moment.

'The Devil. That's what did that girl… The Devil.' And with that, he turned, disappearing into the mist.

FIFTEEN

Elsbeth closed the front door of her two-storey house on Montpelier Road, a sought-after area in Brighton. The warm aroma of freshly cut flowers greeted her and lifted her spirits as she shut away the world's brutality for a while. She was home. Being a psychic, the gift was both a curse and a blessing and, at times, sapped the energy out of her; she needed to rest, relax, and forget about the troubled ghosts that shared her life and home. She had inherited the house from her mother. She, in turn, had inherited it from her husband. Elsbeth was alone in the world, having lost both parents. Her father, when she was young, had an illness that left him bedridden for months, leading eventually to his death.

Her mother, Anne, her last surviving relative, had passed away from natural causes five years ago. But it wasn't her mother who possessed the gift, but her grandmother, the mother of her father, whom she was close to as a small child. She remembered talking to her in the front room of the house when she had come to visit her father while he lay ill in bed. She was kind and had the eyes of someone with great perception and knowledge. Elsbeth always remembered her grandmother telling her, she was special. That one day Elsbeth would realise she had an ability others did not, that she would go on to help those lost in this world, and the next. Elsbeth still felt the presence of her grandmother, Alice, in the house, at times the perfume of soft violets, the scent she'd often worn was in the air, a sign that Alice still walked beside her, between the shadows and the light.

Elsbeth loved the company of men but not to be controlled by them, so she kept herself free from engagement and marriage. For her, it would confine her; she had her home and income and was independent, which marriage would almost certainly remove. She had been told by many men and women of her beauty. How easily she could enchant a person of wealth and title, but she didn't ever think of herself being attractive, preferring to take an occasional lover when required, which was unrestrained from the entanglements and expectations of a relationship. Those who met her found her charming, intelligent, and well educated, but a person who knew her own mind and was not afraid to speak it. Elsbeth was an enigma to many, frustrating and aloof, a horse that could not be tamed, deep as the oceans and the secrets it kept.

Elsbeth made her way slowly up the wooden stairs to her bedroom, one of three on the top floor. Her room had its own internal bath with a larger, more formal bathroom at the end of the landing. Her bedroom, a large bright room at the front of the house; the design reflected her passion and fascination with exotic plants. Many of which sat in various sizes and coloured pots in every room and on her dressing table. Bookshelves with books of all types lined the walls; she was an ardent reader of fiction and non-fiction alike and loved nothing more than curling up in front of the fire with a glass of wine and a good story. The wooden floor was covered mainly by two ornate Persian rugs, bright red and orange patterns, each thread woven by hand, brought back by her father on one of his many trips away. Her mother had said that it was on one of those trips, toa foreign land, where her father had unknowingly contracted the illness that eventually took his life.

She lay down on the four-poster bed and closed her eyes, listening to the voices in the street, the cart and horses of the cabs driving past her home, the wheels slushing in the rain and snow. Couples strolled by chatting, laughing, planning a future, or discussing memories before they faded. She loved it; for her, it was the essence, the heartbeat of a thriving town. Sleep soon followed, a peaceful, deep slumber that would transport her away on childhood dreams of a little girl mesmerised by the kind words of an old lady. The scent of violets once more filled the room, gentle words whispered in her ear of how special she was, and the strange and magnificent worlds she would one day discover.

SIXTEEN

Seamus Keane made it easy for people to find him, it was good for business. His reputation as a dangerous and ruthless provider of prostitutes was well known, and he revelled in the notoriety. His very name seemed to strike fear into most people, deterring anyone from discussing him and his interests in any detail. But he had made many enemies, other gangs wanting his turf, and he was constantly on guard after many attempts on his life. Most days, he could be found in The Black Star pub, on Ship Street. There, he would hold court, conducting his business of renting out women or boys, money lending, and selling of illicit goods smuggled in from further up the coast.

At the back was a small courtyard, where kegs of ale were stored and Seamus would mete out his kind of discipline to those who had crossed him, using his trusty hammer on their kneecaps, fingers, and toes. It was a far cry from the days of being home to a protestant martyr, a man of conviction, who was burnt for his beliefs in the sixteenth century. Now, it housed the very lowest of the low; men without principles or honour who dealt in the currency of pain. Robbers and thieves frequented the building, going only through Seamus Keane to distribute stolen items.

It had two floors above; the first, Seamus would use to store some of his contraband. The second, housed his brothel. It was also the address where Mary Quinn resided and had been making her way back to the night she was killed. Seamus Keane had been informed he was getting a visit from a Scotland Yard man. Down from London to solve the two recent murders and to question him about his connection to at least one of the women killed. He looked forward to the encounter with the Inspector, helping with his inquiries so long as it didn't interfere with business.

Keane had recently spent the night away from the place, forming an alliance with another gang, but had made his way back at first light. Ship Street was home for him, a busy area open for anything at all hours. He saw the usual traders by their stalls, the street workers and vagrants lying in doorways curled up in balls from the icy conditions, skin blue from the weather, soon to be deceased. But for Seamus Keane, even the dead had value.

As he walked the last few yards and around the corner to the pub, the buildings dirty and dilapidated; the filth in the air bit the back of his throat, and the usual shouts, threats of violence, and foul language could be heard from all directions. Front doors, broken and open, revealed even darker conditions inside them. A young woman was breastfeeding, her baby crying as her milk was exhausted. Women were machines, often having ten or more children. Most of these young mothers died young from disease, ending up in prison or prostitution.

It was hell, much the same as his own childhood, growing up on the streets of Dublin, Seamus had learned, at a very young age, how to survive. It was kill or be killed, a tough, harsh world made worse by the British and their penal laws confiscating land, beatings, starvation and imprisonment of those who showed any sign of dissent. He had watched his father be shot in front of him. His mother and sister raped by the soldiers and from that moment, hate took over, his path of violence and crime sealed.

As he neared the premises, a number of emaciated children, dressed in rags, who worked for him were getting ready to go to the more affluent parts of town to hunt, to steal and rob. They called out to him, waiting for their master to send them out. They admired him; he was their way out of the gutter, a pinhead of hope that their miserable lives might change for the better. To him, they were no more than street rats, useful to get him things to sell; there were many like them. If he lost a few, another dozen would be banging on his door. They were pickpockets, opportunists; the smaller ones could break into fine houses, climbing through the smallest of spaces. But if they lived to work another day, and keep the hope alive that, one day, they would be just like him.

SEVENTEEN

As Abberline walked into The Black Star pub, it felt as if he was expected.

'This is not London, Inspector. Small-town people talk. I knew before you did that you were going to be paying me a visit.'

Abberline recognised he had the right man from his strong Dublin accent. 'I'm sure they do, Mr Keane; hopefully, you're not going to greet me with that hammer you like to carry.'

'Now then Inspector, we are all friends here, and you should know I only use that in self-defence.' A smile came across his face as he adjusted his position, sitting forward, one hand on his knee, the other on a glass filled with ale on top of the bar.

The place was dark inside, with little lighting on purpose, making it harder for any prying eyes to see what was going on. It stank of smoke, stale drink and had little decoration, with only a few basic tables and chairs scattered about. It was rough and ready, with no frills or pretence about it, which was why it attracted the type of clientele it did. Abberline found the wooden flooring sticky to walk on, a combination of booze and blood from the previous evening's festivities, as he made his way across the room. Abberline knew this was Keane's domain. He owned it and ran things the way he wanted, and as long as the punters were buying and paying for his women, he was a happy man. Known to conduct his other business interests at the back in a small office with a door leading out to the courtyard, Abberline eyed him with deep suspicion and caution. Keane was reported to be unpredictable, aggressive, and not averse to killing anyone who got in his way, even a police officer.

'Just on your own then. No Miss Hargreaves hiding behind you, like?'

'No.' He paused, 'she had other things to attend to.' Abberline clocked that Seamus Keane's network of informers had also told him of Elsbeth's involvement, which could put her in danger as well.

'What a disappointment; I hear she's a fine-looking woman. Has she given you a private session yet, Inspector?' He laughed, taking another swig of beer.

Abberline ignored the comment.

'Let's stick to why I'm here, Mr Keane, shall we?'

'What can I do for you?' Keane, a burly man heavily tattooed on both arms and neck. He wore dark trousers and red braces over a shirt that was partly open, revealing a further tattoo of a tall sailing ship; underneath it were the words "The Dunbrody". Abberline knew this was one of the vessels that took people from Ireland to America for a better life. But they were no more than coffin ships; overcrowding and disease killed many before reaching the promised land. He had lean, chiselled features with the scar running down from his left eye to his chin just as Polly Nichols had described in The Crown. Abberline guessed he was likely to be in his early to mid-thirties, with swept-back black hair and deep-set brown eyes that held no emotion. Keane had a coldness about him, and Abberline had no doubt that he was capable of anything.

'Mary Quinn lodged here under your roof. She was murdered in an alleyway on the other side of The North Laine.'

'What's that got to do with me? She likely ripped someone off. Got what she deserved, I'd say. We live in dangerous times, Inspector.'

Abberline didn't rise to the bait but remained calm. He was well aware he was in a dangerous place, on his own with a very violent man.

'She owed you money, Mr Keane. So, I would say from that, and what I've heard about anyone owing Seamus Keane, it has much to do with you.'

Abberline watched him carefully for anything that might suggest Keane was uncomfortable in the conversation.

'Look, Inspector, I'm trying to help you here, so I am. She lived here sometimes and sometimes not. When she did, she would pay her way on her back like the others, or she'd be out on the street. She knew how it worked. My world is a world of endless possibilities, Inspector; if you have the money to pay, I provide a service for anyone, especially for men of position and wealth who don't want their wives finding out. They come here knowing it's safe. They tell me their needs, and I provide them with whatever girl or boy they want. They take em upstairs, do whatever they like, knowing that good old Seamus will clear up after. Things go on here; you couldn't even dream of…Then they trot back to their big houses, respectable jobs, doting wives. Some of whom believe their husbands have been at work, while others turn a blind eye, knowing better than to ask if they want to avoid being thrown out.'

Abberline listened to Keane and could see how he had built the reputation he had. People were just a commodity to him, and if that commodity got damaged or became a liability, he would quickly replace it without a second thought. He could see how someone who crossed him could end up.

'I understand from a good source that Mary Quinn was on her way to ask you for more time to pay the money she owed you for her rent the night she was killed. So, I think you knew she couldn't pay, and that incensed you. The great Seamus Keane had to wait for his money. You were not going to be made a fool of. You know what these women are like, and you wanted to send a clear message to anyone thinking of doing the same. An argument could, therefore, be made that you waited for her outside The Crown, followed her, then cut her to pieces as a lesson to others to pay their debts on time. From where I'm standing, that's very plausible, and it gives you both motive and opportunity, Mr Keane.'

'I resent that, Inspector. Where's your evidence, eh? Oh, what, wait. Is it because I'm Irish, run a pub, and I have a bit of a reputation? How many thousands like that are on this fair isle, eh, or in this town? That don't make me a killer. I'm a businessman, I look after me stock, Inspector. I don't damage it, especially if it has some use to me.' Keane's voice changed and became aggressive, standing up from his seat and pushing his chest out to make sure Abberline got the point.

'Do you have any witnesses who can vouch for your where-abouts the night of her murder, Mr Keane?'

'Here all night, I'm here every night; ask anyone,' he replied under his breath, taking a sip from his beer.

'I don't doubt that. I'm sure there would be a queue of will-ing people to swear on their mothers' lives if only they knew who their mothers were.'

Keane put his glass back on the bar, scowling at Abberline. 'Anyways, as I heard it, she was sliced up.' He moved closer to Abberline to whisper in his ear, even though there were only two of them in the room.

'All that blood everywhere, half her guts hanging out, no, not me. Too messy. Now, if it were me, and I'm not saying it was, of course, she'd be in one of those empty kegs out back sealed up nice and tight, floating out to sea; no one would find her. If it were me, Inspector.' Keane stepped back, smiling.

'You don't like people owing you, especially the likes of

Mary Quinn. She disrespected you by thinking she could just fob you off. That's why you killed her.' Abberline's tone also switched up a gear, now far more forceful. 'I know your type. You can't let someone like her get away with anything that makes you look weak. Suddenly, others hear of it and start doing the same. Soon, you lose your grip, and another gang knocks you off your perch. You, *Mr Keane*, have a name in the criminal world to maintain and are not averse to using extreme violence to protect that.'

'Why would I kill her? How exactly would that solve me problems, Inspector? I would lose any chance of getting me money she owed and any future earning potential. So, I would be cutting me nose off to spite me face, I would.'

'Your temper may well have got the better of you, and maybe you didn't want it to look like a common prostitute could run rings around you.'

'As I said before, I'm a businessman, and her type are two a dozen, so they are. But she was in demand so I would have made sure she fully understood paying me late came with a penalty. She would have received a good beating but nothing else you hear. She was making me money. No, I'm not your man, Inspector. I didn't kill her.'

Abberline still wasn't convinced but moved on to the next question. 'Do you know, or have you ever known a Rosie Meeks, who worked in the baker's in North Laine?'

'Bloody hell, come on Inspector.'

'Just answer the question, Keane, or we can do it in a more formal setting if you wish.'

'I didn't know her. Too fat, too old to be of any use to me. Me punters like them as young as I can get. From what I read; the Meeks woman was well past her prime. However, there are some sick people out there who'll do anything. Some police-men I know, not a million miles from here, use my facilities, you know, present company excluded, of course, Inspector.'

Abberline, disgusted and angry at what he was insinuating, continued.

'You're a nasty piece of work, Keane, a bully, pimp, and smuggler, and God knows what else, but I know you have killed, and I know you have done it for a lot less than what Mary Quinn was indebted to you for. So, we'll have another chat, but next time, we will be at Brighton Police Station. So, make sure you don't disappear, Mr Keane.'

'Oh, don't you go worrying yourself, Inspector? I'll be seeing you, that I will. By the way, be sending me regards to Detective Rawlings when you see him, will ya now.'

Abberline left the pub and wondered what Keane meant by his direct reference to Rawlings. He had endured enough of Seamus Keane; he needed to wash the stink off him. After, he would ensure he followed up on this criminal's story. Keane was a killer and extremely violent, certainly capable of killing Mary Quinn. Now, he had to see if there was any connection to Rosie Meeks, but for that, he would need help.

EIGHTEEN

Abberline walked back along the seafront to the sound of gulls squawking above to his lodgings at Regency Square, where he was staying for the duration of the investigation. The broody, slate-grey skies and strong wind whipped salt air against his face, reddening his skin to a healthy glow. The sea, which was at high tide, angrily churned over grey-green waves, morphing one into another. Further out, he could see a fleet of small fishing boats braving the elements, appearing and disappearing into the troughs of the rollers like tiny corks bobbing about. As the waves reached the shoreline and the depth became shallow, water built up from behind, building them upwards into giant walls. White foam formed at the tops like horses as they thundered down the beach, spraying small pebbles and shells into the air, some landing on the promenade where he walked. He remembered the story of the Roman Emperor Caligula and his war against the sea and thought how he would have loved this moment collecting Neptune's treasure.

He followed the wooden railings until he reached a new landmark for the town, the West Pier, which stood directly opposite Regency Square. Two large turrets on either side of the pier's entrance greeted the visitor, with the Union Jack flying high and proudly upon each roof – a wonder of both

British eccentricity and engineering – Abberline marvelled at its construction of wood and iron stretching out in the depths of the sea from the land. He once studied its designer Eugenius Birch who lived in Shoreditch, London, and had designed the one thousand, one hundred and eleven foot structure, which had cost Brighton twenty-seven thousand pounds. It was commissioned to attract visitors to the seashore and show them that the town was good in fair and bad weather, and they could enjoy the benefits of fresh sea air at any time of the year.

As he approached the first stage, a wide area of wooden boards with cast iron railings going around the outside. Numerous wrought iron lattice girders held up the pier, drilled into the seabed, and welded together to give the strength to support the promenade above and the people who walked on it. Lampposts fuelled by gas with twisted metal posts followed the length of the pier, each topped with round opaque white glass covers to encourage people in the day and depth of winter evenings when the light would fade early. Abberline walked past, crossing the road, weaving around the horse-drawn cabs and over the Regency Square. He continued around a large, grassed rectangle, used as a picnic area in better weather, surrounded by black railings, to his rented room at number nine Brighthelmstone House.

He walked into the building, a tall regency house set on five levels with balconies at the front, reaching the third floor landing he entered his room. It was small but warm, with a coal fire ready to be lit, and always kept clean and tidy. On one side, there was a single bed with a wash basin beside it. A small sash window looking out onto the green gave some natural light and a rectangular pine table to eat and work at with a dresser for his clothes next to it. It was perfect for his needs and didn't require any upkeep, which suited his requirements adequately. He was tired from the day. He removed his coat, scarf, and jacket and placed them neatly on the bed, ready for folding and hanging away. Taking some paper and pen from a drawer under the table, he started writing a letter to his wife.

My dearest Emma,

I hope this letter finds you well and you are enjoying the peace and quiet without me and my annoying ways you have so gracefully come to understand. I miss you and our evening chats by the fire, exchanging stories from the day's events and having your insight, which I love to listen to. I have no other person I would trust so much with my work than you. Brighton is an affable town; my lodgings are comfortable and local to the station and my investigations. The case is a difficult one, and I have never before seen such violence towards another as I have witnessed here. I will, of course, spare you the grim details, I would not want you to suffer the loss of sleep I have endured. But suffice it to say we are dealing with a person of such depravity and extreme hatred it seems, towards women, that there appears to be no bounds as to the brutality they will use.

The local Detective is a man named Rawlings, who, for all purposes, has been demoted and as you can imagine is far from pleased at this development. I have also met Miss Hargreaves, the local woman who so openly criticised the police for their inaction. Monro wanted me to meet with her and be seen to have her on side rather than an enemy, as we have had enough bad press on the crimes already. She is a formidable person who you would admire for her character. Strong, educated, and independently wealthy, she has her own mind. I find her belief in the spiritual work, which I know your strong faith would also find hard to understand, to be the most difficult. She has visions of people who have passed and whom she says appear before her, which is not something I can give any credence to. But there have been occasions where I have to question this, as she does possess a sense of things not seen by the eye, which I cannot explain, and that does perplex me.

The killer is cunning and intelligent; of that, I have no doubt. There is a methodology that eludes me, his thinking, his motive. There appears to be little and no connection between the victims that I can find. So, it seems that the killings are random, and that, my dear, concerns me greatly as there is no reason for them other than hate and rage.

I fear that this maniac's work is not over, and there is more to come. The people of this town are living in fear and are, rightly, terrified. I hope I will not let them down, that I can prevent another death from occurring. The person responsible for these atrocities, I fear, has lost their mind and any humanity they may have once possessed. Whoever they once were has been replaced by a monster.

I will write again soon. I have included my address so you can reply to me if you have time. Take good care of yourself and know I think of you often.

Your loving husband,
Frederick

NINETEEN

Elsbeth received word from Abberline to meet him outside the bakery where Rosie Meeks had been murdered. She checked herself in the mirror, placing a tortoiseshell grip to hold the back of her hair in a bun. She made sure that her black lace dress, which she preferred, was sitting correctly and then went back down the hallway to retrieve her coat, ready to leave the house.

She was still concerned after seeing the ghost of Rosie Meeks at the mortuary and knowing that her spirit was trapped. Rosie was locked in this world, unable to move on until her killer had been caught, and Elsbeth felt a responsibility for that, even if Abberline didn't believe anything to do with the supernatural. She had to find a way to release Rosie and Mary Quinn from their eternal unrest. She stopped for a moment, seeing their faces; they haunted her waking mind and, in her dreams, desperate to find peace, to pass over but unable to. Both chained to this world by the hand of the killer who still roamed free.

A knock at the front of the house snapped her back to reality and announced that the cab had arrived to take her to the meeting with Abberline. At the front door she found a small, dishevelled boy, no more than eight years of age, standing on the steps with a small, plain cardboard box tied up with a string in a neat bow.

'The man, Miss, he said to give this to you, said it was important, like. Said I had to wait until you opened it.'

Elsbeth looked at the boy, then beyond him, to see who he was talking about, but there was nobody else there.

'What man would that be?' Elsbeth smiled warmly, not wanting to frighten the child away.

'Don't know him, Miss. He just told me to knock at this door, and make sure I gave you what he sent.'

'What did he look like, this man?' Elsbeth asked.

'Couldn't see too much as the gentleman was inside a cab, in the corner. He looked thin, wore a cloak of some sort, posh like. Didn't say nothing, his driver said make sure I give it to you.'

Elsbeth was intrigued by what the boy was saying. The lad pushed the small box towards Elsbeth, who took hold of it while he stood waiting as instructed.

'Well, seeing as you have gone to so much trouble, we had better open it then, hadn't we?'

Inside, there was neatly folded white paper; taking it out, Elsbeth slowly unfolded it. A lock of bright red hair was enclosed, matted with blood, along with the note. Elsbeth held the lock of hair, examined it, and then traced the writing with her finger. The words were a deep, claret red. It was written in blood. She felt dizzy, feeling she might collapse; carefully lowered herself down to sit on the step.

She found her mind's eye rushing down streets, the names in large letters: Bucks Row, Mitre Square, Whitechapel. Faces of unknown women flashed through her mind: dark alleyways, smog, screams, then someone under a streetlamp, a man with his back to her, a woman's body at his feet, the breathing heavy from the kill, wild like a rabid beast. She could feel him consumed with hate as he started to turn round. Without warning, she gasped as if drowning, coughing and desperate for air, she quickly tried to regain her composure. The images stopped, and the figure stepped back into the shadows. She awoke from the vision and was back outside her house, looking out onto the street. The young delivery boy had gone, the paper message and hair still clutched tightly in her hand.

I'm watching you
See you soon
Jack.

TWENTY

Abberline took the note and lock of hair from Elsbeth, examining them for every detail. Their warm breaths vapourised into whips of cold air as they stood outside the bakery.

'Did you notice anyone hanging about when you arrived, Inspector?'

'No, why?'

'Just a feeling, that's all. It doesn't matter; after this, it's made me more wary of my surroundings, that's all.' Elsbeth didn't want to say for sure without any proof, but she had a bad feeling, a sense that maybe she had been followed. 'There's something else: the lock of hair when I touched it, I...I knew it belonged to Mary Quinn. It's her hair.'

Abberline looked at the matted lock. 'We'll get Cripps to confirm, but it does look like the right colour.'

So pleased you got my note, Elsbeth, and the hair I ripped out her head. A voice came into Elsbeth's thoughts.

'Look, it's probably for the best, given the current situation, but keep this to yourself for now, don't trust anyone,' Abberline continued, turning the paper again to check both sides. 'There is no mistaking it; blood has been used to write the message and signature. But don't forget that these murders, along with your own views, have been reported in the press.

Anyone trying to undermine the investigation could have written this and put a lock of hair in with the note. The press is more capable of doing this to further their own agenda.'

'Do you really think journalists would stoop so low?' Elsbeth asked.

'I've had dealings with them in London. If they feel things are not moving along the way they want, they have been known to invent stories. It increases the circulation of the paper and the profits for the owners. However, what is more concerning is their control of the narrative and the sway of public opinion. In addition, I have learned that the local Brighton MP's wife, Amelia Stanton, made a statement to the press, criticising the case and making it harder for us to catch the person. Do not underestimate the power of the printed word.' Abberline folded the note and hair back up, placing it in his coat pocket.

'It could be genuine and from the killer. I saw things when I touched the lock of hair... terrible things. He signed it, *Jack*. Why do that if he didn't want me to know it's from him?'

'I know you believe you saw things, but I must work with facts and what I know to be true. It might be from the culprit, but I doubt it. I will keep it for the time being, but I have to be honest; I give it little credibility on its own. Detective Rawlings will speak to the press later today at Brighton Police Station. I've asked him to provide them with an update. Maybe then we will see if any of them seem to know more than they should.'

'Women don't feel secure in this town. I don't feel safe, and all you have so far is Mary Quinn's landlord, who, yes, is a sadistic, violent thug and had a motive to kill her, but can the same be said for Rosie Meeks? Seamus Keane said to you that he didn't even know her. So where does that leave us with two women dead, Inspector?'

'Us?' Abberline questioned. 'No, not *us*, Miss Hargreaves. You mean me and the rest of the constabulary appointed by law to investigate and bring this felon to justice, and that's what I intend to do, I can assure you. We need more than spirit boards, séance evenings, and the dead telling us; we require facts and evidence that will stand up in court. Then, and only then will the person caught for these crimes pay for their actions at the end of a rope. The people of this town want justice and for justice to be seen to be done.'

'Do not misjudge me or my gift, Inspector. I know you pay little credence to my profession, but you should keep an open mind. If you don't apprehend this maniac soon, I have no doubt your superiors will make sure it's your head on a plate.' Elsbeth wanted to make sure the point struck home, frustrated by his mockery and dismissal of her abilities.

Abberline knew Monro held a deep dislike for him and would be only too happy to levy the blame onto him if he were to fail. Abberline was a policeman and deeply suspicious of Elsbeth's psychic claims. He couldn't see how it could be anything other than wishful thinking. It went against everything he believed and had been trained in. He had grown to like her company, but he couldn't bring himself to believe in such nonsense. It would always be a barrier between them. He had been instructed to keep her on his side, so he would go along with it for now. He chose not to inflame the matter by disagreeing any further, deciding it more prudent to focus back on the matter at hand.

'Look, Elsbeth, Seamus Keane is also a compulsive liar; anything he says can't be trusted. We only have his word that he didn't know Rosie Meeks, but he absolutely had a relationship of one kind or another with Mary Quinn. So, until we understand more, he remains a suspect, but that stays between us at this stage. If I arrest him now to pacify my bosses and public opinion, we will have a mob baying for his blood, and I have to be sure. Or, as you said, it will be my head on the block. But one thing is certain: he knows about you, so Keane could also be behind this note, to muddy the waters and throw us off the scent. He would have had access to her hair, seeing as Mary Quinn was staying on his premises and working for him. As I said, he is capable of anything.' Abberline turned and placed the key in the lock to the bakery, where Rosie Meeks had been savagely murdered, and entered inside.

Elsbeth took a moment before joining him and looked up at the apartment. The blooded handprint of Rosie Meeks could be seen, stained on the glass. An oil lamp had been left on, yellow hue emanating from it, and for a split second, she thought she saw a shadow pass across the window. A smash of glass rang out in the street behind her; she turned quickly. She had felt the presence of someone, but then, out of a darkened doorway, a cat hissed and darted across the road.

She promptly followed Abberline into the premises; silhouettes of empty shelves like hungry mouths greeted her, the owners unable to return after the terrible events. It was cold, dusty, and smelled of decay; the silence was only broken by the sound of the bell above the door that rang as it opened. They stood in near darkness, with a half-broken streetlamp outside throwing a small amount of light into the shop. Abberline lit a match as they moved slowly toward the stairs at the back, the wood creaked as he put his weight onto the first step. Stopping in their tracks, the pair heard footsteps walking across the floor above. They were not alone.

TWENTY-ONE

Detective Rawlings took his place in the Brighton Police Station mess hall. He knew the next thirty minutes would be testing; he looked out onto the sea of faces, some reporters he was acquainted with, others he had never met. He had taken questions from press meetings before, but they were always uncomfortable, noisy affairs. People pushing and shoving, accusations of incompetence and criticism of the police being shouted out. Abberline had decided not to attend even though he was leading the investigation, which Rawlings knew would not go unnoticed. He had informed Rawlings that, in his opinion, his time was better spent in the field than speaking at an event like this. This irritated Rawlings and made him feel even more marginalised than he already did. He had not only been demoted, but now was to be the whipping boy for this mob as well.

The room filled with even more newspapermen forcing their way in through the doors, standing shoulder to shoulder; Rawlings realised by the sheer number present that the story had outgrown the local paper, and had gained the attention of more extensive publications. Containment was now impossible; Rawlings smiled to himself; this was the last thing Scotland Yard wanted. Abberline would be held responsible, and not being here to defuse the situation would hopefully mean him being taken off the case. The noise had grown; notebooks waving, foot stamping, and hands clapping, the pack restless and impatient. Rawlings extended his right arm up to address them. 'Now, now then, gentlemen, please calm yourselves, or this meeting will, I promise you, come to a very abrupt end. Order now!' He yelled again. The commotion slowly decreased to a low, disgruntled murmur.

'Listen, this is how this is going to work. Those who know me know that I will speak first, then and only after I have finished, if we have time, can you ask any questions. Is that understood, gentlemen?'

Jeering and more objections to his rules followed, with a flurry of other protests.

'That's the way it is going to be, or we close this now, and you can all leave. It's your choice.' Rawlings raised his voice again and waited, knowing they would eventually have to let go of their egos, stop the tantrums, and settle down. The room fell quiet as Rawlings continued, but he knew only too well they would have the better of him, and any control was temporary.

'So now, as you know, two murders have occurred in and around The North Laine of Brighton. The first victim was eighteen-year-old Mary Quinn, who worked at The Crown.'

'When you mean working, don't you mean as a prostitute?' a voice shouted from the back of the room.

Rawlings, ignoring the intervention for the moment, proceeded with the rest of his brief. 'The second victim, Rosie Meeks, around thirty years of age, was a single mother who worked at a bakery. As far as we know, there was no known association between the two victims. We don't know why these women were specifically targeted, but the manner in which they were killed, the mutilation and the level of anger born out in the attack, and the fact they were both women, it is, of course, understandable why women in the town are feeling concerned. But let me make it clear,' he paused. 'Let me make it clear, gentlemen, I want to assure everyone we are staying vigilant, and I have every available officer patrolling the streets day and night. No one should feel unsafe.' The laughter and shouting from the room was deafening.

Rawlings smirked at the baying crowd as he continued his brief. 'As for Mary Quinn, I am not prepared to comment on her employment other than we know that she was working the night of her murder at the public house. After she had finished for the evening, against the advice of her fellow workers, she decided to walk alone, taking a shortcut through the alleyway to her lodgings in Ship Street. We know that the urgency of this decision was made in some part due to money owed; we believe rent to her landlord, Seamus Keane, an individual well-known to the police.'

A journalist at the front baited Rawlings. 'Are we talking about the same violent criminal Seamus Keane that runs women for sex in this town? Why hasn't he been arrested? If she owed that crazy Fenian money, she was as good as dead, and you know that.'

The crowd erupted again, yelling and stamping their feet so hard it reverberated, shaking the room.

Rawlings, in response, put his hand out to suppress the racket, waiting for them to cease. 'We have interviewed all those who saw Mary Quinn that evening, including Mr Keane, and at this point, we are not making any arrests. But let me stress…They have all been made fully aware that we may well require them for further questioning, and they are not allowed to leave town while our investigations continue, and that includes Mr Keane.'

'So, he's off the hook then cos we all know that he has you lot in his pockets. Ain't that the case, Inspector Rawlings?' More yells of police corruption followed.

'No,' Rawlings snapped back with authority. 'It absolutely is not the case, and if you continue to make such false allegations, I will arrest you myself, and you can consider your position in a cell. Everyone at this point is a suspect, including Mr Keane; no one is above the law.'

A roar of laughter filled the room.

'Unless money is changing hands,' a voice somewhere in the crowd said, which Rawlings disregarded.

'James Harper, *Croydon Gazette*,' a well-dressed man in his late twenties shouted out from the middle of the crowd, waving a document, catching Rawling's attention. 'This document I hold in my hands is from your own Brighton Coroner, Mr Cripps, and covers the postmortem of both victims and makes a sickening read. Cripps says in his own writing that the wounds inflicted on both women were so horrific that it was beyond anything he had ever seen. I put it to you, that this was not the work of a jealous boyfriend or husband; but a lunatic driven by anger and hatred for these women on a scale we have not seen,' the young reporter called out.

'The report, I agree, contains injuries beyond anything any of us has witnessed before, they are deeply disturbing, and it would have made our jobs a lot easier if you lot hadn't gone and printed it on the front bloody page so every man and his dog could see it including the killer—'

Before Rawlings could continue, another journalist spoke out.

'—Well, maybe you lot should do your jobs better. Mary Quinn was stabbed twenty nine times and pieces of her taken for Christ's sake! There wasn't a part of her body left untouched. And the images of Rosie Meeks, ripped open like a slab of meat, her organs cut away and taken, the pictures too horrific even to print—'

'—Leaving her son, an eight-year-old boy, without his

mother and in the workhouse, so what are you doing about it?' a local journalist standing near to the front asked.

The rabble again all started screaming for action at Rawlings.

'I understand your frustration. Every officer feels the same, I can assure you. We will leave no stone unturned, mark my words.' Rawlings drove his point home by hammering his fist onto the desk.

'Women don't feel safe; nobody feels safe in this town, and you clowns are still no closer to catching anyone. Is it the same killer, or are there two? When will you have someone in custody, or is it the fact that you lot are not up to the job? And where is Abberline? Why isn't he here to tell us himself, eh? He's supposed to be in charge, and all we get is his monkey.' A crescendo of laughter and chimp impressions quickly followed.

Rawlings was becoming increasingly uncomfortable at the continued assault on him and just wanted the whole thing to end. 'Inspector Abberline is out in the field doing his job. He has asked me to let you know that on this occasion, he felt his time would be better spent in the detection and apprehension of this criminal rather than attending a press conference.'

'Sure he is, with the help of psychic Elsbeth Hargreaves. Has it come to this? Not even the *great* Scotland Yard can work it out, so they send for a psychic to solve the case for them.' A man was raising both arms up to the ceiling in exasperation. The room ignited in howls, mocking Rawlings again, who felt he was becoming the scapegoat.

'We have not employed Miss Hargreaves,' Rawlings fought back. 'She is not part of this investigation, and any assistance she may or may not be offering is her own doing as a private individual. Also, it is not the practice for Scotland Yard or any other force to seek the assistance of anyone associated with such a profession. I hope that makes her involvement clear, gentlemen.'

'You lot couldn't catch a cold, so stop denying it and telling us things we already know. The problem is you don't have anything, and in the meantime, this madman is still out there, none of you are any closer to catching him?' a reporter from the *Brighton Herald* shouted, 'the wife of our own Member of Parliament, Amelia Stanton, has gone on public record since these murders and insisted that more competent officers be assigned to the case. She has said, and I quote "*If the current investigation led by Inspector Abberline is incapable of giving us an arrest for these monstrous killings of two innocent females, one just eighteen years of age, then we need to look at bringing in people who can. Women need to feel safe, and that right should be extended to all women, whatever class or background. That is why we have a police force; is it not for the protection of its people? The person responsible is an opportunist of the worst kind and preys on women because they are unable to defend themselves. He is a coward who hates women, most likely because he is incapable of having sexual relations with one. In my opinion, he has limited intelligence, and I am at a loss as to why he is still at large. This monster is a stain on society. He needs to be caught, and justice needs to be served.*"'

Rawlings noticed the change. It was becoming more hostile. They wanted answers, their readers wanted answers, and all he could do was tell them what they already knew. Abberline had thrown him to the wolves so he could go to hell in a basket.

'It is, of course, Mrs Stanton's right to make her feelings known if she wishes to do so, but she is not, with respect, aware of all the facts in this case as many have not been made public for obvious reasons.' Rawlings had received no warning or prior knowledge of the article but had to continue. 'We are exhausting all possibilities and knocking on every door, making an arrest likely. The motive is still unclear,' Rawlings answered. 'It might be money owed in Mary Quinn's case. We don't know. But as you can imagine, given the nature of the crimes and the level of injury sustained by the victims, especially Rosie Meeks, someone, somewhere knows who this is. Someone is shielding them. It could be a son, husband, brother, or lover. I stress again, gentlemen, somebody in this town knows, and I urge them to come forward immediately, so we can put a stop to this.'

A scuffle suddenly broke out at the doors into the room with Rawlings ordering the fighting to stop. A young police officer pushed his way through. 'I have an urgent communication for you, sir,' he said, thrusting Rawlings a note, and before he could stop him, the young officer proceeded aloud to inform him, and the rest of the room what it contained.

'It's Joseph Stanton. He says his wife didn't return home last evening and wants you down there to find out what's happened to her,' the officer, out of breath, finished blurting the message.

Rawling's face turned ashen white in shock, as he read the note to confirm what had been said. The room descended into a frenzy, with questions and insults coming from all directions.

'This got anything to do with the murders. Is she another victim?' a person said from the back of the room.

'Maybe she should have kept her posh mouth shut?' Another shouted as the rabble descended into more yelling and shouting.

Rawlings, still reeling, knew he had to try and calm the situation down and minimise damage, he knew in that instant if he was wrong, his career could be over. But he had to say something; he also knew Abberline would be annoyed at not being informed first of this development as he continued his damage control strategy. 'Joseph Stanton is a highly respected and a serving member of parliament, so please leave him and his family alone and let us do our job.'

The crowd taunted the detective as he tried to calm the rabble.

'You can't even find your own shoelaces, but I bet you'll put her highness at the top of the list, seeing she's the wife of a member of parliament.'

Rawlings ignored the statement. 'I...I will keep you all updated on any events, but let's not jump to any conclusions until we have all the information. That is the end of this briefing, gentlemen. I thank you all for your time.' With that, he gathered his papers.

The reporters all tried to leave, attempting to squeeze through the door at the same time and head back to their editors with an explosive headline for the next edition that Rawlings knew they would exploit.

As he left the room, he wondered if he had said the right thing, if Amelia Stanton would soon return. But something came over him like a dark cloud that had blotted out the light, an eclipse of his worst fears. His body felt cold, his stomach tightened, and the back of his mouth went dry as the possibility dawned on him.

What if he was wrong? What if she wasn't coming back? Someone had her, or worse? What then? He needed to speak to Abberline as soon as possible.

TWENTY-TWO

Abberline held his finger to his lips, indicating to Elsbeth to keep quiet as they made their way up the stairs to the first floor, to the place of Rosie Meeks' murder. Elsbeth lifted her dress slightly and followed Abberline's steps, almost on tiptoes to be as silent as possible. They stopped just before the landing, a dark and foreboding passage, and waited, neither saying a word. Abberline looked back towards Elsbeth; then, as he made the last step, the floorboard squeaked. Elsbeth stood behind him; her heart raced as she wondered whose footsteps they had heard. *They could be armed, could be that the killer came back for something.* All these thoughts and more darted back and forth through her mind as Abberline slowly turned the small brass handle and carefully opened the door. Elsbeth held her breath.

A crack of light came through as Abberline crept into the room, pushing the door back further, the hinges creaking as he did. There was an overpowering stench of a rotting corpse, even though the body of Rosie Meeks had been removed to the morgue some days ago. The foul smell had seeped into the walls and plaster of the room, letting no one who entered be of any doubt about what had occurred. Elsbeth found it hard not to gag as she followed closely behind.

'Police!' Abberline shouted. 'You are in a restricted area. Come out and show yourself. I have more officers coming; best you do as I say.' Abberline drew a small wooden truncheon from his coat pocket and held it tight in his right hand. He turned to Elsbeth and whispered for her to stay by the door, in case she needed a quick way out.

The light was not great, just a small gas ceiling lamp illuminating the front lounge and back bedroom. The owners, returning home after a trip away, had discovered the dismembered body of Rosie Meeks. The horrific sight meant they could not step back into the property, unable to erase from their memory what their eyes had seen, the experience too traumatic. Elsbeth, frightened and worried for them both, did as Abberline asked and waited by the open door. She watched as Abberline moved slowly and cautiously, like a cat, into the centre of the front room.

It was sparse, just two old brown leather armchairs stained and torn, each with a hand-knitted throw in red and green hung over the back, and a small open fireplace that had not been cleaned; ash and spent coal still in the grate. To the right of the room, under the only window, sat a small pine table and two basic wooden chairs at either end. Abberline could see towards the back of the bedroom and the blood-soaked mattress where the victim had been killed. He swallowed, moving forward, trying to sense or see any movement. The room had been divided in the middle by a brass rail that ran across wall to wall. Large, dulled brass rings supported a heavy red patterned fabric that ran down to the floor and had been pushed over to the left side to hang free. For a moment, he thought he saw the curtain twitch. Something behind it. He raised his weapon, ready to strike, got closer, and watched intently. As he reached for the curtain, he held out his free hand and very slowly gripped the material before he threw it back in one quick motion. 'Police,' he shouted, his heart pounding. But there was nobody there.

Elsbeth moved away from the safety of the only exit, following him into the room.

'Somebody is in here; we both heard the…' But before Abberline could finish the sentence, the door to the room slammed shut. Someone had been hiding behind it. A man shot across the floor, grabbing Elsbeth from behind and wrapping his arm tightly around her throat. She struggled to get free as Abberline moved towards them both.

'Nah, you don't, or I'll snap her pretty neck. I will. Stay where you are.'

'I'm an Inspector with Scotland Yard; I'm here investigating the murder of Rosie Meeks. It would be best for you, if you let the lady go and surrender yourself to me.'

'I had nothin to do with Rosie's death, nothin you 'ear, I… I needed to see where it happened, that's all.' The man spoke with a northern accent, was middle-aged and, not more than five foot two or three, had a slim build, with thinning brown hair and smelled of oil and coal. The bristles of his unshaven chin rubbed against Elsbeth's pale skin.

Abberline could see Elsbeth struggling, trying to free herself, but the man's grip increased.

'I warned you not to try anythin, didn't I, eh?' He yelled against her ear.

Abberline wanted to keep the man talking, he was obviously dangerous. 'What relationship did you have with the deceased?'

'She was a friend, got to know her from comin to the shop.'

Abberline wanted to calm things down, so he lowered his voice. 'Ok, stay where you are. I'm here officially, and you're not supposed to be here. Understand this isa crime area.'

'I ain't goin nowhere,' he screamed back at Abberline.

Abberline had almost got close enough to risk a lunge for him. He continued to talk, trying to distract the man.

'You know, if you hurt her, I promise you will not see the light of day for a very long time. Now, let her go.'

Elsbeth saw an opportunity, bent her right arm, and in a swinging motion, twisted her body round and, with some force, connected her elbow with the man's head. He yelped in pain. At the same time, she used her left leg to kick backwards into his shin with her boot, hard enough for him to release his grip. Abberline took his chance too and grappled with the assailant. They fell to the floor; Abberline dropped his truncheon, seeing it roll under the table. Several punches were exchanged as he tried to restrain him, but the man was as slippery as an eel, landing a punch on Abberline's nose.

It disabled him long enough for the attacker to run as fast as he could out of the room, down the stairs and into the labyrinth of streets that made up The North Laine. He had gone; all that was left was the sound of the bell ringing above the front door as it swung back and forth, marking his escape.

Elsbeth helped Abberline to his feet and offered him a lace handkerchief from her cuff for the blood coming from his nose. Abberline thanked her, and checked if she was ok, while reaching for his truncheon from under the table.

'We're not going after him?' Elsbeth asked, while noticing a small round object on the floor.

'No, be like hunting a needle in a haystack in these streets; they're like rat runs.'

'Who was he then? Why was he really here?' Elsbeth asked. 'Do you think it was the killer?'

'I don't know, we have to find him first.' Elsbeth listened as she walked over to the item that had caught her attention on the floor.

'Would this help? It must have fallen off during the

struggle. It caught my eye and seemed out of place.' Elsbeth bent down and then handed the object to Abberline.

Abberline examined the small pin badge that had come away from the assaulter's clothing. It was round with the words London Brighton and South Coast Railway around the outside. Its face was divided into four sections displaying the heraldic alms of each region the railway served: London, Brighton, The Coastal Towns, known as the Cinque Ports, and Portsmouth.

'Is it significant?' Elsbeth asked.

'It tells us it meant something to him, and most likely where he will be.' Abberline handed the badge back to Elsbeth to see for herself.

'He works the railways.' Elsbeth declared, looking at it carefully.

'We need to go, now.' Abberline, already halfway down the stairs, slowed so she could catch up.

'Where to?'

'Brighton Station. But we need to make a quick stop first.'

Elsbeth shivered. Somewhere in the shadows that criss-crossed the darkened alleys of this town, a killer watched and waited. She looked over again at the handprint left by Rosie on the glass. The presence of a restless spirit was in the room, the pain and sadness it carried with it. Elsbeth took one last look and silently wished the spirit of Rosie Meeks peace, before closing the door behind her for the last time.

TWENTY-THREE

Seamus Keane sat in his office at the back of The Black Star pub, his feet on the desk, leaning back in his chair as there was a knock at the door. Keane said nothing and waited for it to open, knowing who was behind it.

'Ah. If it isn't Detective Rawlings. What can we be doing for you?'

'You know why I'm here, Keane? I've got this Abberline from Scotland Yard down here taking over the investigation into these murders. One of them, Mary Quinn, who worked for you as a prostitute.'

'Well, as I remember, not such a long time ago, you taking advantage of the same yourself and ya didn't even have to pay for the privilege? And, talking of payment, I'm wondering where my benefit of this little arrangement is with you. I pay for information and protection, but all I get is you down here drinking my beer and expecting the merchandise for nothing, so you do.'

'I'm here to warn you, Keane, that your name is top of the list of suspects in both murders. You knew the Quinn girl. She owed you money; it seems everyone in this town owes you something.' Rawlings thought of the debt he owed this gangster and how his grip on him had tightened over time. He didn't like it.

'You accusing me of something here, Rawlings? I've met your Inspector Abberline; he came down here, so he did, nosing about, threatening this and that, telling me not to leave town. As if I would. This is my town anyways. Best if you and he remembers that. I told him what he wanted to hear, and that's that.'

'I know you, Keane. I know what you can do; I've seen with my own eyes how you dish out punishment. I covered up for you when you beat that girl to death in front of everyone in this very pub because she dared to argue with you. I could have watched you swing from the gallows for that, but I protected you. So, I have no doubt you could have killed the Quinn girl and, for all I know, the other one in the bakery. Sending a message to those trying to muscle in on what's yours, like them Newhaven boys, who would have your head on a spike in a heartbeat.'

Seamus Keane said nothing, watching Rawlings, he took his feet off the desk, slowly stood up, and walked round to face the detective face to face. He was good three inches taller than Rawlings, Keane leaned in.

'You're forgetting where you are, Detective? Who you're talkin' to? You work for me; I tell you what to do and what to think; in short, Detective, I own you. Believe me, you don't know what I am or am not capable of.' Keane's tone did not rise but had a fierceness to it, his eyes glistening, giving away the raging storm within.

Rawlings stepped back, sensing danger.

'Maybe, Rawlings, your Scotland Yard fella would like to know how you help keep me and my business interests safe. See how that does for your long-term prospects.' Keane's voice became louder. 'You better be off before I forget myself. You understand me?'

Rawlings turned away and made for the exit, seething, trying to figure out how to get himself out of the mess he was in. If Abberline ever found out he was on Keane's payroll, it would be his job, then prison, and a policeman inside would last less than a day.

Keane watched Rawlings as he reached the door, feeling nothing but contempt for him. He didn't like bent coppers. He saw him as weak and greedy, but he had many people in this town like him in his pocket, their snouts in his trough and Rawlings was just the same.

'Watch how you go now, Rawlings. It's dangerous out there. Wouldn't want any harm coming to you now.'

Rawlings looked back at Seamus Keane as he leaned against the bar, holding up a pint of beer with a broad smile across his face. He knew it was a veiled threat and thought of saying something but decided against it, but he also knew the day would come for Seamus Keane when there would be a reckoning. He closed the door behind him, stepped onto the street, pulled his collar up against the cold, and disappeared into the crowd.

TWENTY-FOUR

Abberline and Elsbeth arrived back at Brighton Police Station where they met Detective Rawlings in his office. Abberline told him about the incident at the bakery, and Rawlings updated them on the press conference and the disappearance of Amelia Stanton. It was a tense moment as Rawlings tried to explain his reasoning for playing down the disappearance of the politician's wife.

'So, what made you think that the police's view is that there is no connection to a prominent man's wife going missing and the case we're working on? We haven't even visited the house or spoken to her husband, and yet you have already ruled out any link? Maybe you have the same psychic abilities as Miss Hargreaves here; in fact, I'm of the opinion you two could form a double act. I work on facts and evidence. We never make assumptions– is that clear, Detective? Is that understood?' Abberline said, annoyed that Rawlings had gone against police protocol and made matters worse.

Rawlings was still not listening. 'Stanton's wife made this statement in the press. She has been very vocal about the killer, calling him a coward and probably unable to have a sexual relationship with women, which could easily make her a target.' Abberline continued.

'She went to the press as I did because, as women, it was the only way to get people to listen. Maybe she was just fed up with being ignored,' Elsbeth said.

Abberline looked over at Elsbeth before continuing. 'Now she suddenly goes missing. Don't you find that strange, because I do, Rawlings? Stanton is a serving government official; he won't keep quiet about his wife going missing, will he?'

Rawlings shook his head in disagreement. 'Women like her don't go missing, big house, rich husband. She'll turn up soon enough, tail between her legs, mark my words.'

'My God man, have you crawled out of a cave? She could be lying injured somewhere or worse,' Elsbeth snapped, giving Rawlings a disgusted look.

'What if you're wrong, Rawlings? Then, we look even more idiotic than we are already being portrayed,' Abberline continued. 'Sorry, no, I stand corrected. You will look even more stupid. I know the press, and if they smell a story, nothing will stop them from inventing and speculating, making it fit their narrative. In future, please say no comment on anything unless I tell you otherwise. Do you understand? We have to solve these two murders. Preferably without the press all over us making it even more difficult.'

Rawlings reluctantly agreed, but Abberline could see he was seething at being spoken to in such a manner, especially in front of Elsbeth. Abberline knew Rawlings hated having the case taken away from him and was set in his ways; but that was tough, he was in charge and Rawlings reported to him whether he liked it or not.

'I will visit the husband, Joseph Stanton, later, and you better hope his wife has reappeared. I want you to follow up on the lead we have on the Meeks murder.' Abberline then explained to Rawlings in more detail about the encounter at the bakery and the railway badge that was found after the altercation.

'I want you to take some men, go to Brighton Station and find this man. I have a description here, and this badge might give you some luck in finding him. I'm sure he's hiding there, so when you find him, arrest him and bring him here for questioning. Do not let him escape, is that understood?'

Rawlings, annoyed, left the office to collect two uniformed officers as instructed to conduct the search for the man in question.

Abberline rolled a large chalkboard over and started to write down the main points of the case so far.

'Do you trust Rawlings to find this man?' Elsbeth asked.

'I have no choice; I need people on the ground. If this man is our killer, we need to apprehend him soon. The press will love the fact we had a suspect and let him get away.' Abberline was still reflecting on his conversation with Seamus Keane regarding Rawlings. It bothered him. Keane was more than capable of bending officers to his way of thinking, especially if there was a financial incentive. There was widespread corruption in the force, and he didn't need an officer taking bribes, especially from a well-known criminal who was also a suspect in the murder of two local women.

'Do you think Amelia Stanton's disappearance could also be linked to the killer and the man who attacked us?' Elsbeth questioned.

'It's possible. Amelia Stanton was very outspoken, called the killer a lot of names, and maybe he took her to teach her a lesson. But first, we need to know how long she has been missing, if she still is, and where she was going when she disappeared. It's all about timing, motive, and opportunity. We won't know until we have all the details.' Abberline continued to write down all the points on the blackboard, making sure each line was spaced, and each word was the same height. 'Now let's go over all we know, then we'll go and see Joseph Stanton.'

Abberline started writing down bullet points of the case on the left, with the known or potential suspects on the right-hand side of the board. He pinned photographs of the dead bodies taken at the scene and during the autopsy on the right with an additional margin for any notes. Everything was aligned neatly and in order.

'So, we have two murders and possibly a missing person that may be connected to this case. Our first victim; eighteen-year-old Mary Quinn. On her way back from The Crown to see her landlord, Seamus Keane. She owed him rent and was going to ask him for more time to pay, taking a shortcut through a twitten to The Black Star pub. But she never made it; she was attacked near to the exit and stabbed twenty-nine times with such ferocity that the blade fractured bones in the process. Her body, mutilated and discarded on a rubbish pile in plain sight to be discovered. A vagrant and a potential witness said he saw the attacker and spoke to him but was only able to give us a vague description. Now, given the fact that the witness is an alcoholic, anything he told us could be considered problematic at best. Do you remember, Elsbeth, what the old man said when asked if he could describe the killer? He said it was the Devil he saw. He was scared, really scared. Maybe he's worried the killer will come back for him. Seamus Keane is very much a man capable of murder; I've met him. He has a very weak alibi for the night of Mary's murder, and I am sure would for Rosie Meeks as well. Most people in this town know him and would be too frightened not to vouch for him for fear of reprisal. He runs a brothel along with several other illegal activities, and he is known to have a violent temper and has, I'm certain, killed before. Could he be responsible for the death of Mary Quinn? Yes, he knew her, and she owed him money and didn't have it to pay him.'

Elsbeth thought back as Abberline spoke to the time in her home, when she had consulted the tarot cards for guidance and asked who the killer was. When she had turned the card over, she was presented with the Devil. The card had many interpretations, but in this instance, it was accurate given the horrific nature of the crimes and the evil intent behind them.

'Do you believe in evil, Inspector? I'm not necessarily talking about the evil people *do* to one another; more the evil inherent, in a person's soul.'

Abberline looked at Elsbeth, taken aback by the sudden question. 'I'm not quite sure how to answer that. I'm not certain what you are asking, but I suppose the only way I can explain it is through my job. I have come to accept that there are people who do wrong or evil deeds, which I think have been instilled in them, through their upbringing or the experiences they have gone through. Do I believe in a person being born evil? No, I see no evidence for that.'

'Those people who have committed crimes of such violence, you believe they were coerced towards doing so by a set of unfortunate circumstances?' Elsbeth wanted to question him more.

'You've had a privileged life, Elsbeth. You've never been poor, and you never had to steal or pick up rotten food off the streets to eat. You've never felt the pains of starvation or had to sleep on freezing pavements with nowhere else to go. Poverty can drive a person to many things, and they'll end up doing anything, even kill. It's a basic instinct. People will resort to the most depraved ways to live, and soon enough, that way feels normal. That's what I've seen.'

'So, you think people are made evil by circumstance?'

'In my experience, yes.'

Elsbeth pondered on his answer for a while. 'The current murders of these two women, if we are to follow your train of thought, would be that the perpetrator of such horrific crimes was driven by the necessity to survive, yes? So, tell me, how does the killing of Mary Quinn and Rosie Meeks help anyone survive? They were not killed for food, money or property. They were savagely and brutally attacked, and then their bodies mutilated for what appears to be no real reason at all. So, what circumstance in the killer's life could motivate such a crime?'

'Statistically, murders are committed by someone who knows them or a close relative. People can, at times, under the right conditions, be capable of doing the most terrible things to each other in a moment of madness. It doesn't mean they are born evil; it just means they were evil at that moment, driven by certain conditions. The murders of these women are different as they display a hate I have not seen before, so the reason for such attacks may be new. But it is my belief that conditioning of some kind will be found to be responsible for the actions of this individual.'

Elsbeth was unconvinced and sensed that he was trying to find a way of explaining a deed so senseless and so dreadful that the only answer lay in statistics. He was not open-minded enough to even consider that there are, on occasion, there are those who are simply are born that way. Evil.

'Both women I have seen after death, Inspector, and have told me of how this person killed them, and both say that he will continue, as did the witness in the alleyway. This is not an instance of insanity; we are dealing with a genuine example of the most depraved and sick mind possible. In my opinion, the killer is not going to suddenly stop and throw themselves at the mercy of others for forgiveness. This person is, without doubt, possessed and fuelled by their pathological hatred for women that will *not* end, Inspector, unless we find him, and he is dispensed back to hell from where he came.'

'You know my feelings on spiritualism. I can't, I'm sorry, come to terms with this. I don't. I…can't bring myself to adhere to your practices. I am a policeman; that is what I am, and that is what I do. There are procedures and rules and ways of doing things, and we…I can't be seen to go down that road of an unproven and much-faked profession that would draw us even further away from public trust. Our reputation is fragile at best, and we must be seen to do everything by the book, especially now in the midst of these killings. We are faced with a new type of adversary, one that demands we approach this with a system that is tried and tested and that works.'

Elsbeth realised they came from very different worlds. 'I can see I'm going to have trouble with you, Inspector.' Elsbeth smiled.

'Not at all. I know that following a systematic approach to crime will ultimately pay off, and I don't know any other way. To start believing that someone is bewitched by some evil entity that has driven them to do such things is, I'm afraid, the stuff of books and writers of strange fiction. As I understand it, even the church is deeply sceptical about this subject of people being born evil.'

'Well, you know what they say, Inspector: The trick of the devil is to convince us he doesn't exist. And as far as the church is concerned, if they publicly renounce that a person can't be inherently evil, why then do they have exorcists to cast evil out?' Elsbeth studied Abberline as he mulled over what she had said. She could see that probably nobody had ever questioned him before or given a good enough argument to make him consider his views.

Abberline hadn't expected a conversation on this subject and wanted to get back on track with what they knew so far on the case. He quickly took back control, moving the discussion forward.

'Our second victim, Rosie Meeks,' Abberline said, looking back at the board, 'she worked in a bakery, in her early thirties and was a single mother with a son aged eight at the time of her murder. She had served customers all day, as she usually did, including some of her regulars, whom we still need to speak with to see if they saw anything untoward. We know she was working alone at the time because the owners were out of town, away on business, and this has been verified. They didn't return until the next day, so it was Rosie Meeks' responsibility to open and shut the shop. It was the owners on their return who discovered the body in their living quarters above the shop, and it was they who raised the alarm. As we can see from Mr Cripps's coroner's report and photographs, the killing of Rosie Meeks had taken on a far more violent turn. What was left of her was so disfigured it was hard to identify the remains as a body at all, and some of her organs, as with the first victim, had been removed.'

'I saw the ghost of Rosie at the mortuary when I left the examination room for a moment. She said she knew him, the attacker. Given your dismissal for such things, I didn't say anything then, but it was as real as you standing here. She must have crossed paths with him somehow for her to say that.'

Abberline looked suspicious; he dismissed any supernatural evidence but conceded the victim could have known her attacker; that much was true.

'Well, she worked in a shop, so it's plausible that our killer met her that way as a customer. Seamus Keane,' Abberline continued, feeling uncomfortable with Elsbeth's spiritual encounter, pointing to Keane's name on the board. 'He claimed he had never met Rosie Meeks, and to date, there is no evidence to say that he did or didn't know her, but this is a small town, and he is a well-known money lender. If Seamus Keane wanted to send a message "This is what happens if you don't pay what you owe" to look strong and in control it would remind anyone thinking of taking his business that there will be consequences. Then, yes, he is more than capable of such butchery. I understand from Rawlings that there has been trouble with a rival gang looking to extend their territory, and that has caused tension. Mary Quinn owed him money, and Rosie Meeks, a single mother, suddenly finds herself in need of additional funds. It's not out of the question she could turn to the likes of him. So, he stays a strong suspect; he has the means, and a man like Seamus Keane doesn't need a motive.'

'And what of the note delivered with a lock of Mary Quinn's hair? It was signed Jack,' Elsbeth asked.

'The lock of hair we know belongs to Mary Quinn, Cripps compared it to the victim's, it belongs to her. The note is worrying because if it is real, it leads to the conclusion that we are dealing with one person, one killer. But to sign their name to it?' A pause. 'No, I don't trust that; that is where I think this could be all part of some deception here. As I have said before, the press is not above this type of stunt.'

Elsbeth thought for a while. 'You know, I think the killer wants us to know it's him. He's making an announcement: this is me, this is my name, and by giving me the note with the lock of hair, he's making sure of that. I understand you have trouble believing me, but I just feel his presence.'

'Then why not just kill you?'

'I'm not sure; maybe he knows I have this gift, is playing with me, and sees me as some sort of adversary. I don't know,' Elsbeth said, frustrated. 'But something tells me it's him. The delivery boy, his description of the man in the carriage who gave him the box with the note, and then the witness who saw the killer of Mary Quinn. Both descriptions have very similar characteristics.'

Abberline listened to Elsbeth but didn't want to write off any possibility at this point. 'Seamus Keane could have also invented it to put us off the scent, so let's not take anything too literally at the present moment. Cripps said that the killer was left-handed in both murders and that a long, thin, serrated knife was used like the one a surgeon would use.'

Elsbeth looked visibly sick at the mention of his name. 'Cripps is a Jackal, and I don't like him for many reasons; he has something dark and soulless about him and too much time spent with the dead. And he certainly doesn't want or like an independent thinker around him, especially a woman.'

'Oh, I can testify first-hand how independent you are, Miss Hargreaves,' Abberline commented, turning around from the blackboard with a slight smile. 'But this is not about who we like or don't like. It is about facts and motives. We have the facts as I have outlined above, but the *why* for the killings still eludes me.'

'What about the man who attacked us at the bakery? We still don't know why he was there or how he knew Rosie Meeks, but he used her first name, so he had some connection to her?'

'Yes, he's interesting, we scared him; he knew her, admitted to that, but how much and why he felt the need to visit the place where she was murdered, I'm not sure yet. I have despatched Rawlings down to Brighton Station. I'm sure our man works there, and if he does not give them the slip, I will be asking him those questions myself. Then, we have the possible disappearance of our politician's wife, Amelia Stanton. This might be nothing, but we can't assume anything. It may or may not be related, but she had said some very damning and outspoken things about the killer. Keane would have had dealings with our illustrious Joseph Stanton somewhere along the line, of that you can be sure, but we have to be careful accusing a serving parliament member of mixing with known criminals.'

'Amelia Stanton stood up for what she believed was the right thing to say. Another strong woman with an independent thought outside her husband's, Inspector. What's the world coming to?' Elsbeth's caustic remark did not draw any fire from Abberline.

A uniformed officer knocked at the office door. 'Sorry to trouble you, sir… Madam. I've just received some information I think you will be most interested in hearing.'

'Go on,' Abberline instructed.

'Well, sir, we've just had a report at the front desk. A fishing boat hooked a body out from under the pier. They knew instantly who it was.'

Abberline's world crashed as his worst fears thundered in his mind like a runaway train. He looked at Elsbeth and saw she was also thinking the same thing.

'Tell me, was the body a woman?' Abberline asked the young officer. 'Has it been identified?'

A silence that seemed to hang in the room, as Abberline and Elsbeth waited for the answer.

'No, sir,' came the reply. 'Not a woman, a man. Seamus Keane.'

TWENTY-FIVE

Cripps had arranged everything for the evening's event at the morgue where he worked. The people attending had come from all corners of the country and represented the finest private collections in the land. He had sent out the invitation's weeks before, and been hard at work harvesting body parts and placing them into glass containers of various sizes to be displayed in the greatest possible light, and in turn gain the best possible price.

He had gained a reputation and done his utmost to make sure that all the exhibits had been carefully catalogued and embalmed, giving the purchasers years of pleasure. It was a small, but exclusive club, where most of the potential buyers he knew in person, or by reputation. They were the rich, the famous, and the successful, but they all had one thing in common, to possess the greatest collection, and they were fiercely competitive.

Cripps noticed one person he hadn't seen before, a tall, lean man standing at the back of the room holding a small, black doctor's case. Whoever it was didn't want to be recognised as he wore a mask covering his eyes and nose. But he had a presence about him that made Cripps inquisitive, and he made a mental note to be sure he made contact before the evening had concluded.

The products were kept in a separate room in the morgue and Cripps had each one in order and by catalogue number. Organs of every type, gender, and disfigurement were available to be purchased, even a complete foetus that was horribly deformed, a rare and unique item, which he expected to do well in the auction.

The evening ran smoothly, and was, as always, a success, making Cripps a handsome profit. The event came to its natural conclusion with the usual empty pleasantries exchanged, the guests filing out with their new possessions, content until the next time. Cripps noticed the man who had been standing at the back earlier was still there and decided to go over to make his introduction.

'Good evening, Mr... sorry I didn't get your name?' Cripps put his hand out, waiting for a response that didn't come. 'Well... er of course never mind, I do hope that you enjoyed this evening's little soiree, but I have to say I didn't see you partake in any of the sales. So, I was thinking now, he's a man who's after something else, something special. Er, would I be correct in that assumption, sir?'

The man said nothing but stared at Cripps which made him feel suddenly very uneasy. Cripps stepped slightly back, looking towards the door and working out if he would have enough time to make a run for it.

'Don't worry, Cripps, I'm not going to harm you; on the contrary, I believe we have much in common, maybe enough to work together.'

'Well... that's interesting and you seem to know me, but I still don't know who you are. As you can see, I already have a successful business and a full-time position as the town's Coroner, so I am a bit busy at the moment to consider anything else.' Cripps watched the stranger for a reaction, his mask hiding any expression but his eyes black and dull seemed to look right through him. 'May I ask how you got to hear of this gathering, did you receive an invitation?' Cripps asked, the awkwardness becoming worse. There was no reply. 'Well, if that's all, I *really* do need to be getting home soon.'

'What if I could double, treble, your takings, Cripps? I'm sure a man of your business acumen would jump at such a proposal?'

Cripps stopped in his tracks, rubbing his bony, clammy hands together as greed took hold of his better judgment.

'Well, if you put it like that, maybe I have been a bit hasty, perhaps you can enlighten me, providing, of course, there is no risk to life or limb. Well, mine, I mean.' Cripps grinned at him trying to bring some humour into the conversation, but there was none. The stranger's stare was ice cold.

'You sell body parts to those who will pay well to have them in their private exhibits. But you are, of course, limited by what comes through your door. As you have said, you are the town's coroner, and most of the dross that passes through here does not hold any value, so you sell those on for medical examinations. That's unless you come across any that may be considered unusual in your world. They will, of course, command a reasonable price, and you keep them back until you have sufficient stock to hold a sale, as tonight demonstrates.'

'How do you know all this?' Cripps' eyes narrowed in suspicion.

'Oh, Cripps, I know everything about you; it is in my interest to know. People always talk, and you would be surprised how much information you get from a person with a knife held at their throat.'

'Indeed.' Cripps swallowed hard, realising he was in the presence of an extremely dangerous man. He was clearly well-educated, his public school voice was low, calm but had at the same time an intensity about it. His clothes were of the finest cloth, so money was clearly no object, but as to his identity, he clearly wanted that kept secret.

'The death of that local prostitute who went by the name of Mary Quinn, I believe,' the stranger continued.

'Yes,' Cripps replied. 'She was walking alone late at night through an alleyway in The North Laine and was stabbed twenty-nine times, her body ripped open and parts cut away. Looked as if a wild beast had got a hold of her. But since then, there's been another murder, a woman who works in a bakery, Rosie Meeks, they found her, well they found what was left of her, on a bed above the shop. The killings have the whole town on edge, people saying there's a monster running loose on the streets. They sent someone down from Scotland Yard to take over the case; an Inspector Abberline, I do believe. And the local psychic Elsbeth Hargreaves, who's now helping him, says she's had a visit from the ghost of Mary Quinn at her home.' Cripps concluded with a derisory smirk.

'Yes, I know about them. Elsbeth Hargreaves has a gift; I read her article in the local newspaper, and I feel a connection with her; likewise, she at times feels my presence. They will both have their part to play in my journey, I'm sure of that.'

Cripps noticed he seemed to be lost in thought for a moment.

'As you say. To be honest, I'm not a believer in all that sort of spiritual stuff but to each their own. You have an interest in these murders then?'

He moved uncomfortably close; Cripps wondered if he could smell his fear as he whispered his reply.

'You could say that. I am the one who killed them.' He reached inside his coat pocket and withdrew a serrated knife. Cripps immediately recognised it as a medical instrument used for surgery and dissecting cadavers.

'You have them here in the morgue?' he asked Cripps.

Cripps, feeling very concerned for his safety, replied. 'Yes, I have them here on ice,' he said cautiously. 'Just finished the autopsy on them, both will end up being dumped in a shallow grave somewhere.'

'I sense you are not quite believing me, Cripps.'

'No, not at all. I can assure you; I believe every word you have told me.'

He placed the small black doctor's case he had been holding on a table, opened it, and removed two jars containing parts of an intestine, lung, kidney, and genitalia. These are from those two you have over there; I cut them out myself. You can have these as a gift.' He stroked the sides of one of the jars before putting it back down next to the other. Now you need to help me in return.'

'How, exactly, can I do that?' Cripps asked nervously.

'Let me explain. I am independently wealthy; my parents are both dead and left me very well provided for. I don't expect you to even come close to understanding, but I intend to make society better, by removing the vermin that has infected it. My work is very, very important to me and I need someone I can trust, someone who appreciates the skill involved. You also work with the police and are, as you say, the coroner for the town. You will have access to inside information that will be a distinct advantage to me.'

Cripps tried to change the subject. 'The loss of your parents – was that recent? You must miss them as you are still a young man?' Cripps knew he could be making matters worse, but he thought it best to show some empathy even if he had none himself.

'My father was a doctor but when he wasn't bringing women home, he was a useless drunk; my mother was just weak, who did nothing and just accepted it. I used to hear him snorting and grunting like a pig in my room with those women.'

Cripps could see he was becoming more and more angry like something had switched inside him, his voice had changed to one of anger.

'They made the appearance they cared and wanted the best for me, but they didn't. I hated and despised my parents. They had me put away in a secure hospital after an incident with a local girl. She deserved it, I gave her something to remember me by. I made sure my time away was useful, I read books and learned as much as I could, as well as the layout of the place. The inmates were frightened of me and the doctors, even more so. I found I could get people to do what I wanted, and one day I used that to my advantage and took a guard hostage to aid my escape.'

'But what of your parents?'

'Let's just say I visited them late one night. That's where I first used this.' He held out the knife again close to the face of Cripps.

Cripps stopped asking questions – he didn't want to antagonise him. 'So how can we help each other?'

'As I said, I need to continue my work. I have just begun and there is much to do, I am still perfecting my craft you might say. I need you to be my eyes and ears, especially around Abberline and Elsbeth Hargreaves.'

'What's in it for me?' Cripps quizzed.

'These jars; use them to move suspicion away from me. I have someone in mind. I saw him while I was selecting the Meeks woman at the bakery. He knew her well and would make a good scapegoat. Abberline will be under pressure to solve these murders, while these two meaningless, unknown women have become famous, thanks to my work and the local press. So, think about it, Cripps. Think what this means. Think about how this affects these two jars on the table in front of you.'

Cripps stood silent for a moment, then the penny dropped. 'They become more valuable, and even more so if they don't catch you. If they catch the wrong man, hang him only then to find out they had it wrong. These items increase in value even more. Then anything else associated with your work has value, and the more you do, the more you're feared, the more they make. Wonderful. I…I can make a fortune. These alone will make a ton of money once I write to my clients and tell them what I have. It's a win-win situation.'

'Now you see. I get to do my work, you get rich.'

'Where are you staying?' Cripps asked.

'I have a place. Don't worry, it's out of sight and safe. I need you to get a map of the entire sewer system for Brighton as soon as possible. I can't tell you why now, but later, later it will all become clear.'

'By the way, the missing politician's wife, Amelia Stanton, who chose to vent her frustration out in the press about me. She's not missing; I will tell you more in due course.'

Cripps looked at him, considering his options; this man was on some kind of mission and would not be stopped. No one was safe and what fate Amelia Stanton faced was almost certain to be a painful one. Should he turn his back on this deal, as the man was clearly insane? Something inside him told him not to; this was a once-in-a-lifetime opportunity, and he wanted money, lots of it. But he also realised that if he rejected the offer, he would be lying on a mortuary slab himself.

'If we are to work together, should it not be prudent that I know your name? How do I get in contact with you? I don't even know what you look like.'

'I have no name. I will find you when I need you.'

Cripps thought for a moment and called after him as he left the mortuary.

'I will call you, The Ripper. That will be your name.'

TWENTY-SIX

Detective Rawlings arrived at Brighton Railway Station with two uniformed officers. The station, built in 1840, was used for passengers and as a locomotive depot where repairs were carried out. The front of the building was impressively large, rendered in white, a grand rectangular, balanced building set over three floors; two sides sat slightly higher than the central elevation. On the ground on each side was a raised balcony to the height of the first floor, which wrapped around to the back. As passengers arrived, they would see nine Romanesque columns and arches, before taking them through into the main station with a large ornate clock suspended from the roof above where the trains would arrive and depart.

The second floor had fifteen windows facing out towards Queens Road and the sea, with the final elevation having three windows on each side. Inside the station, there were a number of booking and parcel offices for people to buy tickets or collect and send goods. Initially, the station had three separate roofs, but due to the popularity of railways and the expansion of platforms, a single iron and glass roof now covered the entire building. It was most impressive, with thousands of glass panels held in place and supported by huge iron beams and arches. The massive roof curved across the expanse, shimmering in the sun.

Rawlings and the two officers entered the main concourse. It was a bustling, noisy, area, excited children ran around, moving their arms around like wheels, mimicking the chuffing sound of the locomotives. The smell of coal and steam from their chimneys rose as high as the glass roof. Engine drivers released pressure by pulling a valve inside their cabs, giving a cacophony of sound whistles, screaming through the air. The owners of newsstands strategically placed by platforms were shouting over one another, giving the day's headlines. Ticket collectors, station officials, and porters with luggage piled high, tied on wooden trolleys with leather straps, weaved through the crowds, all playing their part in a fast, vibrant, colourful environment with its own rules, autonomous to the outside world, it was a town within a town.

Rawlings and the two officers made their way to the Stationmaster's office to the left of the concourse. It was a large room with several staff beavering away through mounds of paperwork piled on top of their desks. A large board at the back displayed times for trains departing and arriving, and another to the side of it with ongoing repairs to train and track.

'I'm Detective Rawlings from Brighton Police Station. Are you in charge here?'

'Yes, I'm Stationmaster Lewis,' replied a man in his fifties sitting behind his desk in a London Brighton and South Coast railway uniform of black jacket, trousers and black bowler hat. 'What can I do for you, Inspector? As you can see, I'm extremely busy, and I don't have a lot of time to give you.'

'We are on official business, so I insist you make the time. We are investigating the recent murders of two women in town. I'm sure you know of them. There are a few newspaper stands out there selling stories about the crimes.' Rawlings' method of communication was both curt and aggressive. He didn't believe in the niceties afforded by others.

'Yes, yes, of course I do, Detective, it's a bad business, a bad business indeed.' Lewis lowered his head. 'Those poor women and one so young as well,' he replied, shaking his head in a perturbed manner. 'How can I assist you?'

Rawlings showed Lewis the badge Abberline had found after the altercation with the suspect at the bakery. 'This belonged to a man who was found at one of the murder scenes. It's, as you can see, a railwayman's badge from a service that operates out of this station, I believe?'

'To be honest, Detective, the London, Brighton, and South Coast Railways operate out of a few stations, and this man whom you seek could work at any of them. What makes you think he is here?' Lewis looked up at Rawlings, perplexed.

'He's, most likely, a local man, said he knew the deceased Rosie Meeks, the woman who was brutally murdered at the bakery not far away from here, so it would not be unreasonable to assume he also works locally, seeing he must have used the shop on a regular basis.'

'A badge isn't much to go on, Detective? I know every man on this station, and I will need more than that to help you identify him if he is to be found here.'

'He's about five foot two inches of thin build, middle-aged, apparently had a strong smell of oil and coal.'

'Well, he wouldn't be working on the platforms or as a conductor, that's for sure, they keep their uniforms clean. So, it looks like he works in one of the engine or coal sheds. Any other information?'

Rawlings looked back at the notes given to him by Abberline at the station of a description of the suspect. 'He spoke in a northern accent.'

'Hmm, the only one I know like that is Jack Robertson, came down from Leeds way. Been here for about five years. Works in maintenance fixing the locomotives next to the coal sheds.'

'I'll get one of my men to take you there. Be careful. It's

dangerous with lots of heavy machinery and inspection pits that are deep enough to kill you in an instant if you fall in one. So stay close together and don't wander off; you're in my world now.' Lewis motioned for one of the platform staff in the office to escort Rawlings and the two officers to the engineering area on the other side of the station yard.

Rawlings acknowledged the instructions and followed the man out of the office and towards the back of the station, where a narrow path ran alongside, taking them past the trains out of the cover of the roof and into the open. They crossed some tracks until the man pointed to a large shed with a sizable rectangular wooden sign above the entrance saying, "Engineering". 'That's where you'll find him.'

They advanced toward the entrance to the shed and stepped inside. Rawlings would do things his way, find this man and take him back to the police station one way or the other, dead or alive, regardless of what Abberline wanted.

TWENTY-SEVEN

The colossal shed stretched and twisted back into the dark like an underground tunnel. As wide as it was high, four locomotives were parked next to each other, with men clambering around every part of them. Hammering, hissing from vented steam shooting up to the roof, people shouting over a cacophony of sound, wrapped up in the smell of oil, coal and water vapour that mixed with the unfiltered smoke. The heat was intense, with molten metal being poured into moulds from forges that were placed to the side for the repair of large cast iron parts. Orange and yellow sparks flew into the air like fireflies coating Rawlings and his men as they walked through, asking everyone if they knew the whereabouts of Jack Robertson.

A welder pointed towards a forge further down into the shed and said he recognised the description of the man they were looking for. He told them he could be found there fixing a "bogie" as the axles on one of the locomotives had become loose. As they approached Robertson turned and saw Rawlings and his men. Sensing something was wrong, he dropped his tools and ran. Rawlings and the other officers started to follow, but this was not their world and it was pitch black, so they lit three oil lamps that were hung on the shed door before going after him. 'Be careful,' Rawlings told the two officers. 'There's all sorts of debris here, and inspection pits are difficult to see. Fall down one of those, and you're not going dancing with your wife for a while. So, watch your step.' The two uniformed officers, neither one of them over twenty years of age, new to the job, listened intently to Rawlings as they moved forward.

'One of you keep to the left, the other on the right. I'll take the middle.' Rawlings pointed to where he wanted them. 'Use your lanterns, and he might be armed, so truncheons at the ready, boys. Abberline wants this dog alive, but you've seen what he did to Rosie Meeks, so watch yourself. Don't take any chances; he's an animal.'

The darkness quickly swallowed all three men, the sounds of the works slowly evaporating behind them. Rawlings could see the lanterns behind him on either side. They didn't give out much light, so he reminded the men to walk steadily. He squinted his eyes as he moved cautiously, his shoes crushing the stones underneath. 'Best you come out now, Robertson, if you know what's good for you. You're not going anywhere. Give yourself up, and we can chat about this mess at the station.' No response came, only the grinding sound from boots on gravel on either side of him.

Rawlings held his lantern higher; something lay in front of him, maybe a pit sunk into the ground; then, from nowhere, a man shot in front of him, and a punch to his face sent Rawlings falling backwards towards the hole. He turned his head as the inspection pit loomed. He was losing his footing. He felt himself free-falling backwards into it, unable to stop the motion. Just as he thought he was gone; a hand grabbed his coat collar and pulled him back to safety.

Jack Robertson's face, black with soot and sweat, stared at Rawlings, his eyes sore and red, bulging out like a frog. 'I didn't kill anyone, you 'ear. I never had nothin to do with Rosie's death. I've been fitted up by you lot cos you can't find the real killer. Now it's your turn to feel scared.' Robertson pushed Rawlings back, his body teetering on the edge of the abyss.

'You'll hang without any doubt if you drop me, Jack. Be sensible, don't do it.' Rawlings glanced down behind him, facing his own death, as he felt his body once again falling towards it.

'Goin' to hang anyways, you lot will make sure of that, so got nothin left to live for 'ave I?'

Rawlings could see the lanterns of his two colleagues approaching, creeping up behind Robertson.

'Look, Jack, we can sort this out. Pull me back up, and let's talk about it.' Rawlings wanted to keep Jack looking his way so as not to see what was coming up from behind him. Robertson knew Rawlings was playing a game and twisted his body around. But before he had a chance to take any action, a wooden batten struck him firmly across the face, opening a large gash and then another blow across his forehead. Robertson yelled out in pain as blood streamed into his eyes. One of the officers took hold of him, while the other quickly caught Rawlings from falling.

Rawlings breathed a massive sigh of relief. He punched Robertson hard in the side, then in the face again. 'You're going to wish you let me drop. I promise you that, you sick bastard. This is just the start of your problems. I'm arresting you for the murder of Rosie Meeks.' He handcuffed him and threw him to the two young policemen to take him into custody. Rawlings dusted himself off and adjusted his coat, annoyed at a tear in his jacket. He felt good at arresting Jack Robertson and was sure they had the man for the murder of Rosie Meeks, and maybe he could tie him to Mary Quinn as well, then he would be the hero of the hour. Abberline and the interfering witch, Elsbeth Hargreaves could run off into the sunset together. He watched as they dragged the suspect by his feet out of the engine shed into the light.

Rawlings picked up the lantern that had fallen onto the ground during the struggle. He looked back; he was sure he saw something move in the shadows and the sound of whispers. He stood still. A feeling of being watched came over him; holding the light higher, he moved it from side to side, but it was so dark that little could be seen too far ahead. He had done enough today; he shrugged his shoulders, turned, and walked back towards the entrance and the sound of workmen. As he reached the exit's safety, he looked back once more. Something back there had caught his eye, but whatever it was it disappeared, melted into the inky space as if it was never there.

TWENTY-EIGHT

Elsbeth and Abberline arrived at the home of Joseph Stanton in Carlyle Road, Hove. A beautiful and elegant double-bay white-fronted property over four floors, it was as much a statement about wealth and power as it was Victorian architecture. A butler in his senior years wearing a black tailcoat, matching trousers and a starched white collared shirt with a black bow tie answered the door and took them to the library where Joseph Stanton was waiting. The room was what you would expect of a well-heeled man of money and standing. Row upon row of leather-bound, gold embossed books, many first editions, greeted the visitors. A deep textured carpet, beautifully handmade, most likely shipped from abroad, lay across a waxed oak floor with a leather settee and a single reading chair positioned on it. The room had the feeling of a masculine enclave.

A ceremonial sword exquisitely engraved with a gold braid wound around an ivory handle hung on a wall, next to a box of framed medals showing a past he was proud of. Stanton was a military man who had served most of his time in the army as his father and grandfather before him. He had been posted overseas for most of his career, where he had met Amelia. He had retired as a Major and was highly decorated after the Crimean Campaign and the short-lived Indian rebellion in 1857.

A distinguished and handsome man, Joseph Stanton stood six foot two inches tall of medium build with salt and pepper hair. Immaculately dressed in a tailored suit, he stood against a large, ornate black mantelpiece above which hung a portrait of himself, his wife Amelia and their two young children, Sophie and John.

'Mr Stanton, my name is Inspector Abberline from Scotland Yard, and this is Miss Elsbeth Hargreaves, who is assisting me.'

'Yes, quite indeed, Abberline. I know your chief commissioner, Sir Charles Warren. Good man. We attend the same club in London we often share a brandy after the business at The House is concluded.' Abberline knew Stanton was not a man to drop names unless there was a purpose behind them; after all, he was a politician, Abberline understood the veiled threat. *I know your boss, so you had better not disappoint me.* Stanton appeared bemused by the presence of Elsbeth.

'You look surprised to see a woman, Mr Stanton?'

'I'm an army man, a traditionalist, you might say, Miss Hargreaves. It's my firm belief that women should be at home raising their children, not working, unless, of course, they come from the lower classes.'

'Well, being of independent means and having no children or husband to tell me what to do with my time, I am free to engage in any activity that appeals to me.' A simmering dislike marked Elsbeth's reply to the misogynist in front of her reinforcing her views on men who sought to control women.

'Well, my wife appears to have taken it upon herself to, also, busy her time with matters of little importance. If she led a simpler life and followed her husband's lead, you would not be here, and she would not have gone missing.'

'I understand sir, that your wife, Amelia Stanton, has not returned from a visit to Brighton, and that's what you are rightfully concerned about given the recent events in town.'

Abberline wanted to change the tone of the meeting. They were not here to antagonise Mr Stanton, but to find out what had happened to his wife.

'You mean the murders, Inspector. You don't have to dance around me; I've seen much worse serving my country. These women, as I understand it, were of a lower disposition. Indeed, one of them, I believe, a common prostitute, the other a single mother, so there is no doubt in my mind why they attracted violence. I see no connection or, indeed, any reason why this killer would want to harm a well-educated and highly positioned member of the community such as my wife.'

Elsbeth could no longer contain her displeasure at his conceited views. 'That is your opinion, Mr Stanton, and certainly not the opinion of the female members of your constituency that you say you have so much concern over. I hope that you are correct in that assumption. However, the killer's motives are not clear currently. Women don't feel safe in Brighton, the town you are elected to serve. They feel at risk, as your own wife made abundantly clear to the press when she criticised not only the police, but the killer as well.'

Stanton's displeasure at Elsbeth's remarks was evident, the corner of his mouth twitched slightly as he turned to address Abberline.

'Inspector, I did not invite you here to my home to be reminded of my duty to the members of the electorate. You are here, at my behest, to look into the disappearance of my wife and mother to my two children. To locate her, return her, so things can return to normal.' Stanton's face reddened in indignation at being spoken to in such a disrespectful manner by not only a woman but also one he clearly considered outside his class.

'I completely understand, sir, and I apologise for any misunderstanding Miss Hargreaves may have given you,' momentarily looking over towards Elsbeth, willing her not to say anything else that might offend Stanton. 'We take the murders and your wife's disappearance very seriously. Her article in the press regarding the killer does concern me; however, at this point, there is no evidence to suggest your wife's temporary absence and the killings are linked, but we have to, as I am sure you appreciate, keep an open mind. Hence my visit to you today, to assure you every effort is, and will continue to be made to find Mrs Stanton and have her safely returned to you and your family.'

Stanton walked away from the mantlepiece and started pacing the room like a caged animal. 'I can tell you it's causing me considerable problems; I've had to ask our governess to step in for additional days to mind the children until my wife decides to return. I have important matters of state to attend to, don't you know. I also have my constituents, as well as Parliament, to consider, Inspector. This whole ordeal is most inconsiderate, and I can assure you that serious words will be had with my wife upon her return; she had no right, no right at all, to speak to the press about these murders or anything else. But as you know, idle tongues, Inspector, it doesn't look good if people start talking, and the longer she is missing, the more they gossip, so speed is of the essence here. I have my position to think about.'

Elsbeth found it hard not to laugh out loud and found it incredible that he seemed to care more about his job and the opinion of others rather than his wife's welfare. She had been missing for three days now which was out of character and fast becoming a matter of urgency.

Elsbeth said nothing but shook her head in total dis-agreement at how Abberline was conducting the interview in such a submissive way. Stanton was talking about his wife's restoration to the family like a piece of lost luggage.

'So, can you shed any light on why your wife may have

gone astray, Mr Stanton?' Abberline had his pencil and note-pad ready to record any details.

'Not really. She left here three days ago to meet friends in Brighton, one of her so-called society events, they usually see each other at a coffee shop in Meeting House Lane. They get together once a month to help with the plight of the poor and impoverished in the town. Of course, it is a pointless exercise; you can't help those who will not help themselves. Discipline is what these malingerers need. But it's a cause she gets a modicum of satisfaction out of, so I gave my permission for it, albeit reluctantly.'

'Your permission?' Elsbeth said with amusement.

Abberline quickly intervened, seeing a potential flash point. 'So, has she ever gone away for such a length of time before? Or is this, would you say, unusual behaviour?'

'My wife has never or indeed would never, leave the children for more than a few hours at a time. She is devoted to them. So no, is the answer to your question.'

'Now, this is difficult, sir, but I have to ask this to get an overview of Mrs Stanton and her sense of being, her state of mind if you will, the last time you saw her.' He paused. 'This is not intended to offend in any way, and I apologise in advance if it does.'

'Carry on, Inspector.'

'How were things between you and Mrs Stanton? Were they on a good footing, so to speak? Did she seem preoccupied with something? Did she seem on edge, perhaps of a nervous disposition, worrying about anything unduly to you?'

'I'm not sure what you're getting at, what do you want me to say exactly? She seemed quite normal as far as any man could make out a woman's mind.'

Abberline watched for Elsbeth to say something, but thankfully, she decided not to add fuel to the fire. He thought about how else he could approach the question, but realised he had little option but to face it head-on.

'Was your wife happy in your marriage? Was there ever a moment when you thought she was not and sought the company of another—'

'—Was your wife having an affair?' Elsbeth interrupted, frustrated with Abberline walking on eggshells.

'Good God, of course not. We had differences like any married couple, but she respected me, my position within this community and would never jeopardise that or her children. Why on earth would she want someone else?' Stanton said, raising his arms in protest.

Elsbeth looked over at Abberline. 'Why would she, indeed, Mr Stanton? You are clearly a loving, caring husband who only has his wife's best interests at heart.'

Abberline knew Elsbeth was being sardonic and moved the conversation on. 'Can we see her room, please, sir, to see if there might be any indication other than the reason you have provided? It's just formality, well, my own way of doing things to make sure we don't miss anything that might be significant. "Leave no stone unturned" as they say.' Abberline smiled, trying to take the heat out of the situation.

'Well, yes, I suppose if it helps, but don't go taking anything unless you ask me. I want everything left exactly as it is.'

'Of course not, sir. It will be just a cursory look, that's all. Thank you.'

Having been reassured, Stanton went over to the side of the room and pulled on a long silk cord. Within a minute, a knock at the door to the library came, and the butler arrived.

'Williams, take the Inspector and his…his *assistant* to Mrs Stanton's room and remain outside until they are finished.'

Yes, sir, of course, sir.' Williams opened the library door wider and signalled Abberline and Elsbeth to follow him upstairs.

As Abberline followed Elsbeth out of the room, he watched Stanton look back at the picture of his wife and children. Abberline saw he was a cold, hard man with little sentiment and no doubt this was, in all but name, a loveless marriage. He wondered if this was a domestic disagreement that had caused the temporary departure of his wife. But the fact that she was devoted to her children bothered him, and raised questions about why she would have been gone for so long. Something had made her not return, which was one of two things. It was either her choice or it was not. Whichever it was, they needed to find her. Fast.

TWENTY-NINE

As Abberline and Elsbeth entered Mrs Stanton's bedroom, they were greeted by a beautiful aroma of fresh flowers, which Elsbeth loved. It reminded her of her own home, and the decoration of floral wallpaper and matching curtains. The room had a style and consistency that mirrored her taste. She already liked this woman she had never met. There was an air of gentleness about Mrs Stanton, who seemed very different from her husband. Williams, the butler, did as instructed and waited outside the room and Abberline closed the door for some privacy. Elsbeth noticed the scent bottles on the dresser with a simple tilting mirror on top. Her jewellery box and sil-ver-handled hairbrush, the beautiful quilt on the four-poster bed and admired how the balance of the room worked. Next to the dresser was a wardrobe and, on the other side, a writing bureau. A chair with a cushion that matched the curtain material sat under a sash window. All the furniture was made of dark wood, which contrasted well with the décor. It was peaceful and light, and Elsbeth recognised it as a place for Amelia Stanton to retreat to and have time alone.

Abberline looked for anything that could indicate where or what may have happened. He went to the writing bureau and opened the drawer, rifling through the contents. He found some letters bound together with a red ribbon tucked at the back. He drew the chair out from beneath the bureau and sat down, untied the ribbon, and started to read through them one by one.

'You know I'm not sure Amelia would be too pleased you're reading through her private letters,' Elsbeth remarked.

'If we are to find anything to explain her disappearance, we must examine everything as it may later prove something vital that we were unaware of. Interestingly, these letters were deliberately hidden at the back of the drawer.'

'Maybe she didn't want her husband finding them and going through them like you are now. Maybe she saw them as private and didn't concern anyone else. Women need their own space, Inspector. Especially from a man like her husband, who seems remote and cold and more in love with himself than her.'

'Not all men are cut from the same cloth, Elsbeth, but I agree with you as much as it might surprise you. He is like most men from the military; their manner does not always lend itself well to normal civilian or married life. Everyone has secrets, and sometimes, we need time to look at them on our own. Maybe Amelia Stanton found that expression in these letters. Somewhere to put down her thoughts and to confide in others.'

'Hmm, so there is another side to you, Inspector, underneath that prickly demeanour. There's hope for you yet.'

'By the way,' Abberline continued, 'Rawlings sent word that he arrested a man called Jack Robertson at Brighton Railway Station, most likely the man who attacked us at the bakery and our suspect in the Rosie Meeks killing. I didn't want to say anything with Stanton standing there as I'm interviewing the suspect with Rawlings tomorrow. I don't want a hanging party outside the station with Stanton at the head of it.'

'Of course not.' Elsbeth nodded in agreement. 'You said

the man Rawlings has arrested; his name is Jack Robertson. Someone called Jack signed the note to me with the lock of Mary Quinn's hair, remember? Maybe it's the same person?'

'Possibly, but it would be a bit of a coincidence, and I don't believe in coincidences,' Abberline replied. 'We will know more soon, but as I said before, I don't think the note came from the killer. It's more likely from the press or someone else playing tricks.' Elsbeth didn't look convinced. 'Anyway, I can't let you attend the formal interview with Robertson, you understand. It's a police matter, and you're a member of the public and not allowed, so at this stage, we can't have anything going wrong and all this work to be thrown out in court if it is our man.'

'I understand, it's fine, Inspector. You can update me afterwards if anything comes of it.'

Abberline looked across at her and smiled as he continued to sift through Mrs Stanton's correspondence. 'This is interesting,' he said out loud to Elsbeth. 'Most of the letters are from friends, and some seem to be almost like diary entries to herself, as I expected, reminders of moments she wanted to capture and return to. But there is one that isn't any of these which most intrigues me.' Abberline carefully examined the letter that had caught his attention as Elsbeth moved over towards Mrs Stanton's dressing table.

Elsbeth picked up the hairbrush, turned it over to reveal the bristles, and slowly teased some hair away. They were light brown in colour and felt thin and wispy in her hand. The noise of paper shuffling from Abberline at the bureau distracted her momentarily. She held the hair tight in her palm, concentrated and made a connection. She could hear Abberline, but it was distant, muffled, as if it were a dream.

She was transported to somewhere dark, a grim place that hollowed the heart. There seemed to be little light, a room damp, and confined, the area smelt of stagnant water; smelt of death. A steel-plated door was up ahead, heavy, one you kept secrets behind. Elsbeth sensed herself floating towards it. *A guttural cry for help from behind, a tormented weeping, of a woman in pain and in despair.* Elsbeth pushed hard against the cold metal, but it didn't move. *It was sealed like a tomb.* She wanted to reassure the woman but could not; the words stuck in her throat; she was mute. As a hand touched her shoulder, Elsbeth stepped back, frustrated and terrified. Paralysed to the spot, a figure from behind leaned close to her ear; the cold feel of a serrated blade against the skin of her neck, his whisper slow and controlled masking something else... *Rage.*

Your destiny is mine.

'Elsbeth? Elsbeth what's wrong? Wake up.' Abberline shook her shoulder as she snapped out of the trance-like state, her eyes watery, still bleary, her focus going in and out.

'I think I know who this is from,' Abberline excitedly announced, holding the letter he had been examining. Elsbeth looked around at Mrs Amelia Stanton's bedroom, holding tight onto the strands of her hair, her palms still sweating.

'Mrs Stanton... I've seen where she is. She is in great danger; we must get to her.' Elsbeth's words were hushed, and she trembled with fear.

Abberline looked at her, confused, almost ignoring what she had just said. 'Look at this. It is just one line; I found it amongst the other letters, but it is different. It's from someone who means her harm. Look at what it says.' Elsbeth reached up and slowly took it from him; her hands shaking, she read it.

'"Your destiny is mine."'

An arctic wind swept through her soul, and Elsbeth instinctively knew who this was from. She shivered, looking back up at Abberline.

'Amelia Stanton is not missing. She was taken.'

THIRTY

Abberline hailed a cab along the Hove seafront, giving the driver an urgent note for the attention of Detective Rawlings, Brighton Police Station. The note, first instructing Rawlings to go to the coffee shop in Meeting House Lane and talk with the staff to see what they do and don't remember about Amelia Stanton. Then, to take some officers and undertake a thorough search along the seafront to make sure she was not lying injured from a fall or worse.

As Elsbeth considered things, they started to walk past the West Pier and along the front towards the town centre.

'You're not going to find her on a beach, Inspector. I know she's somewhere else, I saw…She's being held against her will.'

'I can't go to my boss and tell him that you had a vision. Believe me, he's not the sort of man who would take kindly to such a suggestion. I'm a Detective. I need evidence, facts, and proof. Do you think Stanton will be happy if I tell him what you have just said to me about his wife? He has powerful friends, one of whom is the Police Commissioner for Scotland Yard.'

'You still don't believe me, even after all I have told you so many things. Such as the killer was left-handed, your late wife who died young from a chest infection, Polly Nichols at The

Crown? Where I told her what her husband did for a living, and what her future would be if she returned to Whitechapel. All this, and you still think I'm nothing more than a circus act, a fraud, that I'm making it all up!' Elsbeth's frustration was plain to see as Abberline stopped to listen.

'I didn't say that. I don't understand this gift, as you call it. I can't explain it, nor do I arrest people based on dreams and intuition alone. It just doesn't work like that. The public doesn't like the police and has little trust in us. I'm already feeling pressure from having you assist with this. Look I appreciate the support and assistance you have given me, but people are quick to judge, especially when it comes to the police.'

Elsbeth put her hands in her coat pocket to keep them warm. 'People don't have confidence in you because of men like Rawlings. He's a neanderthal, and as long as you have that type in the police, people will have deep reservations about it.'

Abberline ignored the remark but knew she had a point. He had his own suspicions about Rawlings and just how close he was to Seamus Keane and other known felons in the town.

Elsbeth leaned against the wooden railings, looking to the sea, watching it churn in its winter womb. She turned back to face Abberline, the salt wind playing with her hair, frustrated by his unwillingness to have an open mind.

'I was born with this. I didn't ask for it. I understand it's outside most people's comprehension of what is considered normal. I'm not asking you to abandon everything you hold as the truth, but there are things in life that can't be explained by science and logic. I don't know how I do this; I just know I can. Amelia Stanton is being held against her will somewhere, and time is running out.'

THIRTY-ONE

Rawlings went over the arrest details and detention of the suspect Jack Robertson, primarily for the murder of Rosie Meeks. Robertson, held in a four-foot by six-foot cell on the basement floor of Brighton Police Station, waited to be interviewed. With possible formal charges being brought against him. He sat locked in the cold, and alone on a wooden bench with a table and chair to one side and a small opening in the wall. Iron bars obscured his view of the outside, allowing only a tantalising glimpse of the sky. It was freezing as he rubbed his hands and arms to keep warm, waiting to be seen.

'Look, before I go and get Robertson, you know they fished the body of Seamus Keane out of the sea, so he can't have been our man. Also, as far as the missing Amelia Stanton. I did, as you said. I took officers, we searched all the beaches from the West Pier to the Chain Pier, and nothing. We looked in all the fisherman huts: again, nothing. Even checked the cafe – they said she hadn't been there in some time,' Rawlings reported as he made himself and Abberline coffee before the suspect was brought up from the cells.

'It appears Miss Hargreaves may be correct, and Amelia Stanton has been taken. Do we have a cause of death for Seamus Keane yet?' Abberline questioned.

'Dr Creeps, as we call him, has the body. I went down there this morning thinking it would be your first question and turns out that he took a beating. Quite a good beating from the evidence, and then he was drowned. Sea water in his lungs. Very different from the recent murders. My way of thinking is that has more to do with his criminal dealings than anything else. The Newhaven gangs have had a long feud and a number of run-ins with him, and I can see one of them doing for him.'

'What did Cripps determine the murder weapon to be?'

'Something heavy and wooden; he found splinters in the man's head and body. Cripps said it would have left its mark on the weapon used. Inspector, this has all the hallmarks of a gang-related murder; he had a list as long as your arm of those wanting him out the way. I doubt we'll l ever find the culprit, but he's done a lot of people a favour in this town. Not many be crying over the grave of Seamus Keane.'

'Yes, I'm sure you're correct.' Abberline stopped there.

The remark that Seamus Keane had made about Rawlings when they'd met in his pub had stayed with Abberline. Keane indicated that Rawlings was on very friendly terms with him, which could mean many things, corruption was one of them. So, if he was taking money from this gangmaster, and now he was dead it would be a clean slate for Rawlings, with no one to accuse him of anything. It was very convenient for Keane to wash up dead, and not out of the realm of possibility that Rawlings had killed him either.

Abberline continued. 'It doesn't mean Keane didn't kill Mary Quinn; he had motive and opportunity. But something tells me it wasn't his way of doing things. He would have made sure people knew it was him somehow. If she were on her way back to ask for more time to pay her rent, then maybe he knew there would be little point in killing her and cutting off an income, as he so candidly put it to me. He was a violent thug, and no doubt would have reminded her with a beating not to be late again, but kill her? On reflection, no I don't think Seamus Keane was our man. We're looking for a different type of creature. Get Robertson up here, and let's see what he has to say for himself.'

With that, Rawlings did as ordered and went to bring the prisoner up from his cell.

THIRTY-TWO

The interview room was, in fact, the office of Detective Rawlings as it was the only suitable place to carry it out. Rawlings brought Jack Robertson in and sat him firmly in a chair opposite Abberline.

'You know me, Jack, you attacked Miss Hargreaves and myself in the bakery, the place where you butchered, without remorse, a single mother. So, you know why you are here and what you were arrested for, it'll be best for you to come clean. Tell us what happened, what made you kill Rosie in the way you did. Maybe, just maybe, I can save you from the rope. But don't cooperate; I'll throw you to the wolves. We clear, Jack?' Abberline waited for his response.

'I ain't done nothin wrong, I liked her, that's all, nothin more, so what's the crime in that then?'

'You're no better than an animal. Ripping her apart like a piece of meat, what kind of man does that? Answer me, you northern bastard.' Rawlings, who stood next to the suspect, moved around and started banging the table in front of Robertson with his fists. 'Or God as my witness, I'll be having a word with you *one to one* back in your cell.'

Abberline carefully watched the reaction on Robertson's face, who seemed genuinely frightened at the prospect.

'As you can see, Jack, feelings are running high, and no wonder, given the nature of the crime.' Abberline continued speaking in a softer tone to take the heat out of the situation for a moment. 'Before we get into the details, let's get some background. You came down from the north, Leeds, as I understand it, five years ago to work at Brighton Railway Station. Is this correct?'

'Yeah,' replied Robertson. 'No work up north unless you want to die in them mines, so I came down south, better pay, more work like.'

'Where do you live?'

'At the yard, been kipping in one of them sheds, nobody knows. It does for my needs. Anyway, it ain't a crime far as I know.'

'Well, I doubt your employer would be so congenial about your living arrangements.'

'Yeah, well, I don't really give a damn what they think, they get their pound of flesh from me.'

'So how did you come to meet Rosie Meeks, Jack?'

There was a pause in his reply, almost as he thought through his response.

'I go to the bakery every mornin for me buns to ave later with me supper. I got to know her a bit. We'd talk sometimes on our own, you know about life; she was nice to me, made sure I was ok, you know. She would give me extra, even some soup on occasion. She…She, I think, had the eye for me.'

'Something you're not telling me here. Why were you at the bakery where Rosie had been killed? Why attack me and Miss Hargreaves?' Abberline grabbed a pen on his desk, twisting it through his fingers.

'I knew the place would be empty, and bein the owners couldn't face goin back, not after what happened. I wanted to see…for me self where it happened; maybe I don't know. You could have been anyone…' He paused. 'I reacted, that's all, just wanted to get away from the place.'

'So, you say she had an eye for you; what do you mean by that?' Abberline continued.

'It's a northern term, sir, for her having a fancy for him. As if,' Rawlings interrupted, sniggering.

Abberline ignored Rawlings and carried on. 'So, Jack, you were under some illusion that you had a relationship with her? You just purchased some buns from her, as did many others; what makes you think you are special? She had a child, did you know? A child who is now in the workhouse without a mother to fend for and protect him. How does that make you feel, Jack, now you've taken his mother away from him?'

'I didn't take anyone away from no one, you 'ear, I know she had a nipper. She spoke of him often like.'

'Did you see yourself being the father? Moving into the home, a readymade family? No more sleeping rough in a coal shed for Jack. No, you could be under a roof having dinner by the warmth of a fire, feet up and Rosie to comfort you in bed.' Abberline was stepping up the pressure, trying to find a way through to see if he was hiding a terrible truth. If he confessed to killing Rosie, then maybe he would do the same for Mary Quinn; he needed to keep digging away. 'Then something went wrong. You tried it on with her. Maybe you went around after work when the owners were away and tried to kiss her, but she pushed you away. You get angry, don't you; only natural, Jack? Saw that dream you had slipping away?'

'No, no…I never hurt her. You fuckin lot are trying to pin this on me cos the papers are calling you all useless. I ain't done nothin, you hear me, nothin. You're lookin in the wrong place. She told me at the time, someone was worrying her, some bloke standing in the queue, posh-like; she said she ain't never seen him before. Well dressed, out of place, just stood there looking at her. Something about him, she said, made her skin crawl. I told her I could hang about, make sure he didn't cause no trouble. But she said she could take care of herself and not to worry, like. I took a look when I left the shop, but he had gone whoever he was.'

Abberline remembered Elsbeth saying the ghost of Rosie Meeks had told her she knew who killed her. He didn't believe in the dead coming back but wondered if the killer could be this so-called stranger or the man before him.

'Come on, Jack, you're making this up. Some gent turns up at her bakery and stands there staring. No, I don't see it. I think the truth is that things got out of hand, didn't they, Jack?' Abberline leaned in across the desk, his voice now turning harsher, increasing the pressure. 'You saw red; she told you she wasn't interested. You get jealous as she tells you she's got some other bloke, and that's something you couldn't have, aren't I right, Jack? You're not going to let another man move in on the woman who had an eye for you? So, you thought if I can't have her, no one will. Look at these images. This is your work, Jack. This is what you did to her, the woman you say you liked, the woman you say fancied you.' Abberline spread out the photos of Rosie Meeks' dismembered body taken at the morgue. 'Do you own a long-serrated knife, Jack? Is that what we will find when we go over the hovel you've been held up in?'

'No, you're mad.' Jack turned away from the images. 'I don't have any serrated knife or any other knife, come to that. I'm tellin you idiots, I didn't do nothin to her,' Jack screamed at Abberline; his fists clenched so tightly that the knuckles turned white. He was trying to get out of his chair as Rawlings pushed him back into the seat.

Abberline continued the onslaught of questions and accusations; he knew Jack Robertson was a cocky, nasty piece of work who fancied his chances with women and maybe didn't like it when they didn't reciprocate. He changed his approach and went back to the first murder of Mary Quinn, turning the screw tighter and tighter.

'You have been living and working in Brighton for a few years. If I go down The Crown, you know, the place where working men like you go to get sex and I ask around, is anyone going to say they know you?'

'I never been to that pub; it's a dump.'

Abberline watched Jack carefully.

'I'll tell you what I think, Jack. You think women are there for just one thing, and you don't like it when you don't get what you want. Maybe you weren't getting anywhere with Rosie and became frustrated. I understand, I do. So, you go to a place where you can find someone willing, and there she is, young Mary Quinn, working at The Crown; maybe she smiled at you, gave you the nod? But the problem is, Jack, if you want her company, you're going to have to pay for it. Did she laugh at you? Was that it, Jack, took your money and made fun of you? Maybe you couldn't perform? Humiliated, you followed her down that alley, didn't you, *Jack*.'

Rawlings, seeing Robertson on the ropes, joined in the assault. 'That temper of yours got the better of you, didn't it? You're not going to let someone like her laugh at you cos you can't get it up, especially as you had to pay for it, so you stab her repeatedly, leaving her body slumped up against rubbish like a sack of shite.'

Abberline then slammed the morgue photograph of Mary Quinn's naked body covered in slashes and stab wounds, on the desk in front of him. 'Take a good, long, hard look at what you did. She was just eighteen years old.'

Jack shook his head violently, his face turning puce with rage, the veins on his forehead stood proud pulsating, as spit sprayed out with his words. 'You bastards, you ain't doin this to me. I ain't goin to swing for this; I told you I've never been to that place, and I never hurt Rosie, I'm telling you the truth.'

Abberline continued as Rawlings stood back.

'Then you go back to Rosie Meeks when you know she's alone, looking after the shop while her employers are away. You're not going to take no for an answer. So you spin her some yarn about how much you want to be with her.'

'No, you're wrong.' Robertson shook his head violently. 'Yes, I went to the shop in the morning to get some buns as always…Then I left, had to get a train. I needed to get back up north, had to sort some stuff out. I never went back.'

'Oh, how bloody convenient for you,' Rawlings shouted at him. 'Where's your ticket then?'

Robertson frantically searched his trouser pockets. Then he threw his hands in the air. 'Dunno, I…I must have thrown it.'

'Of course you did, Jack,' Abberline said sarcastically. 'No, I think you went back and told her again you're really interested, thinking she'll come around. But she isn't so keen; she just wants to be friends. Then, the penny drops. She has someone else. You think she's been playing you, making a clown out of you just like Mary Quinn did. You feel that rage within you again, but this time, it's worse; the devil has ahold of you. You don't just kill her; you want to show her no one does that to you, so you rip her to pieces.'

'We get involved, as the newspapers to start building it up, and then some parliament member's wife shouts her mouth off. You start to get worried. What if someone talks? What if someone points the finger at you because you've been going around telling others at work that you're on a promise with Rosie? And let's not forget, you're down her shop every day, not looking good for you, Jack. You start thinking maybe you needed a distraction, so you kidnap Amelia Stanton to throw us off the scent. She's the wife of a prominent politician who you figure is going to come before a street walker and a shop employee. Am I right, Jack?'

'No, no, no.' Jack slammed his fists back down on the table

in protest again. 'I never killed anyone I told you; I weren't there. I didn't take any posh man's wife, neither. You two, are you insane? Where's ya proof? This is all just rubbish, and you know it. I ain't done nothin to no one, and you have nothin to say I did, or I would be on the end of a rope by now.'

Rawlings slapped Robertson across the back of the head. 'Watch your mouth.'

'I ain't confessin to nothin. I get plenty of women, and I don't need to pay for it neither. It's you lot who is makin this all up cos you have nothin, and ya desperate to have anyone for it. But I ain't goin quiet, you 'ear me, Inspector Abberline.'

'Own up to what you've done, Jack; you'll feel better. Look, I'll talk to the judge; no public trial, it'll be all over nice and quick, I promise.'

'I'm innocent. I didn't do either of them women,' he screamed, his face red with fury.

'Ok, Jack, have it your own way, but we are going to search every inch of that dump you've been living in, and you had better pray that we don't find anything.'

'I'm sure you will make certain to find somethin. You're a laughin stock you lot, and everyone knows it. Now, some stuck-up politician's wife gone missing, and on your watch.' Jack Robertson leaned in closer to Abberline across the table. 'Not lookin that good for you, either, Inspector.' Robertson grinned, leaning back in his chair.

'Oh, Jack, one last thing,' Abberline said, ignoring his comments. Still fiddling with the pen in his hand, he suddenly threw it at Robertson, who put his hand up to catch it.

'Take him back to his cell, Rawlings.'

Abberline sat back as Rawlings escorted the prisoner as instructed. He had interviewed many suspects in his career and could usually tell if he was being played for a fool. Jack Robertson was a sad, lonely person who saw himself as a lady's man and didn't like it when they told him to sod off; he had a temper, fancied one of the victims, so he was a prime candidate. And then there was the pen.

There had been two murders and no conviction, and now, another woman had gone missing. Scotland Yard wanted answers, and soon, especially when they discover he had someone in custody. The room felt icy cold as his thoughts suddenly turned to that of the missing wife, Amelia Stanton. Maybe Elsbeth was right; maybe Amelia Stanton was being kept somewhere, and if Jack Robertson was their man, he wasn't going to tell them; he would take his secret with him. Amelia Stanton was being held against her will, possibly injured, and he knew time was running out.

Rawlings came back into the office.

'Why did you throw that pen at him? What was that about?' Rawlings asked.

Abberline smiled at Rawlings. 'Because we know the killer is left-handed, and Jack Robertson instinctively caught the pen in his left hand.'

THIRTY-THREE

Her arms had been extended above her body, wrists bound with two leather straps so tightly that they cut into the skin, fresh blood streaming out whenever she moved. A heavy metal chain looped back up to a pulley system where Amelia could be raised or lowered, her feet barely touching the ground, the tips of her shoes scraping back and forth against the dirty, wet brick floor, her arms taking the weight of her body. With both shoulders and wrists screaming in pain, Amelia's skin twisted and tore as she swayed from side to side, unable to control anything. Blindfolded, but she could still smell and hear her surroundings.

The room echoed as water seeped through the roof, dripping down and forming a small pool. There was a smell of dampness, mould and seawater; cold air brushed against her skin as she heard the sea thundering, and close by, a door swung on rusty hinges, banging back and forth in the wind. There was chatter, two people whispering, and then one left. She heard footsteps, the door being slammed, its hinges creaking.

'Please let me go; my husband will be missing me. I have two children who need me. If it's money you need, my husband's rich. He'll pay whatever you want.' Silence met her words.

'I don't know what you want from me, why I'm here, but I

assure you the police will be out looking for me.' Still nothing. 'I know you're there. I can… I can hear your breathing. Just talk to me, please, just tell me what you want from me.' Her voice trembled and broke, bowing her head, her chin resting on her chest. She sobbed uncontrollably. It seemed like a day or more had passed, but she couldn't be sure time didn't exist in this place. It had been sucked into a void. She felt weak and hungry and thirsty, her lips dry and chapped. She licked them with her tongue, trying to moisten them, but they felt rough, the skin broken.

'Please, may I at least have some water? I'm so thirsty. Just a drop will help, anything, please.' She wanted to keep speaking. She thought by communicating, whoever had taken her might feel something. She wanted to scream, to shout, to get them to listen; she was so petrified she would never see the faces of her children again. Her heart tightened, her breath short, gasping, her lungs tight; she felt as if she was suffocating. A scraping and dragging noise in the room filled her ears, she turned her head to one side, trying to locate it. Then footsteps traversed quickly and steadily, back and forth in a most urgent manner. There was a loud noise and the sound of an object rolling along the floor. There was a pause and then the footsteps got closer, walking around her, a gloved hand brushed her face. It felt like soft leather. *They are wearing gloves, leather gloves.*

'Thank you, thank you. I know you are a good person. I know you don't mean anything bad, just some water, please, and then maybe we can talk; you can tell me what I have done to find myself in such a place. I want to help. I want to understand. I'm sure we can sort this out. I know you don't want to hurt me.'

A hand reached out from behind and gently wrapped around under her chin, lifting her head slowly, carefully back. She felt her hair being stroked, accompanied by deep breathing. She felt the air move and the presence of the person.

She needed to make contact to look them in the eyes, try to reach them and show them how frightened she was. The grip moved to the front of her neck and tightened; her airway blocked. Her mouth opened, and she gasped for air. She felt something metallic with sharp edges being rubbed across her face, causing deep lacerations. A metal can was forced into her mouth, and with it, stagnant sea water with the stench of urine flowed like a rapid down the back of her throat, some dribbling out down the side of her mouth and onto her dress. She retched, trying to turn her head away, but fingers moved into her mouth, pulling her jaw down further and wider as more of the putrid liquid was forced down. She wanted to vomit, the bile rising up from her stomach. She could hear the other person's breathing get faster; they were excited.

The person moved behind her, pulling the chain attached to the pulley. Her arms shot upwards in excruciating pain as they popped out of their sockets; then she was released to the deafening sound of metal links clinking and rattling as she crashed back hard onto the floor. Tears of agony streaked down her cheeks, making a path through the dirt and grime that stuck to her face like a mask. She thought of her children, back to a moment when they were all happy, their faces smiling and laughing, playing on the beach, the sun glinting like diamonds off a flat endless sea, and the bond only a mother can have in life and in death.

A small black doctor's case was placed down on the floor, opened, and a thin razor-sharp serrated knife taken out. Her blindfold was cut free, but her bloodshot eyelids had inflamed and welded together. She forced them open, the skin stretching, tearing, the pain all too much; her vision clouded, coming in and out of focus. She turned her head to one side.

'I didn't look. I didn't see you; I promise.'

The silence was deafening, broken only by the water dripping and the slight shuffle of feet in front of her. She closed her eyes to the sounds of summer waves gently breaking on the shore and the laughter of children, feeling the sun on her face and the warm breeze through her hair. She wept.

THIRTY-FOUR

Elsbeth and Abberline met outside Brighton Station and made their way towards the concourse and the Stationmaster's Office. Inside, they met the same man Rawlings had, and he directed them to the shed where Jack Robertson had been living. They walked along the narrow path that led out into the yard and then over to the engineering division where Robertson had been apprehended.

'What do you suppose we might find in there?' Elsbeth enquired.

'I'm not sure, but we have to do a full search; we need evidence, and without it, it's going to be circumstantial, and that, in my book, is not good enough to hang a man, whatever he is being accused of.'

The shed lay at the back of the main engineering section, a small wooden structure no bigger than eight feet by six feet with a single door that had been padlocked.

Abberline took out a small pocketknife and inserted it into the lock, twisting it a number of ways before the lock sprang open.

'There you go. My time as an apprentice watchmaker sometimes comes in handy, understanding how mechanics work. A padlock is a simple movement, and almost all of them work by the same principle.'

She watched him wipe the blade, freeing any residual dirt, before folding it and placing it back in his pocket.

They entered the shed. It was dark and gloomy and smelt of oil and coal just as the suspect had done. Abberline removed and lit an oil lamp which was hung off a nail. The yellow light revealed a messy area, a long bench to the left running the length of the shed, and a single makeshift bed on the floor in the middle covered in sack cloths with a torn and grubby pillow. Elsbeth noticed the only window at the back, but it had been boarded over, presumably by Robertson, to stop prying eyes.

'Inspector, look, if we can try and pry that board off, we can get some natural light to see by–' pointing towards the window.

Abberline looked about, finding a long metal bar, and prised the panel covering the glass off, the glass itself covered in soot and dirt. Elsbeth fetched some of the sackcloth off the bed and wiped a few panes.

Abberline felt deeply uncomfortable in such a disorganised mess which grated on him. 'Let's get started. You take the front; I'll start at the back, and we will work towards each other. Look for anything that could be used as a weapon, anything out of the ordinary.'

Elsbeth went towards the front as instructed and worked across the room; she kept the door open to add more light to the search. The front was littered with rubbish; tin cans, beer bottles, and clothing just strewn across the floor.

'I'll be lucky to be able to find my way out of this place, let alone come across anything of significance.' She paused, found a wooden pole to move more questionable items around instead of picking them up before continuing.

Abberline worked quickly and thoroughly he had conducted searches many times before. 'If there's anything here, it will most likely be hidden, maybe wrapped in some clothing or something like that, hidden from view.' As he stepped towards the centre of the room noticed a loose floorboard. He bent down and held the lamp lower to see the nails had been removed. There were four holes in each corner; someone had deliberately taken them out. 'Elsbeth, come here. I might have found something. See if you can bring another lamp over. If I'm right, we're going to need it.'

Elsbeth found one on the long workbench to the side and made her way over to Abberline. He thanked her, lit the lamp, and put it beside the gap in the floor where he had removed the board. He took his coat and jacket off and asked Elsbeth to hold them as he rolled his shirt sleeve up on his right arm, before slowly lowering it into the abyss, feeling his way with his hand as he went. 'Not sure how deep this goes before I reach the bottom.' His arm was now more than halfway sunk into the hole.

'Can you move it about, feel anything?' Elsbeth was curious and thought she had the slenderer frame out of the two of them so it might be easier for her.

'Nothing yet. I might have to remove more boards for better access, but that will take time. Hang on, there's something here. I just brushed the top of it. We need some more light. Can you attach one of the lamps to something so I can lower it? See what this might be before I put my hand on it.'

Elsbeth fetched the wooden pole she had used earlier to move the detritus about, and some coarse twine wound up into a knot hung off one of the wooden beams. 'Will these do?'

'Yes, perfect. Tie the lantern handle to the pole, please.'

Elsbeth did it in quick time and waited for Abberline to remove his arm out of the gap. He took the pole and slowly lowered the lamp back down until it reached the bottom. He peered down, his head angled to get a better look. It was tight, but there was an old rag wrapped around an object. I will put my arm back down to try and get it out. He was confident he could retrieve it but, at the same time, slightly concerned at what it was he might find.

Elsbeth moved closer and leaned over. 'Be careful, who knows what it is.'

Abberline didn't reply as he concentrated on the task.

'Nearly there. I'm just going to try and grab it.' His breathing was quick, sweat appearing on his brow. He gradually felt the cloth with his fingers and cautiously started wrapping them round, getting a better hold. 'I'm just…I'm just going to very slowly…' A pause. Then, before he could do anything, he felt something move under the material. It was large and warm and hissed and squealed a high-pitched sound. The head of a large rat appeared. Its black, beady eyes stared up at Abberline. Within an instant, it quickly scurried into the black abyss, disappearing further under the floor space. Abberline jumped but grabbed the cloth and object as fast as he could, bringing it back to the surface.

'Are you alright, Inspector? You had me worried there for a moment.'

'I'm fine; it was just a rodent.'

Elsbeth watched as he carefully undid the package until its contents were revealed. 'Is that what I think it is?' Elsbeth said, not quite believing her eyes.

'Yes, it most certainly is.' Holding it up, he examined the long, thin, serrated knife, inspecting the surface. 'There's dried blood on the blade, and it fits the description Cripps gave us in his autopsy report, so I would say it's a good possibility this is the weapon that killed Rosie Meeks and Mary Quinn. But without further examination, I can't be sure; we need to match the wounds on both bodies to be sure.' Abberline felt a sense of achievement but wanted to make sure of his find before re-interviewing Jack Robertson and charging him formally.

Elsbeth thought back to the conversation in the morgue with the coroner, remembering what he said would happen to the two murdered women. 'Cripps would have let the bodies go for burial by now?'

'Maybe, but I can have them exhumed. It's easier as there is no family. Rosie Meeks' son is too young, and Mary Quinn had no one here. But it will be a last resort. It should be more than possible to determine if this is the knife used in the murders from the photographs and the dimensions Cripps has provided, but we will need his professional eye as well to substantiate this. I want a second opinion to make sure. I don't want any surprises, especially as I will have to report this to Scotland Yard. He should have kept the bodies back as he knows we are still investigating their deaths, but there is only so long they can be stored at the morgue with limited ice. Maybe two to three weeks at most before the bodies start to decompose to be of any use, and we are reaching that upper limit soon.'

Abberline put the flooring board back in place and asked Elsbeth to untie the lantern from the pole and put them both back on the workbench. If they needed them again, they would at least know where to find them instead of grappling about in the dark.

Elsbeth placed them both back as asked; as she went to turn the flame off, something on the shelf above her head caught her attention. The light was reflecting off some glass. Two large jars were pushed back towards the wall. She checked for something to stand on while the Inspector was busy putting his jacket and coat back on. She found an empty wooden crate and used that to reach up, edging the jars slowly towards her. She couldn't immediately see if they contained anything, but they were heavy as she brought them down. She stepped off the crate and stood in absolute silence, shocked by what she had discovered.

Her words came out as a whisper; she wanted to shout but was unable to, her voice quiet and trembling. 'Inspector… Inspector, I think you need to look at this.'

Abberline heard her calling and rushed over to find her standing rigid, her gaze fixed. 'What is it? What have you found?' He watched her slowly raise her arm, pointing at the containers before her.

'What the hell is that?'

Abberline didn't answer her but picked one up, recognising exactly what it contained. 'Organs. Heart, liver and intestine.'

'Why would anyone want to keep animal parts like this?' Elsbeth questioned, still disgusted and shaken, finding her voice.

'They are not animal organs.' Moving the jar around and examining the contents closely before he confirmed: 'They're human.'

THIRTY-FIVE

Cripps prepared everything for the impending visit of Inspector Abberline and Miss Hargreaves. He set out the photographs and reports on both women and waited for their arrival. He had been informed by an officer from the police station that the Inspector had discovered what he believed to be the murder weapon, and some missing organs contained in two jars. This brought a smile to his face, knowing that the items were coming back to their rightful owner. He had been an avid collector of the macabre and knew many private collections that housed some magnificent specimens. To Cripps, they were works of art to be celebrated and sold to those who shared his passion for such strange things. He kept his own private assemblage behind a secret door to the back of the morgue. The construction was paid for with his own funds, so the purpose of it remained a secret. He would often go into the room by himself and sit in silence, looking at his prized possessions for hours.

He had decided to hold another one of his gatherings, people who understood quality, and all prepared to pay handsomely for it. Cripps was an opportunist, void of morals or ethics and would take any measure to advance his collection and bank balance. He saw the dead as products, and even when mourners came to view their deceased, he thought about how he could make a profit out of the departed. The poor offered rich pickings as nobody knew them, and they could be sold off for medical experiments. But his main stock in trade was the unusual; any age, sex or colour made no difference to him, providing they possessed some unique oddity; he would prepare it for sale as a part or even a complete body for those clients with the room to exhibit them.

Business was booming as he had a never-ending supply in Brighton to see him through to retirement. The two bodies that had landed on his slabs from the recent murders presented him with a predicament. They were not worth very much on their own, but together, double murder victims that had been violated beyond anything seen before, they had become collectable items. And to the right person, they could fetch a nice sum. He had stored them away in the back and kept them on ice for another time. The body of Seamus Keane was also lying in the corridor, waiting for his attention. But Keane was a cheap penny gangster beaten to a pulp by his own type. He had little value, so Cripps had already decided to sell his body for pig food or dissection; either way, he would turn a small profit.

As he looked about the mortuary, checking nothing suspicious could bring any unwanted attention, he heard knocking at the front door. He knew it had to be Abberline and the awful Hargreaves woman who seemed to follow Abberline around like a puppy. He wondered how she would look dead on one of his tables, staring up at him. He smiled as he put on his jacket, looked in the mirror, slicked his hair back, and left the room. Walking down the corridor, his footsteps echoed on the hard floor as he made his way to the reception at the front of the building, ready to greet his visitors.

THIRTY-SIX

Elsbeth decided to take a cab to the morgue, after the last time walking up St James Street had not been a pleasurable experience, and the weather had not changed much, still only just above freezing. As the cab drew up outside, she waited a few minutes for Abberline to arrive, but after a while, she alighted from the cab, paid the driver and knocked on the door to The Dead House. Already, she was feeling her stomach turning. Cripps was a frigid man void of any emotion, creepy and disconnected from both the dead and the living. She loathed him intently and hoped she would not be alone with him for long if she had to wait for Abberline.

The door opened, and Cripps stood at the threshold, bowing gently, posturing for her to enter.

'Good morning, Miss Hargreaves. I do hope you are well?' Elsbeth knew he didn't mean a word of it; his voice was oily and insincere.

'Is Inspector Abberline here yet?'

'No, I'm afraid he has yet to grace us with his presence. I've had word he's been held up at the station, but no matter, I'm sure he won't be long. Please come through, we can wait for him together.' He parted his lips in a half smile, a sneer as a wolf would just before the kill.

Elsbeth followed Cripps down the corridor, the sickly embalming smell of amber reminding her of the first visit. She wondered if she would ever come to like that scent again. They reached the examination room of the morgue, where he offered her a seat. 'Please make yourself comfortable, Miss Hargreaves. May I offer you some tea while we wait?'

Elsbeth could think of nothing worse than any refreshments being prepared by his hands. 'No, thank you. I'm sure Inspector Abberline will be here shortly.'

'Hmm, I understand that the Inspector has found the murder weapon?'

Elsbeth watched as Cripps slithered around the tables where he performed the autopsies. 'He has, and we need to demonstrate if the blade found is a match for wounds on both of the victims who are, I presume, still here?'

'Oh yes, indeed, sorry, I'm sure Abberline wanted me to keep them back, but I had them removed not long after your previous visit. They had started to decompose so I sent them off to a plot especially put aside for those who are… shall we say, financially embarrassed? You understand?'

'You mean a place where there is no other use for it other than a dumping ground for those that can't afford a decent funeral. Just somewhere to put them without any marker, just so long as they are gone from this place.' She felt her anger rise at Cripps and his complete lack of empathy, which was a world away from her own feelings, but it seemed to come very naturally to him.

She started to become more uneasy as he moved closer towards her, only the last embalming table between them and the body that lay on it. A starched white linen sheet covered the form as he rested his hand on it. Taking the edge of the cloth, he lifted it back to her waist to show the corpse of a young female of about twenty years of age.

'Now here we have a good example, Miss Hargreaves, of

a young person sadly taken too soon by the overindulgence of opiates. She had come from a good family; her father was a local solicitor. He had informed me that she had been educated at the finest schools and given every opportunity to marry into society. But as is the way of the young and careless, she fell foul not only of her family but the law, which greatly embarrassed her father. She had become involved with a ruffian who introduced her to this addictive drug, becoming dependent on it and him for the supply, until it ultimately resulted in her untimely death.'

Elsbeth sat in silence; she hated that women should be educated and taught about the fine things in life just to be married off to the first available socialite who had a healthy bank balance and a large country house. There was something of a cattle market about the entire process that didn't sit well with her. But she suspected Cripps knew this and was playing on her moral standards.

Cripps moved his hand onto the body of the young woman, his expression changing. His hand was on her chest, her breasts still firm and pert. Taking his time, he slowly traced the contours of them, enjoying the moment, then advanced down to her navel. 'Beautiful skin, such a waste, don't you think, Miss Hargreaves.' He rolled the sheet further down, revealing her vagina. 'I doubt very much if she left this life a virgin, don't you agree, Miss Hargreaves?' Looking up, smirking.

Elsbeth, sickened, turned away.

'Oh, come now, Miss Hargreaves. Surely, you're not the squeamish type? I wouldn't have put you down as one of those at all. No, you misunderstand. I'm merely giving you a lesson in a day in the life of a mortician. This is an example of the tragedy one has to deal with in my profession. Perhaps you might demonstrate your skills by conversing with this dead specimen. I am always eager to learn.' His sarcasm was not disguised.

Elsbeth was not going to let this continue; she knew exactly what he was trying to do. 'You don't shock me, Cripps. I will not be provoked for your amusement either. Quite frankly, you disgust me. This person had a life that had meaning, and her body deserves respect, Cripps, which you clearly have little of.'

Cripps noticed that she had dropped the title Mister in her address when using his last name, which amused him.

'Oh well, as you please.'

As he covered the body, he noticed a black leather glove at the bottom of the slab; he knew instantly who it belonged to and quickly removed it. *It was unlike him to be so forgetful.* The door to the room opened, and Abberline stood at the entrance. Elsbeth was more than relieved to see him.

'I apologise for my late arrival. I had some business to attend to at the police station. The front door was unlocked, so I hope you don't mind I came straight down.' He looked over at Elsbeth, who looked unwell and nodded.

Abberline handed over the knife found at the living quarters of the suspect, Jack Robertson. 'These two jars are internal organs. Maybe you can confirm if any of these belonged to the victims?'

'Of course, Inspector, I'll check my records and let you know. Unfortunately, as I was saying to Miss Hargreaves, I don't have the bodies, they had to be despatched shortly after our last meeting, but don't worry, I can make a professional opinion based on what we have. People do keep the oddest of things, don't they, Inspector?' he said, looking at the jars of organs. Cripps took the knife and examined the blood stains, moving it up and down in a stabbing motion. 'Right, let's see first if this is indeed the murder weapon.' Still holding the knife, he tilted his head to one side so only Elsbeth could see his face and smiled.

THIRTY-SEVEN

Elsbeth returned home from the mortuary after picking up some supplies from town. She had agreed with Abberline to wait after the meeting with Cripps until he had returned the results of the knife and contents of the jars found at the suspect Jack Robertson's living quarters. Elsbeth remembered the last time she met the suspect was at the bakery, where he had threatened her and Abberline but had got away. Since his arrest, Abberline had told her that he had a strong motive for killing both women since Seamus Keane was now out of the picture after having been found floating in the sea, so Jack Robertson would remain in custody. If it turned out that the knife was, in fact, the one used in the attacks and that the human remains belonged to one or both victims, then they had their man. Then, there was a motive and a good chance if he was their killer, he had abducted Amelia Stanton, so they would need to find out where he had hidden her before it was too late.

Elsbeth felt some relief that the person responsible for the murders would, in most probability, now face justice and pay the ultimate penalty for his despicable and horrific crimes. She walked through into the front lounge and remembered back to that night when Mary Quinn had appeared to her. She removed her coat and bonnet and undid some ribbons in her hair so that her long dark locks fell about her shoulders. She felt exhausted by it all and wondered how Abberline could keep up such a pace. But it was his manner and his profession, his unquestionable commitment and sometimes direct manner she strangely admired, even if it grated on her at times.

She lit two candles on the table and bowed her head as the wind howled and rain moved almost horizontally against the house; it was not a night to be out. Her thoughts turned to the young Mary Quinn and single mother Rosie Meeks, who committed no crime other than to be two women in the wrong place at the wrong time. Now their spirits roamed lost and tormented, unable to rest until the person who took their lives had stood trial and joined them. She asked in her thoughts that Amelia Stanton be found soon and reunited with her family. She decided to consult the cards as they would give more insight and direction as to where Mrs Stanton was being held. She had seen something when she held a sample of Ameila's hair in the lady's bedroom when they went to speak with her husband about her disappearance. What she had seen was shocking, and the overwhelming sense of fear she got from Amelia worried Elsbeth greatly. Elsbeth's skills were old, formed many generations ago by her grandmother and hers before that. Elsbeth would do everything in her power to use all she knew to find Amelia and bring her back safely.

To have a successful reading of the tarot, she knew she had to be totally free of any distractions. Be still and present in the moment, both in mind and body. She felt many emotions from the day's events and needed to completely relax before attempting to consult the cards. She left the lounge and made her way up the stairs to her bedroom, which was on the first floor at the front of the house. She lit the fire in her room, prepared by Mrs Shoesmith, her house help who called three times a week, and after closing the curtains the room was now snug and warm; she felt safe and cosy. Elsbeth undressed, placed her clothes on the bed, and put on a pink hand-embroidered silk gown that had a Japanese pattern on the back over her naked body. She used water to cleanse body and soul, so proceeded into her own private bathroom, which had been divided off in the bedroom behind an elegant panel screen. She ran a hot bath, adding orange and rose oils, lighting several candles in the room to add to the ambience. She knew she was lucky to have such luxury.

Only the finest homes had fitted bathrooms, most separate from the bedroom. But Elsbeth was single and wealthy, loved her bed and her bath, and was never one to follow convention. She had the tub and toilet built to look like furniture and the wash basin of the finest porcelain hand-decorated with wildflowers. It was feminine and exuded style and elegance. She dropped her gown and looked at her naked self in the mirror, turning each way and checking her figure, looking at the imperfections that in her mind she had, never seeing, or understanding the beauty others saw in her. She slid into the hot water and submerged herself, releasing all the day's stress and problems.

It took an age to relax, her skin, soft and smooth as the warm water lapped over her every muscle, her breathing steady and rhythmic. She was at complete peace, semi-awake, almost in a trance-like state, the scent of orange and rose in the room, twisting and dancing with the steam that rose from the tub. The candles shone a soft light, tears of wax dripping down the sides, building one on top of the other, forming a beautiful and unique sculpture. She sighed slowly and, closing her eyes, slid beneath the warm water, totally immersing her face. She raised her arms, putting her hands on each side of the tub, ready to pull herself up and opened her eyes.

The faces of Rosie Meeks and Mary Quinn stared down so close that only the thin skin of the water separated them.

Their faces seemed untouched by death, hovering, both looking terrified. Elsbeth, her body and face still submerged, didn't know what to do. She couldn't hold her breath any longer. Her chest ached as searing pain tore through her lungs. She had to come up for air. She quickly pulled herself up, water streaming off her body, ready to jump out of the bath and run into her bedroom.

'Get out now. He's in the house.'

A deafening, high-pitched scream came from their mouths. Then both faces vanished, and she was left in the tub, terrified and alone.

THIRTY-EIGHT

Elsbeth lifted herself out of the tub, reaching for her gown. Her wet skin clung in patches to the silk as she tied it around her waist. Blowing out the candles in the bathroom, she crept softly into the bedroom. If someone was in the house, she'd lock the door, open a window to the street below and call for assistance. But the thought that someone had entered her home irritated her, and she was not the running kind. She went to the fire grate and lifted a black cast iron poker from the set of fireside tools. Only the hallway clock broke the silence as she moved gradually out onto the landing. Two further bedrooms were on this floor, plus a smaller additional bathroom at the far end of the landing. She had to be sure. She slid along, her back to the wall, her wet gown leaving a smear like a snail, grasping the weapon tightly in both hands, raising it, ready to strike. Each step she made was careful, and considered, her bare feet feeling the carpet against her skin. She reached the first door, releasing her grip of one hand on the poker; she reached out and slowly turned the handle. It creaked.

She entered, leaving the door open so the light from the hallway lamp followed her. The room was slightly smaller than her own bedroom but decorated to the same standard with style and elegance. Floral wallpaper matched the curtains and a small open fireplace, which was unlit. It was dark inside, but the light from the hallway helped her to see the double four-poster bed, dressing table and mirror, and a large wardrobe in the corner. She put both hands back on the poker as she crept to the end of the bed. It was high off the ground, and she bent slowly to ensure nobody was hiding underneath it. Nothing. She walked to the other side, each step measured, her heart racing, still nothing. Maybe the warning Mary Quinn and Rosie Meeks had given her in the tub was wrong, but somehow, she didn't believe that. The next room proved to be the same, with nothing unusual; only the bathroom remained at the end of the landing. A noise downstairs caught her attention. It wasn't a loud, crashing, banging announcement. It was more synonymous with a gentle knocking sound emanating from the back of the house. But it was out of place. It didn't belong.

The narrow hallway from the front door led, first, to the lounge. There was a further reception room next to this room and then the kitchen, which had a back door into the garden. Elsbeth made her way down the stairs, glancing back over her shoulder every now and then just to be sure, as she hadn't checked the other bathroom. The weather pounded the house, the rain sounding like small stones being showered against the roof and the glass in the windows. The smell of the beeswax from the candles that were still burning reached her as she got to the bottom of the stairs, with the lounge in front of her.

Her skin now felt clammy against the fabric of her gown, uncomfortable and clingy, her feet cold against the black and white chequered floor tiles. She listened. There was the sound again, towards the kitchen and the back of the house. A dull thumping. *What is that? Should she shout or run while she had the chance?* Her wrists and arms began to ache from having to hold the poker. She moved past the lounge and the reception room, the door slightly open. She carefully closed it shut, not wanting another surprise like the one at the bakery where Jack Robertson had attacked her and Abberline. Not this time; this time, she was ready. This was her house, and she would not give them the satisfaction of running. She wanted to see the intruder head-on and would do whatever was necessary to protect herself and her home. But for all the bravado, one thing remained, as bright as a full moon on a clear night, she was afraid. She got nearer, and the sound became louder. The sweat from her hands loosened her grip slightly. Her mouth and lips were dry. She swallowed with each footstep; arriving at the kitchen door, she pushed it open cautiously.

Stepping in, there was little light; she stopped again, standing rigid on the spot, trying to control her breathing. Unable to see clearly, her mind started filling in the blanks, seeing motion when there was none. Shadows crossed her path, and the rain continued to fall so intensely it distorted sound. She was sure she heard a voice, a whisper. She twisted her body round, the hairs on the back of her neck standing up, her eyes fixing on any movement, trying to see what or who was in the room. Squinting, she had to get further in; she recognised the outline of the large pine rectangle table that stood in the middle of the kitchen. Above, a large pot rack hung filled with various-sized blackened pans for cooking. In front of this was a sink and window looking out onto the garden. She worked her way around the table, feeling her way; to her left was a black cast iron range, and to the right, a dresser housing plates, cups, cutlery, and crisp white linen for the tables. As she reached the back door, she saw it was ajar but didn't seem broken. It was moving, thumping against the frame, causing the noise she had heard. She could see the key was still in the lock on the inside. The wind suddenly blew so strong that the door flew back, hitting the wall, glass flew through the air, and onto the floor. Two large pans hanging off the rack fell, bouncing across the room.

Elsbeth dropped the poker quickly, covering her face with her hands as shards of glass shot past her, missing her by a hair's width. She ran forward, slamming the door shut with her shoulder and turning the lock; as she did, she felt a shooting pain in her right foot; she had been cut, the blood seeping from the wound. She went over to the sink and tore two towels into strips, picked her foot up and tied the strips around, stopping the blood and partially covering the wound. As she looked up and out of the window towards the back of the garden, the silhouette of a figure, a tall man wearing a cloak of some kind, holding what seemed to be a small black case, stood watching. She jumped back, her spine hitting the side of the table; she let out a cry. She quickly moved forward again and grabbed a box of matches on a shelf just below the windowsill; her hands shaking, she broke one and then got another out, lighting the lamp fixed to the wall next to the sink. The gas ignited; its flame shot upwards towards the ceiling before settling down. She stared out of the window into the blackness of the garden, but the figure had gone, just the rain lashing down where the person had been standing.

I can get to you anytime I want, Elsbeth.

As she walked carefully backwards, still looking out of the window, any pain from her injuries she was feeling was quickly replaced with horror. On the middle of the kitchen table was a gift, an organ, its colour a reddish brown, wedge-shaped with two lobes of unequal size and shape. She recognised it immediately, having seen the very same thing in the mortuary; it was the liver, a human liver. But what turned her stomach, what made her feel like vomiting, was the blood oozing from it onto her table. It had been removed recently. It was fresh.

THIRTY-NINE

A knock at the front door broke the silence as Elsbeth navigated around the kitchen table, her eyes fixed on the bloodied organ. Worried who it could be calling, she tried to be as quiet as possible; *what if it's the person who left that...that thing?* Making her way back out to the hallway, she hopped as quickly as she could into the front lounge, putting on some slippers to help protect her cut foot and any blood weeping through the makeshift bandage. She waited at the front door, her heart beating; she had no idea who it was on the other side. Opening it a bit at a time, she nervously called out, 'Who is it?' Before any answer came back, the door was suddenly pushed open. Abberline stood shaking the rain off his coat.

'For Christ's sake, aren't you going to let me in? It's a biblical storm out there.' He moved into the hallway, drenched, as Elsbeth stood back. 'I have something to tell you. I've heard back from Cripps at the mortuary regarding the knife and organs found at Jack Robertson's shed at Brighton Station.' He stopped, noticing the look on Elsbeth's face.

'Please...please go to the kitchen, go, look.' She pointed towards the room. 'There's something there. Somebody was in the house. They told me, they warned me.' Elsbeth was shaking, her face drained.

Abberline didn't understand but could see how shaken she was. 'Who warned you? What are you talking about? Look, stay here; I'll take a look around.'

'The kitchen,' she insisted. Elsbeth stood back as Abberline made his way down the corridor, listening for any sounds from upstairs. He knew he would have to search the entire house to ensure the intruder, if there was one, had gone. Abberline rushed to the kitchen, noticing the organ lying on the table; he checked to make sure there was nobody else there. Then, he went to the back door and peered out into the pitch-black garden. Elsbeth had quietly followed him and stood in the doorway.

Elsbeth shared her thoughts. 'I'm no expert but my basic understanding is this is a liver; however, I have no idea if it belongs to a man or a woman. But one thing I'm certain of is it was inside a person not that long ago or has been preserved somehow as the blood is still liquid and has not formed a clot. It makes me feel sick.'

Abberline looked at her in a questioning way. 'Okay, don't worry, I'll get it collected and taken to Cripps for confirmation and identification to see if this, too, has come from one of the victims.'

'I saw him. The intruder was at the back of the garden, just standing looking at me, and then when I looked back up, he had gone, probably through the back gate that leads into a narrow alleyway back out onto the main street.'

'Did you see what they looked like?'

'It was dark, so not really, just an outline. But it was a man, I'm sure of that, and tall, he had a cloak on of some kind and I think he was carrying a small case but that's all I'm afraid, I'm sorry, as I said, it was difficult to see.'

Abberline wanted to bring back the conversation to something she had said earlier when he had arrived. 'What did you mean they warned me? Who told you someone was in the house?'

'Mary Quinn and Rosie Meeks told me.' Elsbeth could tell from his cynical expression that he didn't believe a word of what she was saying.

'Hmm, well, as you know, I find all this spiritual stuff hard to believe, and even though you have been able to provide me with information which, I have no explanation for...' He paused. 'I still find it just too much for me to accept. You understand I hope?'

'I understand, Inspector. It's not something you can put in a test tube and get an answer as to how it happens. It's something within me, even I don't fully understand how it all works. All I know is that those women warned me, and they were as real as you are standing here.' They had come to know each other well enough to have equal respect for one another, which was good enough for her, but she wasn't going to give up on him.

'Cripps has confirmed the knife we found at Jack Robertson's matches the wounds inflicted on both Mary Quinn and Rosie Meeks. I came round to let you know. It seems a good thing that I did,' he smiled at her. 'So, we can safely say that it is our murder weapon. The two jars of organs also match the ones taken from both victims. He's checked them against all the information and his notes, and there is no doubt. So, it looks like we have our man.'

'If that's true, Inspector, and Jack Robertson is in custody, who could have left that disgusting deposit in my home, and why?'

'Well, Jack Robertson has a lot of explaining to do, especially in the light of the knife and the jars having been linked to both victims and found where he's been staying.'

'It doesn't make sense; he couldn't be here if he's locked up in your cell.' Elsbeth lowered her head in thought. There was a pause. 'Unless...'

Abberline finished the sentence: 'Unless Jack Robertson was working with someone else. There are two of them. This is even more of a reason to return to Jack Robertson with the evidence. If we push hard enough, he'll give us the other name. But if we are correct and Jack Robertson was working with another, then that person is still at large and most likely is with Amelia Stanton. Rawlings found nothing on any of the beaches or fishermen's huts. Her husband is not happy and has been making his voice heard in Scotland Yard, and I've been summoned to a meeting back in London.'

'When do you go?'

'Tonight.'

FORTY

Abberline arrived back at Scotland Yard H division for a meeting with his boss, James Monro, Head of CID. He wanted a complete update on events in Brighton and an explanation as to why there still had not been anyone charged over the two murders. His meetings with Monro were never easy affairs, as his boss had a deep-seated dislike for him. Abberline, as usual, waited outside Monro's office to be called in. He could see Monro was not alone. There was another man with his back to Abberline, gesticulating with his arms and hands in the air. The raised voices in the office were suddenly shattered by the fierce, bellowing scream of Monro.

'Abberline, get in here now.'

Abberline quickly gathered his briefcase files, hat and coat and entered the lion's den.

'Shut the door and sit down,' Monro barked at him. Abberline did as he was told and sat next to the other man, whom he recognised immediately as Commissioner Charles Warren. Warren, from Bangor, Wales, was a military man and a general who served in the Royal Engineers and found civilian life difficult and frustrating. He didn't like the fact that the Metropolitan Police Force for which he had been tasked to put right at forty-three years of age was being scrutinised by the recent murders in Brighton. He was annoyed that the local press was making the whole police force a laughing stock.

'Abberline, I want you to explain to Sir Charles and me what exactly you have been doing down in Brighton and why no one has been charged with these appalling murders.'

Before Abberline could answer, Sir Charles Warren quickly intervened, turning to face Abberline. A medium height man with a pot belly and a large walrus moustache immaculately dressed in a black suit, highly polished shoes, his back straight, he had a commanding presence.

'Abberline, you were dispatched to sort this mess out, and the press is having a field day. What on earth are you doing down there, man? To make matters worse, Joseph Stanton, the Minister for Brighton and a personal friend of mine, has written to me this very morning, making it clear that your efforts to locate his missing wife have been woeful at best. According to him, you visited him once with some woman in tow. You asked a few questions, went and rummaged around in the lady's bedroom, and then left. Stanton has not heard a word from you since. His wife is still missing. We have a murderer running around killing people, and the press is making us all look like clowns. What do you have to say for yourself, man!'

Sir Charles, incandescent, rocked back and forth as he shouted at Abberline. Monro sat back, grinning from ear to ear, unable to hide his pleasure at seeing Abberline being torn apart.

'Sir Charles, if I may please speak for a moment, I shall, I'm sure, put your mind at ease.'

Sir Charles huffed and withdrew, sitting back and turning his head from side to side, waiting to hear Abberline's pitiful excuses. 'Well, get on with it. I am due in Parliament in an hour. And let me tell you, I'm not going to keep the Prime Minister waiting, so let's hear what you have to say and make it fast.'

Abberline knew he had to make a good report, as two very annoyed people, one his direct boss and the other the head of the police force, were waiting impatiently to hear his explanation. If it weren't more than satisfactory, he would be out of a job and pulling pints in his local pub by nightfall.

'First and foremost, Sir Charles, please let me absolutely reassure you that I am in control of the situation in Brighton, and there is no need to concern yourself.' He watched the reaction to his opening statement as Sir Charles, his eyes watery with rage, listened impatiently.

'I will come back to the missing Mrs Stanton in due course. But first, as you know, two murders occurred in the North Laine area of Brighton. The first was an eighteen-year-old, Mary Quinn, a prostitute from Ireland who worked at a drinking establishment. She owed money to her landlord, a man well known to the Brighton police as a violent money-lending thug who had many illegal businesses. One of them was prostitution, which he ran from The Black Star pub in the town.'

Abberline waited to see if any questions or more likely criticisms were forthcoming, but for the moment he was free to continue his brief on the case.

'I have interviewed him myself and found him to be more than capable of murder, especially if anyone were in debt to him. Mary Quinn's body was found in an alleyway near where she was working. She had been stabbed twenty-nine times; her body was ripped open, organs removed, and the body left on a rubbish tip. A homeless man, who says he was a witness to the attack, gave us a sketchy description of the killer, but it must be noted he was some worse for drink. The second victim, Rosie Meeks, thirty years of age, was a single mother who had been working at a bakery in The North Laine for a few years. The night she was killed, she had been left alone to run the shop as her employers were out of town on business, a fact we have, of course, verified. Her attacker, I believe, knew this and took advantage of it. Her body was mutilated beyond anything I have ever seen in my career to date. Far worse than our first victim, Mary Quinn, it was torn to pieces, and again, internal body parts had been taken.'

'But you have no one charged for either offence, is that correct, Inspector Abberline?' Monro now interrupted with almost joyful glee.

'It was my initial thinking that the murders were separate, sir, as they did not seem necessarily connected, but I'm not so sure now that is the case. Having interviewed Seamus Keane, it was not implausible that he knew both women and both owed money to him. So, he could have been responsible for their killings and was setting an example of what might happen if you didn't pay him back. His world was a savage one; it's all about fear and control. But the problem is, did he do it? As Seamus Keane said to me, he would lose the money and future earnings, especially with a prostitute like Mary Quinn, who, as I understand it, was in demand.'

Monro put his glasses on the end of his nose and opened a folder that contained a report. 'Hmm…But even so, you saw fit not to arrest him at the time, a man you, yourself, admit to being violent and more than capable of killing. Doesn't that show a lack of judgment on your part, Inspector?'

'If I was to arrest Seamus Keane for the murder of Mary Quinn or Rosie Meeks, I needed solid evidence, sir. As it happens, he had a water-tight alibi. A number of people were prepared to swear on oath that he was sitting at The Black Star pub all day and night when the killings were committed. Now, I know if he wanted, he could provide an army of people to testify to the judge; in that case, without any physical evidence, he would certainly be acquitted. The case would be thrown out, and you and the commissioner would be even more aggrieved as we would be back to square one, with the press having even more fun at our expense.'

Monro interrupted, 'But this is all irrelevant anyway as it says here that Mr Keane's body was found floating in the sea off Brighton beach, so his innocence or guilt is now one of conjecture? So, we will never know.'

Abberline knew that Monro was enjoying every moment of this. Monro wanted him off the force, and this case was a perfect situation to discredit him. He often wondered if he had sent him down to Brighton for this very purpose, to fail.

'Yes, that is correct, sir, but Seamus Keane was a victim of a violent attack with a wooden object, as Doctor Cripps, the coroner, found splinters in the man's head during the autopsy. Keane had many enemies, and I am as sure as I can be that this death was gang-related and at the hands of another like him. I don't believe he was responsible for the killings of these two women. It is easy to see how people could jump to such a conclusion given his long list of violent offences, but Seamus Keane was a businessman, albeit a crooked and vicious one, and it would make no sense for him to lose money.'

'It's reassuring that you are certain of something, Inspector,' Sir Charles said, almost mocking him.

Abberline continued, not rising to the remark. 'Cripps, has made his autopsy report very transparent on both women that the killer is left-handed, using a serrated blade, the type used by surgeons, and has a good understanding of human anatomy to locate and dissect the organs from the bodies in such a fashion. So again, this goes to confirm that Seamus Keane was not responsible for these killings as his knowledge of the human anatomy was, I would wager, poor, to say the least. So, we can say now with conviction that the murder of the two women is, by the same hand, the same person.'

'The report that somehow got leaked to the press?' Monro said, looking over to Sir Charles.

'Anything to do with this Hargreaves woman you have been taking with you? A bloody psychic, I believe here, says so in the paper!' Sir Charles repeatedly pressed his index finger at the column about Elsbeth's criticism of the way Brighton Police were managing the initial case. 'No wonder we are a joke. Whose idea was this?'

Abberline suddenly saw an opportunity to get into Monro's good books. It was, after all, his suggestion that he should work with Miss Hargreaves, so she didn't go to the press again.

'Of course, Sir Charles, the leak was most unfortunate, and it has to be said it did not do us any favours. I have not yet ascertained who leaked the report, but I have my own suspicions. With regret, I fear it can only have been someone within our own ranks. Either way, it was a betrayal of trust, and I will find out who is to blame. Miss Hargreaves has been a valuable asset to the investigation for her local knowledge and speaking with women who would otherwise not be so compelled to help the police. I, of course, do not use or have any confidence in her so-called psychic ability. Her involvement, as I have mentioned, is only for support. That is all I can assure you.' Abberline did not want to go down the rabbit hole and say how much Elsbeth had been involved. It would not do either of them any good and would receive more than a frosty reception, to say the least.

Sir Charles became restless as he checked his pocket watch. 'I hear a lot of assurances from you, Inspector, and precious little else. Like a suspect being charged.' Abberline could sense the atmosphere in the room becoming worse.

'Yes, indeed, sir, if you will allow me to continue…' Abberline felt the heat rise under his collar, causing a slight redness to the skin as the inquisition continued.

'I can now tell you that we have a break in the case. We are currently holding a local man in custody at present who knew the second victim, Rosie Meeks, and I have reason to believe there is enough circumstantial evidence to make a good case he encountered Mary Quinn, our first victim.'

'Why haven't I been informed of this?' Sir Charles moved to question Monro.

'Well, I…er,' Monro stammered for an answer, now looking to Abberline.

Abberline saw another opportunity to save his boss. 'To be fair, Sir Charles, it is early days, and I thought it unwise to commit to making any public announcement until we had solid evidence. The suspect is one Jack Robertson, he works at Brighton Railway Station as an engineer and has been living in one of the empty huts, which I should point out is unknown to his employer. But after conducting a thorough search of his quarters, I found a knife and two jars containing human parts. On further examination and with the help of Dr Cripps, we were able to ascertain that the knife and the body parts were linked to the murders of Mary Quinn and Rosie Meeks.'

'This is fantastic news, Abberline. Why didn't you tell me this at the beginning, man?' Sir Charles had gone from a man wanting to throttle him, to one of exuberance.

'So, we can charge this… who did you say, Jack Robertson, without any delay? I can tell you there won't be a judge in the land who won't find him guilty and sentence him to hang. Don't worry, I'll make sure of that.'

'Well, before we make this public, sir, there are a couple of things we must take into consideration. First of all, Jack Robertson says he's innocent and adamant he had no involvement with any of the murders, and I'm slightly uneasy as to why we found both the murder weapon and the remains so easily. My other concern is he might not be working alone.'

'What?' Monro interrupted, shocked at the revelation as Sir Charles stood up from his chair in exasperation.

'Listen here, Abberline, you made it very clear to both me and Monro here that the killer was one person responsible for the murders. Now, you tell us that's not the case, and there could be another. What are you saying, man?'

Abberline had to calm the situation quickly before it got out of control. 'Please, gentlemen, hear me out. We have secured items from Jack Robertson's residence, as I explained. We have a serrated knife which exactly matches the wounds on both bodies and two jars of human remains that have come from both women. We know he definitely knew Rosie Meeks, and if she rejected his advances, maybe it was enough for him to want to take his rage out on someone like Mary Quinn, who happened to be walking back from her job at the pub. Later, he returns to Rosie Meeks; when he knows she is working alone, he pleads with her, but she refuses him again. He tells her what he's done because she spurned his advances. She's disgusted and says she is going to the police. He can't let that happen; he loses his temper, kills her, and mutilates her body beyond recognition. He has a motive, and we have found evidence to suggest this is possibly what happened.'

'So where is the problem then, Inspector? It seems like a very open-and-shut case where I'm sitting,' Monro asked.

'With the best will in the world, sir, Jack Robertson can't be in two places at the same time. Elsbeth Hargreaves had an intruder in her home just before I left to come here. They left a human liver on her kitchen table, which must have been cut out recently because it was still bloody, but Jack Robertson was in custody.'

Sir Charles was becoming more agitated at the bad news. 'So, tell me, Inspector, *how* is that relevant?'

'If Jack Robertson is guilty and acting with another, he must know who this accomplice is. Amelia Stanton, I believe, is also caught up in all this and has been taken and is being held against her will in Brighton. If I'm right, then we have to find out the name of his accomplice first before condemning Robertson to hang if we are to have any hope of finding Amelia Stanton alive. I'm sure her husband, your friend, would want us to do all we can to secure his wife's safe return. As I'm sure you do, Sir Charles?'

Sir Charles muttered something under his breath that sounded like an agreement with what Abberline was saying, but through gritted teeth.

'I am confused, Abberline, like Sir Charles. How does the liver Miss Hargreaves found in her house relate to the case at hand?'

'Think of it like this: a house cat leaves a dead bird in the home for its owner to find. This organ was meant for Miss Hargreaves.'

'To what purpose? And who does this…this organ belong to?' Monro questioned.

'I believe whoever is working with Jack Robertson left it as a clear message that they know about her. Maybe in their sick mind, it was a gift.' Abberline thought for a moment before answering the next part. 'The liver could have come from one of the two victims; we may never know that for sure as the bodies have now been disposed of. However, the blood was still fresh, which would most likely rule out that theory.'

'Or it could have come from someone else, another victim. Is that not possible, Inspector?' Monro commented.

Abberline knew this could be true, and it had crossed his mind that it could belong to the missing woman Amelia Stanton, but without a body and no evidence to positively conclude this was the case, he was reluctant to say anything. It would be too incendiary at this time.

'Yes, that is possible, sir, and we will keep an open mind, but we have not had any more reported murders, so I am optimistic in my conclusion.'

Sir Charles, who had been listening to the exchange, turned to Abberline.

'You say that with confidence, Inspector; however, I do not share your enthusiasm. I hope that you are right, but wherever the truth is, it could also have been left as a warning.

FORTY-ONE

Rawlings entered the examination room where Cripps was cleaning up one of the mortuary tables. His leather apron and hands were covered in blood.

Cripps narrowed his eyes as Rawlings stood waiting for instructions. They knew each other; they had a history, and the air was already so heavy you could cut it with a knife. 'Put the organ on one of the spare tables. I will take a look at it after I have washed up.'

'Abberline wanted this looked at as soon as possible. He's back from London soon and is coming down here with the Hargreaves woman about midday tomorrow, so he'll expect some information from you.'

'You do your job, Rawlings. I'll do mine,' Cripps snapped while walking over to wash his hands off in the basin at the back of the room.

'You still owe me, Cripps'.

'I don't owe you anything. You're lucky I give you the scraps, as I do. With all your other interests in the town, I'm surprised you need my work.'

Rawlings put the liver from Elsbeth's house on one of the spare mortuary tables as instructed and walked over to confront Cripps. He moved right up to him and pulled him by the scruff of the neck, so his face was right up next to his.

'Listen to me and listen well, you freak. I'm not a patient man, and I know all about you, collecting body parts to sell off to your so-called friends.'

Cripps pushed Rawlings back.

'Don't threaten me. You're no more innocent than me. You're corrupt, just like all the rest; got your greedy snout in the trough? You're up to your neck in it. I wonder how Mr High and Mighty Abberline would like to know how you earn money on the side, eh? All the bodies going out of here and down to those less fussy about where they came from. Don't expect he would be too pleased to know that, would he?'

'I'm warning you, Cripps; you breathe a word, you will end up joining them. Now pay me what you owe, or I'll ring that scrawny neck of yours. You probably love this bloke who butchered those two women in the town. Well, I have him locked up in a cell as we speak.'

'Do you now? Do send my regards, won't you, from one artist to another.'

'I'll be sending you to hospital you keep this up, Cripps. You know me, and you know I mean what I say.'

'Violence is not the answer, Rawlings. Surely, we have evolved and surpassed the basic instincts of cavemen. If not, then we are no better than mindless thugs like Seamus Keane, are we? Oh, but I forget myself, he was an associate of yours, wasn't he? But somehow, he came to be found dead floating in the sea with his brains hanging out of his head. You, of course, have no idea how he met such an untimely death, do you?' Cripps asked in an impertinent tone as he reached into his cupboard to retrieve a small tin box and some papers. He considered Rawlings nothing more than a neanderthal. But as a serving policeman, he had proved cheap and available.

Rawlings grabbed a surgical knife off a tray with other sharp instruments and held it against the neck of Cripps.

'One more word...' he pushed the blade just enough to break the skin as a trickle of blood ran over the steel. Rawlings's eyes glistened with fury. 'Don't think I won't, old man.'

Cripps slowly backed away. He knew Rawlings had a temper and would do severe damage or possibly end his life right there if he pushed him too far.

'Now, now, then, Rawlings, let's not ruin a good thing. There's really no need to argue. It's not good for business. I have two more to go down to the usual address.' Cripps pointed to two bodies covered with sheets towards the back of the room. 'When can you arrange collection?' Cripps tried to take the heat out of the moment, his hands shaking, and took hold of a clipboard with documentation on it. Licking his fingers, he went through the pages until he reached the one he wanted. He took it out and handed it to Rawlings.

Rawlings snatched the paper from him and looked over the details of the corpses he was to transport. 'I'm not your dog, Cripps. You pay me before I collect from now on or get someone else.'

'Of course, of course, no problem, we're partners.' Cripps smiled at him, opening the small tin box he had taken out earlier, counting out the money he owed plus the additional amount for the next shipment.

'There you see. A man of my word. Now you have the money owed and the payment upfront.'

Rawlings checked the amount carefully and then put it in his trouser pocket.

'Have these two ready to go tonight, and leave the back door open as usual. Don't forget to have that report for Abberline on the liver by the morning.'

'No, I won't. You get on your way; everything is in hand,' Cripps snarled as Rawlings left the room. *If only he knew who put it there.*

FORTY-TWO

Abberline returned from his meeting in London with Monro and Sir Charles and arranged to collect Elsbeth from her home to go to the morgue. The encounter with his superiors was difficult and he felt bruised and tired by the constant doubt and questioning of his methods. He arrived mid-morning outside her home looking forward to seeing a person who had come to admire and respect. She was already waiting outside as the driver got down from his seat at the back and went around the horse to the front of the carriage, opening two small doors to allow Elsbeth inside to take her seat. Abberline knocked on the roof of the cab with his hand to let the driver know to move off. The single horse slightly jolted and then moved along the street, joining the procession of other cabs and pedestrians.

'Good morning Abberline.' Elsbeth said warmly while arranging her dress to be comfortable.

'It's good to see you, Elsbeth.' Abberline replied relived to back with someone who was happy to see him.

'It's nice you are calling me by my first name at last.' Elsbeth smiled in soft surprise before looking out of the window, studying a woman's dress as they carried on into town. 'How did your meeting go at Scotland Yard?'

'Not particularly well. My boss, Monro, isn't a great admirer of my methods, and he is coming under pressure from his boss, the commissioner, both impatient for results. I explained that I was running a double murder investigation and a missing person case all at the same time, so resources were somewhat stretched as Brighton is not Scotland Yard force with its numbers of officers.'

Elsbeth knew the answer to the next question, but she asked it anyway. She was curious and pleased that Abberline was finally taking her into his confidence more.

'And how did the commissioner take that? I wonder. Not very well, I would imagine.'

'Yes, well, I gave them some good news that Jack Robertson is in custody, but they didn't seem interested so much in the facts of the case, only that the knife and jars found in his place link him to the murders of the two women. As far as Monro and Sir Charles are concerned, it's good enough to hang the man. They didn't seem overly concerned with the details or my reservations as to how they came to be so easily found.'

'Did you inform them that you think there may be two of them working together and that if they hang Robertson, you've lost the name of his associate and any hope of finding Amelia Stanton? And, if Robertson is working with someone else, that person may have decided to work alone and put those things for us to find, getting rid of the only person who knows his identity. It's clever; he doesn't have to kill Robertson, doesn't have to lift a finger; the police will do it for him.'

'It doesn't put Jack Robertson in the clear. He's guilty of something here, if not the actual murders. When push comes to shove, I think he will roll over and give us the name of the other person to save his own skin; at the end of the day, Elsbeth, nobody wants to die, do they?'

Abberline stopped for a moment looking out on to the street thinking back to his meeting at The Yard and how he was expected to deliver a result at any cost, it bothered him that his professional standards were being compromised. He turned back to Elsbeth and continued the conversation.

'However, Monro and Sir Charles have made it perfectly clear there are no deals on the table. They need results, and the public needs to see the police are in control and are making the streets safe again. They want to contain the damage this case has done to the force's reputation as much as possible, so we need to get Jack Robertson to confess and give us the other name; that way, I get both of them. Then, God willing, we will get to Amelia Stanton in time.'

Elsbeth was interested to know how his bosses had reacted to her assistance in the case. 'How did they react to me helping you? I'm sure the Commissioner loved the idea of women working alongside the police, chiefly one who is also a psychic.' Elsbeth laughed, knowing only too well how most men felt threatened by her independence and spiritual gifts.

'I reminded Monro that it was his idea for me to work with you to stop you talking to the press and making matters worse. I was doing what they asked. For once, I was following orders, which in this case is rather strange because I don't think Monro really knew what he was saying when he suggested it.'

'Hmm, well, let's not forget the first time I met you. I overheard your idea of combining our strengths when you told Rawlings that you were only going to pay me lip service and then dispense with my advice.'

Abberline looked sheepishly at Elsbeth. He was changing his view of her and had come to like and admire her, but he could not yet bring himself to understand her otherworldly abilities. 'I apologise for that. It was wrong of me. I have to say I have found your intervention at times helpful.'

'Intervention! Oh well, I'll take that as a compliment, Inspector.' Elsbeth smiled at him. 'Who knows, maybe we will work together again when this is all over.'

'Let's not get ahead of ourselves, Miss Hargreaves.' Abberline smiled back at her as the cab came to a halt.

'We're here, sir. The morgue,' the driver of the cab called down.

Abberline helped Elsbeth alight onto the pavement. 'Right, let's see what Cripps has to say.'

FORTY-THREE

Cripps met Elsbeth and Abberline, as usual, at the main entrance to the morgue and took them back to his examination room. Nobody spoke along the way, and the atmosphere was tense. As they entered the room, they saw a large metal bowl sitting on one of the dissection tables, covered with a white linen cloth stained with blood. Abberline broke the awkward silence. 'I need to get back to the station after this and re-interview someone in connection with these murders, and it would help me to understand if this organ left at Miss Hargreave's has anything to do with the case.'

'Hmm, well, I am not a magician, Inspector, and the science of post-mortem examination is still in its early days. We have a lot to learn, but each day teaches us something new.' Cripps sighed and moved towards the container, past Elsbeth, purposely ignoring her.

'You say this was found lying on your kitchen table, Miss Hargreaves?' Cripps eventually asked Elsbeth as he removed the covering sheet, not looking at her.

Elsbeth, repulsed by him, was nevertheless forced to answer the question. 'Yes, that's correct, a man broke into my home and left…This thing in my kitchen. Why, I have no idea. But there was blood coming from it, so it must have been taken recently.'

Abberline moved closer to inspect the organ as Cripps carefully removed it, placing it on the table.

'The organ is healthy, and if there was blood present at the time you discovered it, this has now clotted due to the time exposed, and there are no other visible signs of deterioration. I believe we can say with some certainty that the person to whom this belongs was not suffering from any long-term organ failure, nor is there any proof of malnutrition abuse such as alcohol. If there were, there would be fatty deposits, which I have not detected. So, this person had led a healthy and well-nourished life.'

'Can you tell us anything else?' Abberline needed more information to question Jack Robertson later about whether his theory about two people at work was right.

'The liver grows at about one and nine inches a year from birth, so fully grown by the age of fifteen. This specimen has reached its maximum growth, which I can deduct from the weight and size. So, it belongs to someone over fifteen years of age.'

'Is that it?' Elsbeth asked.

'Well, if you had the rest of the body, of course, I could give you a lot more, but seeing you don't, yes, that is all I can tell you, Miss Hargreaves. Unless, of course, with your powers of spiritual deduction, you can enlighten me otherwise.'

Elsbeth did not respond to his evident intention to irritate her; instead, she turned to Abberline.

'Perhaps the Inspector has something more to ask?'

Abberline seemed engrossed in inspecting the organ, walking around the table, and looking at it from different angles.

'No. As you said, you're not a magician, and I can see that presenting you with just this is not going to give me the answer I was hoping for. Come, Miss Hargreaves, we have taken more than enough time from Mr Cripps, who I'm sure has other pressing matters to attend to. Thank you for the information.'

Abberline held his hand out to Cripps, who took hold of it and shook it with a limp and clammy clasp.

'Not at all, Inspector. I'm glad to have been some assistance to you and, of course, the delightful Miss Hargreaves.'

Elsbeth grinned acrimoniously back at him as she started to walk towards the door, following Abberline.

'Oh, just one more thing before I forget, Inspector.'

Abberline and Elsbeth stopped, turning back to face Cripps.

'The size of a liver for an adult man is roughly four inches and weighs in at the top end of around three and a half pounds. A woman's, by contrast, is smaller at three inches in size and around three pounds in weight.'

'So, what are you saying, Cripps?' asked Abberline.

'What I'm saying, Inspector, is that this liver you presented me with today belonged to a healthy adult woman.'

FORTY-FOUR

Abberline sat in the office and waited for Rawlings to bring Jack Robertson back up for an interview. The information that Cripps had imparted was concerning him as it implied there was another woman's body lying somewhere waiting to be found. Abberline thought whoever had left the liver in Elsbeth's kitchen must have meant it to be a message. Maybe it was a way of announcing the killer had struck again, or it could be something more sinister, closer to home. His worst fears for Amelia Stanton started to resurface. But he decided to keep his thoughts to himself for the time being.

He had been under intense pressure since yesterday's meeting in London with Monro and the commissioner, Sir Charles, to achieve a result and get the confession they all so desperately needed. But Abberline also, importantly, wanted the name of the other man Robertson must be working with, if they were going to find Amelia Stanton alive, and this was becoming more and more urgent.

Rawlings brought Robertson up from the custody cell into the office and sat him opposite Abberline.

'OK, Jack. Well, I hope you have had time to reconsider your position. Honestly, it's not looking too good for you from where I'm sitting.' Abberline waited to see Robertson's reaction.

'I told you, Abberline, and your monkey, I'm innocent of both murders. You got nothin on me, so let me go.'

Rawlings stepped forward and pulled Robertson's head back by his hair. 'Now then, lad, best you be not speaking to the Inspector or me like that. Show a bit of respect.'

'Rawlings, let him go. I'm sure there won't be any need to resort to that.' Abberline thought it best to let Robertson believe he was the nicer of the two, and Rawlings the attack dog, which wasn't far from the truth anyway.

'Now, Jack, we're all adults here? I understand you're not happy. Nor am I. I have far better things to do than sit here waiting for you to confess to these crimes You and I both know you have committed. So please, can we dispense with the theatrics and just get down to you telling us why you killed Mary Quinn and Rosie Meeks? Then Rawlings and I can go home, and you will feel better having this burden off your chest. You owe it to Rosie. After all, I do believe you said she was a friend of yours, wasn't she?'

Robertson stared at Abberline, not saying a word. His expression was one of contempt.

'Ok, Jack, have it your way. Rawlings, please fetch the items for me.' Abberline watched as Rawlings left the office, went into the mess area, took a buff-coloured box off one of the shelves, and brought it back, placing it on the table between Abberline and Robertson.

'Thank you, Rawlings. Now, Jack, these items were found in that hovel you have been staying in.' Abberline thought it best not to mention Elsbeth at this stage as she wasn't officially supposed to be there during the search. Robertson remained silent.

'Now, both Mary Quinn and Rosie Meeks were killed with the same weapon, a thin serrated knife, the type a surgeon would use. Also, both victims had various internal organs removed from them, and what do you think we found tucked away in your place, Jack, eh?'

Abberline took the knife and jars he and Elsbeth had found, from the box, and placed them on the table.

Jack Robertson shuffled on his seat, turning his head from side to side, his face white with shock. 'No, no, this ain't right. I've never seen them things before, you're framin me, Abberline. You and that fancy woman of yours put them in my place cos you ain't got *nothin*.'

'Not so silent now are we now, you northern bastard.' Rawlings stepped forward, shouting into his ear.

'They were found at your place, not planted there by me or anybody else; they were detected during a legitimate search,' Abberline confirmed.

'I told you I've never seen them in me life.' For the first time, Robertson started to look worried.

Rawlings banged the table hard with his fist in front of Robertson. 'Yeah, yeah, yeah. We've heard this all before from scum like you. You butchered those women like a piece of meat, isn't that the truth of it?'

'I didn't kill them, and I don't know how these came to be in my place. I didn't do nothin.' Robertson replied shouting, his voice almost hoarse, Abberline and Rawlings watched as the suspect rocked back and forth in a state of absolute frustration and fear of what he was being accused of. 'You're fittin me up.'

'No,' Abberline replied. 'We don't have to fit you up. You've done this yourself. Now, I might be able to save your neck from the hangman's knot if you tell me who else you have been working with. Like, who broke into Elsbeth Hargreaves's house and put a human liver on her kitchen table? So, unless you want another murder on your hands, you'd do best to come clean, talk about this other person you're working with, tell us who they are, and I'll do what I can, I promise you, Jack. I need to know what you've done with Amelia Stanton. Don't deny it; you have her somewhere.'

Robertson's body seemed to go limp, slouching forward and to the side; for a moment, he appeared to pass out, his head hitting the table. Rawlings had to quickly grab him by the arm before he slid off the edge of his chair.

'Rawlings, get some water, please.' Rawlings did as Abberline asked and went off to get a drink. When he returned, Abberline had uncuffed one of Robertson's wrists as Rawlings put the glass tumbler down for the suspect.

Abberline got up from his chair and walked around to the side of Robertson. 'You're in a lot of trouble here, Jack. I'm trying to help you. You need to help yourself and stop messing me about.'

Jack Robertson coughed and wiped his mouth dry with his free hand.

'It don't make no difference, you ain't goin to believe anythin I tell you. I knew Rosie Meeks, so what? I never did her no harm and never met the other woman Mary…Whatever her name was. Never been to that pub The Crown, I use The Railway pub, up Terminus Road…That's my local, ask those I work with, we all drink there.'

Rawlings, the attack dog, slammed the table again with his fist in front of Robertson.

'Time is running out for you, Jack. We're not running around half of Brighton because you're stalling for time. We found these items in your place. They are directly linked to the two murderers. Admit it now, and as the Inspector here says, we can see what can be done, but we need things from you. A signed confession to the murders of Rosie Meeks and Mary Quinn, the name of your accomplice, and the whereabouts of Amelia Stanton.' He banged the table again to reinforce his anger. 'Now tell us what we want to know.'

Abberline joined in at the end of the conversation, piling

on the pressure as best he could. 'Give us those details, Jack, and maybe I can convince the judge to spare your pitiful life, and you get to see the sun every morning from your cell. Better than having your neck snapped in one of Britain's darkest hell holes.'

Robertson leaned back in his chair, bent his head, and looked at the ceiling.

'Look, I told you lot before, I wasn't here.' He hesitated before he continued. 'I don't want them hounded by this all their lives, but…I ave a wife and child up north in Leeds. I send them money each month, went up to see they were alright. What will happen to them if… If you ave me hung for these murders, eh? They will starve and die on the street, and you two will be responsible. I'm not going to admit to somethin I didn't do, and I don't care what you found. I've been telling you over and over again I'm innocent; you have the wrong man.'

'Strange, how have you never mentioned this family of yours before?' Abberline was unconvinced and was going to call his bluff.

'I'll tell you what, Jack, you give Rawlings here the address where you sent the money, and I'll get someone up there to check it out.'

Rawlings smirked as Robertson shifted in his chair. 'It's not that simple. They have to keep movin about because she has a nipper, and a lot of landlords don't take kindly to kids. So, she has to keep movin to new places and different addresses. I was up there helpin' them.'

'When?' Rawlings barked.

'Now and then, over the last month or so, I don't have exact dates, I just went when they needed. But must have been when these two women were killed, as when I got back, it was all the lads at work could talk about.'

'Oh, how very convenient. Do we look like idiots to you,

Robertson? Do we? You just made this all up,' Rawlings screamed in his face. 'Liar, that's what you are.'

Abberline got up from his desk and instructed Rawlings to take Robertson back to his cell.

'I've done all I can for you, Jack, more than I'm allowed, to be honest. And yet, you still refuse to cooperate or admit to the crimes. You leave me with no other option. You will be officially charged for the murders of Rosie Meeks and Mary Quinn, and further charges of perverting the course of justice will also be made for withholding vital information. You're going to swing for this, Jack. I left some paper and a pen in your cell. I suggest you think about it very carefully if you want any chance to live and see your family again, write a confession before it's too late.'

Robertson struggled, pushing against Rawlings as he was bundled out of the office door. Turning around before being taken back to the cells, he yelled out, 'I ain't confessin to nothin. I didn't do anythin. I'm innocent, and you're going to have to live with that.'

Abberline waved at Rawlings to continue. The items found were damning and more than enough evidence of his guilt. Robertson refused to help them with any information and suddenly, at the eleventh hour, invented a story about being out of town helping his fictitious family. If there were any truth in it, they would find it, but in the meantime, he had no choice but to proceed with the inevitable. Abberline watched as Jack Robertson struggled to free himself while protesting his innocence, eventually disappearing from view.

FORTY-FIVE

Rawlings was in his office at Brighton Police Station when he was called to the front desk. A man was waiting to see Inspector Abberline on urgent business. He was in plain clothes, about twenty years of age, thin, five foot eight inches in height, and wearing round spectacles. Rawlings got to the desk to find the man sitting on a bench by the doors. The young man got up and walked over to the desk.

'I'm here on urgent business. I need to speak with Inspector Abberline.' He got out his warrant card to show Rawlings. 'Constable Miller from Leeds City police, my sergeant told me to get down here with this information in person as it was too important and urgent and to make sure Abberline, I mean the Inspector, got it as soon as possible.' He held out a large buff envelope.

'Well, the Inspector isn't here at present, lad. He's in town meeting with a consultant, so you can wait for him, which could be hours, or entrust me with the information, and I will inform the Inspector on his return. It's your choice, but I expect it's a long way for you to get home, and I'm sure you would like to get going.'

Constable Miller smiled and nodded in agreement. 'We heard you had a few grim cases down here lately. Is this anything to do with all that?' the young officer said, waving the envelope in the air.

Rawlings knew he was fishing, but he just wanted to get rid of him and didn't really want him hanging around the station. 'Look, I can't go into details. You'll hear about it soon enough; we don't want this one slipping through the net. So why don't you tell me what you have to say? I'll ensure Inspector Abberline gets it as soon as possible, and you can be on your way, lad. No point in you waiting around here for God knows how long.'

Miller started to relay the information back to Rawlings. 'Yes, of course, you're quite right. My sergeant said to ensure Abberline also has this written copy for his records. He said–' passing the envelope to Rawlings. 'He said to make sure Inspector Abberline knows that the questions he asked of Jack Robertson were correct. He said they found the woman in question. She is indeed his wife, and she does have a son by him. They're living in temporary lodgings as they have to move about, landlords don't like her having a young'un. I guess it's because they can't charge so much. But anyway, that's what my sergeant said to tell the Inspector.'

'Was that all your sergeant said to say?'

'Err, well, there was just one more thing.' The officer went through some pages. 'Ah, here it is. He said it was important to let you know there was proof that the man you had locked up... Robertson, had been visiting and staying in Leeds at the times Abberline had asked about.'

'No!' Exclaimed Rawlings, who quickly ran back towards the stairs that would take him down to the basement and the holding cells, shouting as he went. 'Stay there, don't move. I'll be back in a minute.' He knew this meant Robertson was telling the truth. He couldn't be the murderer he had been where he said he was, up north seeing his wife and kid.

As he got down to the basement, a row of cells, four on

each side of a narrow corridor, greeted him. Red brick walls were inset with solid double steel doors painted cream with a peephole and a small hatch halfway down that slid sideways to feed or talk with the prisoners. Outside each cell was a rectangle of slate and chalk suspended on rusty nails by a thin rope. The rooms were seven feet high and eight feet wide by thirteen feet long, with a small wooden table, chair, a wash basin, a pot for urine and excrement, and a small window with iron bars. They all stank of damp and human waste, freezing in winter and unbearably hot in summer; it was a deeply depressing and claustrophobic existence. They were mainly full of criminals held for theft or fighting who were usually released by the morning. But cell number two, which housed Jack Robertson, was rare as he would soon be going before the magistrate for murder and other charges.

Rawlings got to the cell and hurriedly looked for the key to the door amongst many others on a chain attached to his trouser belt. He called out, 'Robertson, stand back; it's Rawlings. I'm coming in. Do you hear me, stand back from the door?'

The key slid into the lock, and as he turned it, there was a clunk and a clink. He pushed hard against the door, and as it swung open, he suddenly stopped.

Jack Robertson was slumped against the brick wall of his cell. One end of a bed sheet had been tied to an iron bar of the window, and the other end was around his neck. His tongue was blue, lolling to one side out of his mouth, and his eyes open, but not with life but death. He had hung himself. Rawlings, shocked, looked down to see he had something clutched in his right hand. He went over and eased open the dead man's fingers to retrieve a piece of paper. He slowly opened it up to read the message.

INNOCENT.

FORTY-SIX

Abberline had arranged to meet Elsbeth at a coffee house in Meeting House Lane in central Brighton. Elsbeth wanted to discuss an idea with him as time was running out for Amelia Stanton. With Jack Robertson in custody, she hoped progress had been made on her whereabouts. Elsbeth made her way through the small, cobbled paths that had shops selling everything from clothes to hats to food. They were all busy with people going in and out of them carrying piles of shopping bags, and couples discussing what they were going to buy.

She stopped to stare in the window of one, looking at a bright red dress that caught her attention. In the reflection of the glass behind her, she noticed someone standing watching her. The person was tall with a long dark cloak, holding a small black bag. She had seen this figure before at the back of her garden and felt as if she had been followed since leaving home but hadn't actually seen anything until now. She stared at the reflection, feeling their eyes burrowing into the back of her head. She suddenly felt afraid. The people that were all around her had gone, and she was alone and scared. As quickly as she had turned to face the figure, it had gone, vanished into thin air. The people were back chatting and laughing as they brushed past her. Her heart raced as she looked all around her, but there was nothing.

Elsbeth arrived at the coffee shop to meet with Abberline. He was already there arranging the cutlery to be precisely in line with the edge of the table. They were the only ones in the cafe, so they had a degree of privacy as a young waitress of no more than twenty showed Elsbeth over to Abberline.

'Your guest has arrived, sir.'

'Oh, thank you. Can I order you tea or coffee?' Abberline looked up, smiling at Elsbeth as she sat down opposite him.

'Are you all right, Elsbeth? You look as if you've seen a ghost? Sorry about the pun, but you do look a little pale.'

'Thank you for your concern. I'm fine, just tired. I just had to push my way through the crowds of people; I didn't want to be late. I know how those small things annoy you, and thank you, I will have some tea.' Elsbeth didn't want to say what she had just seen as she knew Abberline would have a hard time believing that the person just disappeared.

The waitress returned to the table to take their order.

'Coffee, for me, please, black, no sugar, and please make sure I have a white cup and saucer, and tea for my guest. Thank you.' The waitress looked oddly at Abberline, writing their order down on a small notepad, and went back behind the counter to prepare the beverages.

Elsbeth didn't mention the cutlery issue and just wanted to know how the interview with Robertson had gone, seeing as they both had a vested interest in the outcome. 'Did you get a confession from Jack Robertson?'

'No, he refused to admit to either murder, insisting he was innocent.'

'So, what happens next?'

'He will be formally charged and appear before the court-appointed judge very soon, as Scotland Yard wants this over and done with. They want me to hold a press conference to announce that we have our man as quickly as possible.'

Elsbeth looked confused, leaning across the table. 'But

Amelia Stanton is still missing, and there must also be another woman's body somewhere missing a liver, and what about the person I saw at the back of my garden, the one Robertson must have been working with? There are a lot of loose ends, and yet it seems to me that Robertson is going to hang anyway, guilty or not.'

Abberline kept quiet for a second but knew he had to share his concerns. 'Elsbeth, as hard as it is, we have to consider that the liver left for you at your home belongs to Amelia Stanton; she could be dead.'

'No, that would mean giving up on her, and I am not going to allow that thought to take hold. I saw her being kept against her will but still alive. You remember I told you when we visited her house, I'm not going to give up on her now. I have not had any feeling of that either, I've not seen her death.' Elsbeth knew it could take time for the dead to come through to want to tell their story, especially if they had met with a violent end. Like the living, spirits had their way of doing things. But she had to stay positive; she had to continue believing that Amelia Stanton was still alive for her children's sake, and for everyone's.

'Yes, I tend to agree that was also my thinking. At the moment we do not have another body to confirm or deny, so we can't give up, we must assume that Amelia Stanton is still alive. Getting back to Robertson, he said he has a family up north in Leeds and had been sending money to them, which I must admit, if correct, doesn't fit with a man who would butcher two women, and then kidnap the wife of a prominent member of parliament. He says he was up north when the two women were murdered. But there's no proof that this family even exists, we only have his word. So I've called in a few favours and got some people looking urgently in Leeds, so let's see what transpires. If they do exist, which I have doubts about, we will have a problem.'

Elsbeth reached for the copy of the *Brighton Herald* she had been carrying in her bag and laid it on the table. On the front page was an article by Amelia's husband, Joseph Stanton. 'Look at this. It goes on about how he has had no progress report about where you are on the case, his wife is still missing, and then he writes about my involvement as a freak show. This is going to ruin the reputation that I have built up over the years.'

'Your tea, madam,' Amy, the waitress, said, placing the cup next to Elsbeth. 'Excuse me, but aren't you that spiritual lady who speaks to the dead? My mother died suddenly, a while back, but I never got to see her, you know to say goodbye. So, I wanted to let her know like... that I was alright, you know. Tell her I love her.'

Elsbeth smiled sweetly at the girl and asked her to write down her mother's name. She would make sure her mother got her message.

'Thank you.' She then placed Abberline's coffee as requested in a white cup and saucer on the table in front of him and promptly left.

Abberline was too concentrated on the paper to hear the conversation with Elsbeth and Amy. He looked pale as he read the full copy. He knew if Monro or, worse still, the commissioner were to hear of this, it would not go unnoticed, and it was possible the commissioner already knew, so he had to take immediate steps.

'The commissioner is a personal friend of Stanton, so this will make matters a lot worse. But without Robertson's testimony of where she is or who has her, we need to think of something else.'

Elsbeth sat listening to Abberline looking out into the street, still haunted by earlier on. Abberline's words faded in and out and echoed like he was in a cave; she felt dizzy and weak. He seemed miles away. She suddenly found herself standing in the alleyway where Mary Quinn had been butchered. Mary was standing, pointing at the wall where her body had been found. Then, from nowhere, another woman's face appeared right in front of her so close she could feel her breath, her eyes full of tears, and red raw from crying, screaming and screaming at her.

'Help me please, dear God help me… he's coming.'

She felt her body jolt and then Abberline's voice registered.

'Elsbeth, are you alright, you're shaking?'

Elsbeth looked up at him; she had to tell him what she had seen this time, whether he believed her or not. It was too important.

'I…I just saw Mary Quinn, the woman butchered in the alley. She was pointing behind her where she was killed. She was showing me something that had been written on the wall. But I …I couldn't see, it was blurred. Then another woman, not Mary, someone else, screamed for me to help her.'

'Who was it? Did you recognise her?' Abberline asked, not knowing what to think.

'I. I'm not sure, but everything in me, everything I know, makes me think it could be only one person… Amelia Stanton.'

Hurry, Elsbeth, if you want to save your little friend. His voice returned to her mind.

As Abberline listened to her, not really knowing what to think, a young man came rushing into the coffee shop. Abberline watched as the man went over to Amy at the counter; they spoke a few words, and then Amy pointed towards him and Elsbeth. The young man approached Abberline and Elsbeth and seemed quite out of breath.

'I'm sorry to interrupt you. My name is Constable Miller from Leeds Police. My sergeant sent me down here to give you some information about a case you asked him to investigate. I came from the train this morning and went straight to Brighton Police Station, but you weren't there.' Constable Miller then took out his notebook. 'I saw a…Detective Rawlings. He told me where to find you.'

'Why didn't you wait for my return?'

'Rawlings told me to get down here while… he dealt with things, sir. ' He hesitated, thinking how to convey the next piece of news. 'It's urgent that you get back to the station now; something terrible has happened.'

Both Abberline and Elsbeth looked shocked at what they were hearing. But Abberline realised what it might be.

'Is it to do with the prisoner in custody, Jack Robertson? What's happened, man? Quickly spit it out.'

Constable Miller swallowed hard. 'Rawlings found him dead in his cell. Hanged himself.'

FORTY-SEVEN

Rawlings was busy carrying the body of Jack Robertson out of the cell with two other officers and removing the sheet from the neck of the deceased when Abberline, Elsbeth and Constable Miller arrived. Abberline asked Elsbeth to wait on a bench at the front of the station to give him time to arrange for someone to take her home and directed Constable Miller to help the other officers with the deceased. At the same time, he and Rawlings went into the office to clarify what had happened.

'What the hell happened, Rawlings? How am I going to explain this to Scotland Yard? He was in your care, and now he's dead. If I find out that you have any hand in this…'

'I had nothing to do with this at all, and I resent the fact that you are accusing me.'

'Oh, come on, Rawlings. You and I know your methods are not exactly by the book, and I've put up with it as it's your station. I'm only temporarily here, but I've seen how you operate. Tell me in detail exactly what occurred and how this man got to hang himself in your jail.'

Rawlings looked annoyed, but he didn't want to be the one taking the blame for this. He could lose his job over it. 'Robertson was put back in his cell the last time you and I interviewed him yesterday, given his evening meal, then later I checked on him periodically. This morning, first thing, this constable from Leeds came in here with urgent information for you. I told him you were out and could be some time. He then told me the information, and then upon hearing it, I realised Robertson had probably been telling us the truth, so I went down to the cells to check on him.'

Abberline paced up and down the office, listening to Rawlings but furious that this could have happened.

'Constable Miller said that you asked his sergeant in Leeds to urgently investigate what Robertson told us about him having family, a wife, and kids up north. And how he sent them money on a monthly basis on account, they had to keep moving from their lodgings. But also, you wanted to know if Robertson's claim of being in Leeds helping his family out at the time of the killings of Mary Quinn and Rosie Meeks was true because if it were, it would give him a very strong alibi.'

'Yes, that's right.' Abberline wanted to know more. 'I asked him because he knows the right people. I trust him to do the job right, unlike you, Rawlings. So, what exactly did Constable Miller say to you, or do I have to get him in here and ask him myself?'

Rawlings didn't show his annoyance at the comment. 'Miller said that the questions you had asked his sergeant to look into regarding Jack Robertson have turned out to be correct. He also gave me this written report and other information for your records. He went on to say that the sergeant knew there would be a backlash against you, seeing we are looking to charge this man with murder and put him in front of the Court Judge soon to answer for his crimes. But it gets worse. It also now transpires his wife is willing to stand up in court and testify he was with her in Leeds, miles away, when the murders of the two women occurred here in Brighton, which, of course, means he couldn't have done it, he's not our man.'

Abberline stopped pacing and stood silent for a moment, reeling inside from the bomb that had just gone off, destroying his case. He sat down at the desk and reassessed the situation. 'So how did he die? Exactly, not how you think; how did he do it?'

Rawlings sat on the other side of the desk. 'He must have used the table in the cell to climb up on and secure one end of the bed sheet to the iron bars on the window. He couldn't reach it any other way. Then, he tied the other end around his body and neck, shortening the length, kicked the table away, and that's the job done, simple as that.'

'Jesus Christ, go on,' Abberline replied, his head down, not really wanting to hear.

'Well, the drop alone must have snapped his neck. His feet weren't even touching the ground, so he was dead soon after, is my guess.'

'So, you're a coroner now as well?' Abberline shot back. 'Just stick to the facts, please.'

'Yes, well, that's all we have. I'm sure Cripps will give you a fuller account, but that is where we are.'

'Nothing else?'

'One last thing, sir. He must have written this note before… before he did it. It was in his hand.'

Abberline took the note, remembering he had told Rawlings to leave some paper and pen in case Robertson had a change of heart and wrote a confession. He stared at it for a moment, then read its contents out loud.

'Innocent.'

'Sir, it doesn't mean he is. His wife could be making the whole thing up to get him off the hook.'

Abberline turned on Rawlings, knowing his dislike for him taking the case over and seeing the mess he was now in. 'You must think Christmas has come early for you, Rawlings, seeing how this is going to go down with The Yard, whom I have yet to inform of this fiasco.'

'That's not true, sir. Yes, I resented you at first, coming down here; using my office, my men, and taking this off me. After all, it's my town, but we…I needed help. Don't forget it's my job on the line here too, sir, so you could say we both have much to lose here.'

Abberline acknowledged what he had said and was pleased they had made some headway between them, but Rawlings was rough round the edges and lacked attention to detail, which had caused him problems. He opened the envelope with the written statement confirming Robertson's claims. There were also several wage receipts from the railway company, Robertson's employer. As he looked closer, a handwritten note was on each month's slip.

Payment deducted as agreed and sent to the spouse at the address provided by the employee.

Abberline threw some wage slips across the table for Rawlings to read. 'Here it is in black and white, initiated and stamped by the railway company. He was telling the truth, and if this was true, then most likely, so was his alibi for the murders. We had the wrong man. He must have known he was going to hang either way, but he didn't want his wife to think he was capable of these murders and took his own life on his terms rather than the state taking it. Jack Robertson was also right about something else.'

'What, sir?' asked Rawlings.

'We are going to have to live with the knowledge he was innocent.'

Rawlings searched for something else to say. 'What of his accomplice? What about him? He's still out there, isn't he?'

'Didn't you hear what I said, Rawlings? Jack Robertson was innocent; he had no accomplice. He had nothing to do with any of this. Whoever committed these murders is a lot smarter than I gave them credit for and is far more dangerous. We. Detective Rawlings, are back to square one.'

Rawlings looked on, not knowing what to say next. Abberline regained control and jumped up from his chair. 'Right, get the body down to the morgue and tell Cripps what happened. I'll speak with him later. We still have a killer on the streets and a missing person. The killer seems to be one step ahead, planting evidence, pointing us in the wrong direction. We've been led a merry dance, but now it's our time to lead.'

Rawlings took notes while asking a question. 'What do I tell Constable Miller? He needs to get back to Leeds?'

'Nothing. Tell him what it is: a death in custody, and we will investigate; he doesn't need to know anything more. The less informed, the better. We don't want the press to get hold of this either, not yet, not until we have some good news, so keep quiet and make sure you tell Cripps the same. I'm going to take Elsbeth back home. She's a target for this maniac now. I'll not be back at the station today. Get this mess cleaned up, and I'll come by your place later to discuss how to proceed.'

Abberline went to the front desk, remembering that he had asked Elsbeth to wait there for him while he talked to Rawlings. But when he got there, she was nowhere to be seen. Only young Constable Miller was there, wanting to see him before he left to go home.

Abberline went over to Miller. 'Where's the lady I told to wait here, the one you met in the coffee shop, who came back with us?'

'Oh, her, sir, she's gone. Went a while back. She left this note for you.'

Abberline,

Sorry, I couldn't wait. What I saw at the cafe, Mary Quinn, pointing at something on the wall… It's too important. I must go back. I have to check. Don't worry. I will send word if it comes to anything.

Elsbeth.

Abberline ran out of the police station, trying to catch her, but she was nowhere to be seen. An icy winter wind blew across the pavement, kicking up some rubbish in the air as it went. He stood still, his body shivering from the cold. The knowledge that this predator was still out there, one more dangerous and manipulative than he could have ever imagined. And worse, Elsbeth had disappeared into the narrow streets of Brighton by herself as the light faded and darkness crept in over the town; remembering what she told him, what she had seen, and what the consequences could be sent a chill through his soul.

FORTY-EIGHT

Abberline left the station and quickly walked down towards town while looking for Elsbeth. She didn't know of the developments, and after the suicide of Jack Robertson in his cell, the whole case had been turned upside down. He had been duped by the killer, who was far more cunning than he had given credit for. Elsbeth's life was in real jeopardy now; she had not waited as agreed, and Abberline was both annoyed and worried. He needed to find her. She could only have had a half-hour head start on him, but the town was busy. People, traders, and day visitors crowded the streets, along with the cabs racing past in both directions. It made it hard for him to see through so many people.

He reached the bottom of Edward Street. The magnificent Royal Pavilion, the playhouse for the hedonistic Prince Regent, the son of the mad King George, came into view. It was the jewel of Brighton and The Old Steine, where it sat majestically. Abberline couldn't help but think that his wife would love such a building with its Asian-style domes, turrets, lattice walkways, and arches. It could have come straight from India. Emma loved architecture, and it would be her dream to go inside and see the luxury of a bygone age. But he quickly put aside such thoughts and sped past the building, weaving through the crowds. Couples holding hands, young and old, single women pushing perambulators, kids playing with sticks and hoops on the road and pavements. It was bustling and became busier the closer he got to the beginning of The North Laine. Stalls shouted offers, row upon row of shops selling everything imaginable: food, clothing, ironmongery, cheese, bread. The smells wafted through the air, tempting the most ardent shopper. The neighbourhood had something for everyone, even for those attracted to the darker side.

He arrived at Church Street, turning right onto Regent Street. Running, he got to North Street, a big, wide road that eventually led back to The Steine. Elsbeth was not there; it was just awash with people. She could be anywhere, and he wondered how she expected the killer to make contact. Then he remembered the vision she told him about at the cafe where she mentioned a message on the wall where Mary Quin's body was found. But he wasn't sure, and time was running out. *Where would you go?* In the end, he trusted his instinct and made his way to The Crown, the pub where Mary Quinn had worked the night she was killed. *Maybe Elsbeth had gone there first; a public place would have been safer.* He hoped he was right.

As he entered the pub, it was as lively as always. He searched across the sea of faces as a woman from the crowd suddenly grabbed his arm. 'I know you. You're that bloke from Scotland Yard come down 'ere looking for the sick bastard who cut up Mary. Where's ya friend, eh? Had enough of roughing it, had she, eh?' Polly Nichols cackled like a witch. 'You kept asking me questions about Mary, she got herself killed, stupid waste. That posh lady you was with, she read me hand, told me not to go back to Whitechapel. What's the likes of her know, it's me home. I goes where I want me,' she cackled again.

Abberline then recognised who she was. 'Yes, of course, we spoke to you as a witness, here in the pub at the table over there. He pointed across the crowd of boozers. 'I'm sorry, my mind is elsewhere. Elsbeth, the lady you met…she's missing. I can't find her, and it's very important, you understand, I find her soon. Have you seen her?'

'Na, not since the last time. But I'm not always about, and when I am…well, you know, I might be otherwise engaged with one of my regulars. So, I could have missed her. A girl has to work, you know.'

Abberline had an idea of how he could get her to help him. 'Look, I'll pay you. You know these streets better than me. I need you to ask the other women who work on them if they have seen Elsbeth. You've met her, so you'll know how to describe her. I need to go and get another officer who's helping me, and I'll be back soon. I'll meet you outside The Black Star pub in one hour. See what you can find out.'

Polly Nichols held out her hand, covered in dirt. 'Coin first, Mister Big-London-Inspector, then I ask. That's how it's done, remember?'

Abberline knew if he paid her, she would be in the bar drinking gin all night. 'A third now and the rest when I meet you. More if you find her.'

Polly grabbed the money and grunted. 'I ain't going inside that pub, bad things happen there. Mary lived there; I told you so. That pig Keane did for her, you see if I'm not right.'

'Seamus Keane is dead, Polly. He was found floating in the sea off the Pier, clubbed to death so that he won't be giving you or anyone else any more trouble. Now, please go quickly; every minute matters.'

Abberline watched as Polly walked off, hoping she would find something out. It was getting late, and he remembered something Elsbeth had once said to him: that some ghosts couldn't be found, and it was as if she herself had become one and had disappeared. He hailed a cab to the other side of town, towards London Road, where Detective Rawlings lived.

He needed him to help find Elsbeth before she met with the Devil and vanished forever.

FORTY-NINE

Abberline arrived at Elder Street just off London Road, paid the driver and knocked at Rawlings's door. It was a typical two-up, two-down rented terrace house where Rawlings lived with his wife and young children. The sounds of screaming youngsters and his wife reached him before the door opened; Rawlings stood in his shirt and braces, drinking a cup of tea. Rawlings moved aside to let Abberline in and showed him into the small front room. The walls were decorated with wallpaper that had a wood grain pattern, torn in places with pictures drawn all over it by the children. It had two dilapidated leather armchairs, one window, and a fireplace, above which hung a portrait of Queen Victoria. The strong smell of wet clothes hanging to dry was everywhere as he watched the family dog eating and licking the last remnants of supper off the threadbare carpet. Two of his kids were jumping around, shouting, and pulling at each other, egging the other one on. It was enough for Abberline to feel quite unwell and that not having a family was a blessing. It was mayhem in any language. Rawlings told the children to get out and threw some wooden toys and newspapers off two chairs for them to sit on.

'I know it's late, Rawlings, but Elsbeth's gone missing. I told her to wait at the station when we were dealing with the suicide of Jack Robertson, but she didn't and took it upon herself to go.' A pause. Abberline thought for a moment before he said any more. He knew Rawlings had strong views, as he did on Elsbeth's psychic abilities, so he decided to tread carefully. 'She went to follow up on a lead to find Amelia Stanton, which was against my instructions, and I'm concerned she is in real danger, so we need to find her as soon as possible.'

Rawlings got up from his chair. 'One thing's for sure: the lunatic who has the Stanton woman is never just going to let her go. Why would they? What's in it for them? There has been no demand for money. No, to my thinking, he has something else in mind for her, and if Miss Hargreaves has taken it upon herself to find her, she could be walking straight into a trap.'

Abberline got up from his seat and got ready to leave. 'Yes, you're right, and let's not forget Mrs Stanton was very vocal in the press about the person responsible for the deaths of Mary Quinn and Rosie Meeks; she attacked the killer's sexual prowess, and that is most likely what got her taken in the first place. I don't think it's about making her an example. I think it's much deeper than that. This killer, I'm sure, likes the attention, but it's the hold of life and death he has over these women, the control, the fear. This is deeper and more personal; he wants these women to suffer before he kills them. He is showing us, me, how unstoppable he is. How invisible he has become; how powerful he is.'

Rawlings looked visibly concerned as he moved outside into the hallway. His wife was in the kitchen at the back of the house, with their three other children and the dog, trying her best to keep them occupied while her husband concluded this business with his boss. Rawlings reached for his jacket, coat, and scarf and asked his wife where his hat had gone.

'I put it upstairs, dear, out of the reach of the kids. You know what they are like. They were using it earlier to play fetch with the dog.'

Rawlings looked at Abberline. 'You don't know how lucky you are, sir, not having them.'

Abberline thought to himself that he did know and was more than pleased that it was just him and his wife at home.

Rawlings's wife walked out of the kitchen to join them. She was a thin woman of about forty with sunken cheeks and grey hair, worn out and looking older than she was. She smiled at Abberline, but her expression couldn't hide the tiredness and exhaustion from the daily grind.

'Glad to meet you, sir. My husband often talks of you.' His wife almost appeared to curtsey as she held out her hand.

Abberline could imagine the things Rawlings had said to his wife about him, and he knew none of them would be good, but he returned the greeting anyway. 'It is very nice to meet you, Mrs Rawlings; you certainly seem to have your hands full.'

'Yes, sir, we do,' she said with an awkward laugh. 'My husband always said he wanted a big family, but he's not here to look after them all. His job keeps him so busy, like.' The shouting and screaming continued in the kitchen as Abberline's smile faded. Rawlings put his arm around his wife's waist and gently kissed her on the forehead. 'I couldn't do this job if it weren't for her. She's me rock, what keeps the family together.'

'Yes, we are indeed very lucky men, and there's not a day I don't appreciate everything my wife does for me.' Abberline smiled, thinking of his life back home.

Rawlings grabbed hold of the handrail and made his way upstairs. 'I'm just going to get my hat, won't be a minute.'

His wife, in the meantime, retreated into the kitchen to resolve another issue with the kids, calling back to Abberline as she went.

'Sit yourself back down in the front room if you please, Inspector, while you wait for me husband. He might be a bit, knowing him.'

'Thank you,' Abberline replied.

As he entered the room, he walked over to the front window. Looking out, his thoughts went back to Elsbeth and how much danger she had put herself in by taking matters into her own hands. She was stubborn, and he admired her for her single-mindedness and strength. But on this occasion, he wished she had stayed at the station; now, he was faced with finding her. His mind drifted for a while, thinking where she might have gone.

'Everything alright, sir?' Rawlings asked without any facial expression.

Not looking directly at Rawlings, Abberline quickly responded. 'Eh, yes, of course, sorry I was miles away. Anyway, let's be going. Don't want to take up any more time from your good lady; I can see she has her hands full.'

'Thank you, sir, very considerate of you.' Rawlings said goodbye to his wife and told her he would not be long but had to help his boss on an urgent matter. With that, he opened the front door, and without speaking, they walked down to London Road to get a cab into town and resume their search for Elsbeth Hargreaves.

FIFTY

The cab dropped Rawlings and Abberline opposite a large statue of the Goddess Ceres, which stood at the entrance of Brighton Corn Exchange on Church Street. The building was once home to a riding school and stables commissioned by the Prince Regent but was now a meeting place for businessmen of the town.

Abberline looked at his watch, conscious of the time; lamplighters were out doing their job. It would be dark soon. 'How far is it from here to Ship Street? I said I would meet Polly Nichols outside the pub that belonged to Seamus Keane. Polly was one of the witnesses who saw Mary Quinn on her last night. She knows the area and the women who work it. Those women wouldn't talk to the likes of us, so I'm hoping one of them maybe saw Elsbeth pass their way.'

'It's a rough part of town, Abberline, she'd stand out, that's for sure. Someone would have seen her,' Rawlings commented. 'Follow me. I know a shortcut.'

Abberline noticed the slight discomfort in Rawlings when he mentioned the pub and Seamus Keane. Even though Keane was dead, it was as if his ghost was still a threat, or maybe Rawlings knew more about his demise than he was letting on. They made their way across North Street down a few narrow alleyways until they emerged at Ship Street, then their destination, The Black Star. Polly Nichols was nowhere to be seen as Abberline and Rawlings waited outside the front of the pub.

'It looks like she just cut and run with your money. I wouldn't put it past her type.' Rawlings speculated.

Abberline was annoyed at his comment. 'I doubt it. I only paid her a third; she'll get the rest if she turns up. These women don't want to have sex in doorways and dark alleyways with drunks, or abusive and violent men, if they can get the money another way Rawlings. Nobody chooses that life. It's not a life anyone would ask for, but it's that or die for them. It is as simple as that.'

'Only God decides what life we get, and they deserve the one they have,' Rawlings replied, appearing quite matter of fact about it.

Abberline looked at the deprivation and hopelessness around him. 'If there is a God, he left this place a long time ago.'

Rawlings said nothing as he spotted a woman rushing towards them. 'Is this her? The one you've been waiting for?'

Polly crossed the road and spoke to Abberline. She hated Rawlings and recognised him from seeing him about town. He was well known for his methods. He was a bully, and it was common knowledge that he was corrupt and kept bad company. Abberline observed her as she stooped over to catch her breath. Her dark hair, curly and matted from dirt, was tied with a red ribbon, which matched the woollen shawl that covered her shoulders. Her dress was long, down to her shoes, grey and torn in parts from age. 'That's the last time I run like that for anyone. Damn near gave meself a heart attack.'

Abberline took her arm. 'Do you have any news on Elsbeth for me? Have you found anything out?'

Polly coughed and wheezed. 'I want the rest of my money before I tell you anything.'

Rawlings stepped in and spoke into her ear, 'Give the man what he wants now, or you won't be running anywhere for a while, understand?'

Abberline moved Rawlings back. 'Let her speak.'

Rawlings, annoyed, stood aside, shaking his head.

'Tell me what you have found out, and you can be on your way.' Abberline took the balance he owed her from his pocket, placing it in her hand. 'There, as agreed, now the information.'

Polly turned away, putting the money inside her dress for safekeeping. She looked from side to side to ensure nobody could see her talking to the Inspector. Her world was a close-knit community, and if she was seen talking to the police, it could look like she was a snitch.

'I talked to the girls, the ones who work most days and nights. I asked everyone I knew, and all of them, other than one, said they hadn't seen this woman. But then I met Erin, Irish, mouthy works off North Street. Anyways, she said she had seen your Elsbeth from the description I give her earlier on. She said she was making her way to the seafront.'

'The seafront, you say. You're sure about that?' Abberline questioned her.

'Yeah, that's what she said. That the woman you're after looked to be in a hurry. She said she seemed worried, but Erin was working and had a punter at the time, so she had to finish business.'

Rawlings huffed loudly, making his disgust clear.

Abberline continued. 'Is there anything else, like the direction she was headed? It's a long stretch going along the coast. Please think, try to remember, it's really important.'

'She didn't say anything more but wait…She did point towards the pier.'

'The West Pier?'

'No, the other one. Chain Pier opposite The Brighton Aquarium over there.' Polly pointed in the direction.

'Right, Rawlings, you go down Ship Street to the front and start walking along from there. I'll walk back and down East Street. Like a pincer movement, we'll cover both ways leading up to the pier entrance. One of us might get lucky and get a glimpse of her.'

'Oi, wot about the rest, you said I'll get more,' Polly shouted at Abberline.

'I said you'll get more if you find her, which you haven't. All I have is a possible sighting. I've kept my part of the bargain.'

'You police are all the same.' Polly kicked the air with her foot in outrage.

Abberline wasted no more time and left to make his way down to East Street, leaving Rawlings alone with Polly, who looked at her with utter contempt. 'You're lucky; I would have beaten that out of you.'

'Don't threaten me Rawlings, I know you were in Seamus Keane's pocket, we all knows. Bet it was you who did for him, put him in the sea dead. It'll be you swinging for that, you mark my words, and I'll be there to laugh as you dance on the end of that rope.'

Rawlings grabbed her tight round the throat, pushing her hard against the wall of the pub. 'Don't even think about it, or you'll end up the same way, you hear me. Keep that dirty mouth of yours quiet about the likes of Seamus Keane, you understand.' He put a hand on her dress and roughly pulled it up as far as he could, revealing her naked body underneath. He tore a small bag that had been tied around her waist with string, knowing that's where prostitutes hid their money.

'This is mine now.' He pushed her hard, making her fall backwards onto the pavement, sobbing, her knees bleeding.

'That's my money, you bloody thief. Give it me back.'

'Not anymore, ain't you heard? Possession is nine-tenths of the law.' He left her screaming obscenities as he walked away, whistling, ready to rejoin the search.

FIFTY-ONE

Elsbeth felt bad leaving Abberline at the police station but couldn't wait anymore. Amelia Stanton had to be found, and after the vision she had experienced at the cafe, Mary Quinn was trying to tell her something. She didn't know Amelia Stanton, had never met her, and yet, she had come to realise that she was a kind, caring, loving mother, and for that alone, she had to do something. Elsbeth had the gift for a reason, she could see things others could not, and she was going to use it.

There was an evil she had never felt before in all her years, a powerful energy locked inside a madman. She knew he had been watching her, toying with her, almost certainly sent the note, and left her a liver in her house. He could kill her at any time, but he hadn't, and she questioned why. Maybe he could see she had the ability to talk with the dead and that interested him, maybe he knew she could feel his presence. Whatever it was, she had a connection with him and soon she would finally meet and look into the soul of darkness.

She walked towards Vine Street and The Crown where Mary had worked but didn't stop, carrying on towards the alleyway where Mary had become the first victim in this series of murders. Elsbeth knew she was easy prey for a skilled hunter, as she traced the steps through the passage as she had done before with Abberline. The brick wall was wet from spitting rain that had just started, making the uneven surface slimy and cold, and the way ahead was as before, poorly lit and gloomy. The familiar sounds of shouting and items being thrown out of buildings echoed out of the dilapidated houses around her. She wondered what life was like in such places. It wasn't living as she knew it. Men, women, and children huddled together for warmth and safety in damp, squalid conditions; every day was a battle. Some of them would wake to fight another day; others, the old, sick, and very young, would not make it through, taken during the night under the silent wings of death.

Elsbeth reached the spot where she had seen Mary Quinn pointing in her vision. It had an air of uneasiness about it; she felt sick and heavy. The rubbish pile where her half-naked body had been dumped was still there like a headstone. On the wall written in chalk was a message that Mary had been trying to show her. She glanced back down the alley through the dim light to check that nobody had followed; her skin prickled with fear. It was clear, but the familiar sense of being watched kept her alert. There was a presence, one she knew. She knelt to read the words that had been left.

Elsbeth,
   Hurry under Chain Pier if you want to save her.
   Yours truly,
   Jack

She went ice cold. The words had a power to them, deep and disturbing. Standing up, she turned around, but there was nothing, just a dog barking in the distance. She looked back at the wall; the letters had started to run down the surface like they were in a dream. Then the rain fell harder, the letters broke up, falling like tears, and then, in an instant, they had gone. Elsbeth pulled her coat tighter and secured her bonnet. She knew where to go now; she knew where Amelia Stanton was.

FIFTY-TWO

Elsbeth made her way as quickly as she could, through the back streets of Brighton, to the seafront as dusk grew closer. She was just short of the pier on Kings Road, picking up the pace; she could see it was just a few hundred yards away. The rain had not relented, and most people had either gone home or retreated into public houses and tea rooms to avoid the worst of the weather until it had passed. But Elsbeth had no choice; she held her bonnet with one hand as she turned off the wide paved walkway and down a slight slope to the beach and lower esplanade. She raced past several fishermen's huts under stone arches that housed the nets and tackle for the boats still out at sea. The fishermen had little choice; if they were to eat, they had to fish even in the rough winter swells. Some never came back, ending up dining at Davy Jones' table.

As she got nearer, she saw the vast four iron towers of the Chain Pier. All had been secured by a number of piles driven several feet into the bedrock. On the pier's boardwalk, the tops of the towers were hollow, and shops were allowed to sell shells and other paraphernalia to the public. Elsbeth had enjoyed many walks along it in happier times, marvelling at the massive iron-linked chains that held the structure up on either side. Getting close, the salt air filled her lungs as huge rollers crashed against the cross braces underneath the structure, the sea testing it, finding a weakness.

She had no idea where to go; all the message had said was under Chain Pier. She reached a series of iron girders crossing each other with the boardwalk and entrance above; she was by herself and had a bad feeling. It was eerie and strange, like a distant world. The smell of seaweed hung heavy in the air as huge swells over the years had twisted the metal into alien shapes. It was a reminder to her how powerful Mother Nature was, as the defending roar of the waves hammered down onto the beach.

She walked further going under the roof of the pier, the light fading fast, she found herself sliding on the small pebbles thrown up by the breakers. She looked around, but there was nothing obvious. *Where was Amelia?*

'Mrs. Stanton... Amelia, my name is Elsbeth, I'm here to get you out, tell me where you are, shout if you can, it's ok, you're going to be okay. I'm here, can you hear me? Make a sound, something to let me know where you are.' Her words lost within the sound of the sea. Again and again, she called out to Amelia like a siren until she turned her attention to the one holding her captive.

'I know you are watching; I can feel you; you know I can. Show yourself. Let her go. I'm waiting... Come on, isn't this what you want?' Elsbeth's voice was mixed with anger and trepidation as she waited for a reply, turning around, looking around for any sign, but only the rain and the wind answered. A metal door towards the back of the structure swung open and shut, caught by the strong gusts; Elsbeth went over and held it carefully, peeping round.

Inside was a room carved into the rock; it was damp like a mausoleum; a chest of some description sat just past the doorway with a lobster trap and an oil lamp on top. The room smelled of rotting fish and urine; it was disgusting. As the gale followed her, there was a crunching sound as she stepped on broken glass and shells that littered the floor. Some matches had been left next to the lamp, striking one; a dull yellow light flooded the room. As she looked up, a large ceiling beam emerged out of the blackness like a ship appearing out of a fog spanning the room's width. The walls were mainly brick with oil and dirt stains; the floor was filthy and full of rubbish. A large rat shot across her path and out the door – not even the rodent wanted to stay. Elsbeth wanted to vomit; the stench was so bad she wanted to run. She was sweating, her heart racing, her breath short, but the thought of Amelia Stanton pushed her forward.

In a corner of the room was a chair facing the wall, and there was a person slumped in it. Elsbeth swallowed hard. She crept nearer, holding the lamp higher. She wanted to speak, call out. She tried, but something told her not to. The person's hair was long, and the head leaning to one side. She got closer and closer until…It was as if a punch had landed hard in her stomach. Slowly, she moved round to the front. Amelia Stanton was dead, her face bloated, blood containing foam leaked from her mouth and nose, her eyes bulging and open, clouding over, fixed to the floor. A large gaping hole at the upper right-hand side above her diaphragm was seeped in congealed blood, her liver had been cut out. Her dress had been torn off the shoulders down to her waist, revealing skin turned blue with a marbling discolouration to it, part of the decaying process. She had been deceased for some time. A small rectangular slate board hung around her neck like an animal in a slaughterhouse with another message.

Too late, Elsbeth.

Elsbeth could no longer contain her horror, screaming out like a mother who had lost a child, a guttural, deep, primeval cry of utter helplessness. All hope now taken. Bile came up through to the roof of the mouth; she bent over and vomited.

The lamp slipped from her hand, dropping onto the cobbled floor, leaving her in complete darkness. She bent down desperately, trying to locate it, her hands shaking, she searched from side to side, trying to find it. Where is it? It must be here …please. The glass cover had broken, a piece sticking out from the floor, cutting her palm. She put her bloodied hand against the wall, weak from retching, frightened; she knew she had to get out fast. It was a trap.

The door to the room, her only way out, suddenly creaked and slammed shut; the silence was broken only by the excited breathing of someone else in the room, someone right behind her. There was a strong smell of amber, a smell she recognised. Elsbeth froze, unable to move; a hand reached around her face, and a cloth pressed hard against her mouth and nose. Her mind started to mist over as she fought to stay awake; her legs buckled and went from under her as she slumped back.

'There you go, missy, don't you worry none, you let Cripps take care of you. He wanted you to see his work close up like,' Cripps said, pointing over towards the body of Amelia Stanton. 'Before he does the same to you. I hope it didn't disappoint; and to think you rushed over here to try and save her, oh dear what a shame,' he added not meaning a word. 'I tell you what, maybe seeing as you can talk with the dead, you can ask her how it felt to have her sides ripped open.' A high-pitched laugh followed, echoing off the walls.

Elsbeth faded in and out of consciousness. Her vision blurred; she was lying on the filthy floor but could just make out Cripps dragging Amelia's body across it and out of the room. He was gone for what seemed like an age; when he did return, Ameila's body was not with him.

'Now, missy, let's be having you,' he said, smirking, lifting Elsbeth. His face pressed up hard against hers. His skin felt cold and clammy as he licked her face. 'Hmm, you taste nice. Oh, you're wondering where I've taken her, the one you couldn't save? We can't have her lying about stinking up the place, can we? So, I threw her rotting corpse into the sea. Don't worry, none. It will wash up in a few days' time after the wildlife has finished with her,' he shrieked, laughing again. Cripps heaved her up further, his grip tightening as he started to move towards the door. Elsbeth tried to move, but her legs were numb, her feet dragging along the floor, leaving a trail in the grime.

'Come on, we really do have to go now. *He* is so looking forward to having some time alone with you.'

FIFTY-THREE

Cripps licked his lips excited at the prospect of watching her writhe screaming for mercy. He quickly exited the room of horrors slithering like snake under the pier to the side of the esplanade, his arm around Elsbeth's waist; he dragged her along with him. There were few people about, but if any on-lookers took notice, it would just seem as if she was drunk and being helped along. After a few feet, Cripps opened a heavy door with rusty bars and a sign on it saying, "Pump Room". Brighton had a maze of tunnels under the streets that most people didn't know about. Miles of sewers and tons of seawater that was pumped into the aquarium. This pump room was a substation that pushed the sea water directly under the beach via two large pipes. The first pipe ran along the length of a tunnel and went right into the aquarium to feed the tanks and the main waterfall attraction. Access to the aquarium from the tunnel was gained by way of a ladder and hatch into the building, which Cripps knew he would have to navigate his way up with Elsbeth.

Once in the aquarium the tunnel carried on taking the second pipe to the main sewage station housed under a Venti-lator building which was about a quarter of a mile away. Cripps was certain the police had no idea about these secret passages so he could move along at his own pace without ever being detected. He gripped Elsbeth tightly as they began to shuffle down the first stretch of the tunnel, which was dark and damp with large pools of stagnant water that had collected on the floor.

'Come on, missy, don't want to be late. I must prepare you for him. Make sure you're all nice and clean. Then, after he's finished with you, if there's anything left, it's my turn. Maybe I'll pluck those pretty eyes out, eh?' His snarl showed his decayed teeth, his breath stale and putrid; she turned her head to one side.

'You won't get away...' her words slurred and broken as she staggered along with him.

'I don't think you are in any position to say anything, dear, do you? Now, you hold on tight, not far to go, then we'll get you settled in.'

Elsbeth struggled, but it was to no avail. Her body went limp, and she lost consciousness once more, sliding back into a deep sleep with only the vision of the mutilated body of Amelia Stanton playing over and over in her mind.

FIFTY-FOUR

Rawlings and Abberline reached the entrance to the Chain Pier almost at the same time. Abberline hadn't seen anyone fitting Elsbeth's description, stopping along the way to ask any shop owners, but they had long gone and had shut for the day. There was little trade in winter months as it was already dark by four in the afternoon, and the bad weather just compounded matters.

'Any luck?' Abberline called out to Rawlings as he saw him approaching.

'No. Nothing. I asked about, but nobody had seen her; the weather's got so bad people don't want to stop and talk, they just want to get to the railway station and go home.'

'She must be somewhere around here. If she came here, it was for a reason. Something or someone told her to, and I'm worried the killer won't be far behind her. Let's get along the pier as quickly as we can. There are a few buildings; maybe she's held up in one.' Abberline knew this was wishful thinking; he knew Elsbeth, and she would not rest until she had found Amelia Stanton, but he had to search anyway, just in case. 'Right, you take one side. I'll take the other. If you see anything suspicious, call out.'

Both started walking along the wooden planks, the rain

and wind becoming stronger the further out to sea they were getting. Neither man found anything. They had gone right to the end, but there was no sign of her. As they walked back, Abberline noticed through the gaps in the boards the beach extended underneath the pier so there could be some space under it, and maybe that's where she had gone. The topside was exposed, but underneath it, she would be hidden, and so would someone waiting.

'Rawlings, follow me. I think she's *under* the pier, not on it.'

Rawlings followed Abberline back to the entrance, then down a slope to the side and onto the lower esplanade, which ran directly beneath the structure. Rawlings and Abberline fervently looked about for any sign, any evidence that Elsbeth had been there.

'Nothing, sir, nothing I can see anyway.'

'Keep looking, Rawlings. I know she was here; there must be something. Call it instinct.'

'I think Miss Hargreaves would call it more of a psychic moment.'

Abberline knew he was being sarcastic and had come to expect that from him. 'Well, she might, but I believe my gut, and that tells me I'm right.'

'Any fisherman out in that must be drowned by now, those poor bastards,' Rawlings commented, seeing the massive rollers pulverising the beach.

'Wait a minute, there's a door of some kind at the back, can you see it? Follow me quickly.' Abberline rushed over to it. The rain poured from above through the gap in the boards, soaking him, his fingers red and frozen.

'Rawlings, help me. I can't open this, it's… jammed.'

He joined Abberline, and the two of them tried pulling together, but it was no use, it was as if the door was welded shut. Rawlings looked about for something to use.

'Hang on. I'll be right back. I have an idea.'

He had seen something that might help and quickly went over and picked up a long iron bar that had fallen off the infrastructure. He rushed back and hit the door several times with it. Something must have loosened; it opened enough for Rawlings to insert the bar and lever it open so they could squeeze through.

Rawlings went in first. 'Jesus Christ, the place stinks like rotting meat.' He coughed and held his hand to his nose and mouth.

Abberline worked through the stench, took a box of matches from his pocket, took one out and struck it on the side. 'Let's see what else we can use to get some light here.'

Rawlings searched and found a small wooden pole and a roll of old sail cloth next to some chains that were used for anchors near the door. He reached into his pocket, took out his pocketknife, cut a few strips off the material, wrapped it around the pole, and lit it. 'It won't give us much light. It's sail cloth and has some tar in it to keep it weatherproof. It won't last long, but the tar will keep it going for a bit. Better than nothing.'

They both went further into the room, the foul smell intensifying as they did.

Abberline stopped in the centre. Hanging down from the ceiling was a large chain on a pulley with two leather straps. He knew this was not looking good as he stared towards the corner of the room… there seemed to be an object like a chair.

'Rawlings, give me the torch for a minute.'

Rawlings did as he was told, and Abberline made his way over to the corner.

'There's nothing here,' Rawlings said behind him, 'just some furniture. The place is empty other than the stench that's making me want to throw up.'

Abberline trod on some broken glass as he walked over and

took the torch off Rawlings shining it down, seeing the broken lamp and then blood.

'Nothing, but this.' Abberline swung the torch towards the wall behind him.

The light flickered as it reached the end of its life, but just before the flame was extinguished, Rawlings caught sight of the small handprint in blood on the side of the wall.

Abberline turned to Rawlings. 'Elsbeth must have cut herself on this glass from the broken lamp. She left us this to find; it's a sign.' Abberline reached out with his finger, smearing blood on his fingertip, 'she was here recently, which means she has to be nearby.'

'How can you be sure?'

'Because the blood hasn't dried yet.'

FIFTY-FIVE

Abberline and Rawlings agreed to split up to cover more ground. Abberline worked back along Madeira Road, following the newly constructed Volks Railway, which had opened in August of that year. He wasn't even sure if they were looking in the right area, but they had to start at some point, as time was running out.

Abberline called across to Rawlings, 'You run back to the aquarium, and, Rawlings, check inside as well. I'll come and find you in thirty minutes.'

The Brighton Aquarium was a large building and about to close to the public. Rawlings thought if Abberline was correct, they couldn't have got too far, and this could be the perfect place to hide. Access to the aquarium was under a large clock tower that stood on top of four arches, then down a twin flight of curved stairs that swept down to the entrance. The staircase was designed to look like the type you could see in a stately home, with beautifully carved balustrades and vases made of stone, giving the visitor the feeling that they were going to see something very special. It was theatre at its best, and the exhibits were among the greatest in the world. Three doors at the front would allow the vast number of visitors in and out of the building. The middle door was still open as Rawlings arrived; one of the aquarium assistants was about to lock up.

Rawlings, reaching the bottom of the stairs, called out to him. 'Hey, leave the door open, Brighton Police. I need to search inside,' he said, flashing his identity card. 'Have you seen anyone in the last thirty minutes coming in here? A well-dressed woman and a man probably in a hurry?'

'We get a lot of well-dressed folk coming here, hundreds a day, mate. So, I have no idea, but in the last thirty minutes you say...' He thought for a moment. 'No, we tell the public well in advance that we are closing, so they are asked to leave by these doors, which is the only way in or out, at least thirty minutes before if we have many people visiting that day. If anyone is left in here, they'll be here for the night with the fish. They won't see the light of day until the morning when I open up at seven to get ready.'

Rawlings was in a hurry and didn't want to be kept talking to this old man. 'Look, just leave me the key. I presume you have a spare. I'll make sure I lock up. You get off home.'

'Well, I... I don't know. It's my responsibility. I'm not sure the curator would approve.'

'The murders of the two women in The North Laine, the ones who were stabbed and ripped to pieces, you read about them in the news, yes?' Rawlings asked the man, who suddenly looked concerned, remembering the awful details. 'The killer is probably in there, so it's up to you. You can stay and help me, and you might get to meet him yourself, or you can be on your way back to the safety of your home; what is it going to be?'

The assistant didn't take long to answer. 'Well, given the circumstances, I'll be on my way; I don't get paid enough for this. I have a spare set of keys at my place. Just make sure you close up afterwards and leave the key in one of the vases on the stairway going out.' His hands shaking, he gave the keys over and moved quickly off before anything else could be said. Rawlings went into the aquarium and closed the door behind him.

He looked up to the vaulted ceiling made up of red bricks. It was almost cathedral-like in its construction and was held in place by a number of granite and marble columns. He looked down the main corridor, which was two hundred and twenty-four feet long, and over at the illuminated tanks inset into the walls that kept all sorts of unique and unseen creatures of the oceans. The tanks, fed with seawater by steam, ranged in size from sixty feet to a hundred and twelve feet in length to house the larger animals. As Rawlings passed the first of the exhibits, he marvelled at what he was seeing. He had lived in Brighton all his life, and although he knew a lot about it, he had never been to the aquarium. As he walked past the first row of enclosures, strange inquisitive fish with bulging eyes swam up to the glass, peering out, then darted back behind the rocks that lined the side and back of the tank. Each one housed something new, exotic, and weird. He found it fascinating and promised himself to come and visit with his kids after this was all over.

The floor was polished stone, the sound of his shoes bouncing off the walls as he walked across it. The long corridor of enclosures ended with a sign and information on how to get to the Waterfall Fernery and Music Room. In front was another set of doors which led to the central hall. Rawlings had followed the aquarium's progress since its opening in 1872. He was excited at the time as it held the largest tank in the world, at 110,000 gallons, up until the time The Royal Aquarium in Westminster was built only four years later, dwarfing it at 700,000 gallons. Even though he hadn't had the time to see either, he would tell stories to scare his children about sea monsters that lay in wait in dark waters.

Rawlings knew the killer was intelligent but had the element of surprise on his side. He proceeded as cautiously as possible, trying not to make any unnecessary sound as he slowly turned the door handle to the central hall, slipping inside. If the killer was in the aquarium, it was an excellent place to hide as there were a number of areas where he could be. He hoped Elsbeth might help him, make some noise, giving him some clue as to her position, but so far, the place was as quiet as a graveyard.

He soon came face to face with the massive tank in the middle that displayed one of nature's most feared creatures, a giant squid. It lay still at the bottom of the tank, its eyes following Rawlings, its eight arms and two longer tentacles moving slowly, uncoiling in the water. He kept his distance, knowing these monsters of the deep were the stuff of myth and legend. Seamen were snatched from the decks of ships by giant arms reaching out of the sea, taken down beneath the waves, never to be seen again. Some squid were said to be so big that entire vessels were lost. He moved around the tank and through another set of doors with no sign of Elsbeth. He was beginning to think they were not in the building at all, and he was wasting his time. Maybe the assistant was right; nobody else had come in here. A lacquered sign on a wooden pedestal with a painted gold arrow pointing to the left said: "This way to Waterfall Fernery and Music Room."

Rawlings followed the sign into another narrow hallway with smaller tanks and exhibits and then into a large conservatory, which held another attraction. A working waterfall built with artificial rocks sat at the back of the room and went from the floor to the ceiling. The magnificent display even had a small cave to the side, creating a sense of wonder and mystery. Rawlings had walked through most of the exhibition without finding Elsbeth or her captor, and he only had this and the music room left to search; he was running out of options. He stopped to see if there was anything behind the waterfall, but the wall of water cascading down made it difficult to see. A small light illuminated the cave entrance, which caught his attention. As he made his way over to it, Rawlings could see that there was something inside, lying motionless on the floor.

As he got closer, he saw what it was. It was a person, the body of a woman. It was Elsbeth.

FIFTY-SIX

Abberline walked briskly along the promenade of Madeira Road. On one side was a high wall with a few benches placed at various intervals below and some steep steps leading up to the main road into the town. On the other side was the Volks Railway Line, and in between, some Japanese spindle trees at a height of twelve feet creating a barrier of soft landscaping. He was a great admirer of the railway's inventor Magnus Volk, an engineer of English and German heritage, who'd been born and lived in Brighton and had read about its opening that summer, but this was not how he wanted to visit it. The line ran for a quarter of a mile from the aquarium, and he set off following it along, crossing the line several times at different points, going onto the beach where small, open fishing boats, lay randomly about after the day's catch. Haul lines, nets and traps were piled inside, ready for the next launch. The boats provided a good, quick hiding place, and he had to search as many as possible. But it was dark and with the wind whipping up huge waves clawing their way closer to him, it was becoming difficult. As he searched each boat, he could hear the steel bones of the pier creak and groan as she twisted in the swell.

He had nearly reached the end of the line. There was no-where left to look and no sign of Elsbeth. He was becoming concerned that he was wrong and that Elsbeth could have been taken on another route. Maybe the killer had a cab waiting, ready to make a fast exit, and the search they were conducting would prove fruitless. But the handprint Elsbeth had left was still not dried, so they had to be close if they were still on foot. He knew Elsbeth was a strong and resilient woman who would not go without a fight, so he was sure whoever had taken her was not going to find it easy. He wished Elsbeth had listened to him; he knew Elsbeth was independent and strong-minded, but she seemed to make herself responsible for saving Amelia. Maybe it was because she couldn't save the other women and had seen what had been done to them, she had to try to save this one. He didn't know, but whatever her motivation, she would need his help.

He reached the end of the track and had not found anything, so was left with little choice other than to run as fast as he could back to the aquarium. He hoped that Rawlings had some better news and that Elsbeth had somehow escaped and had been found. But he knew in his head this was clutching on to hope rather than reality. Abberline hurried down the steps and reached the entrance to the aquarium. He tried the first two doors, finding them locked, but the third one was not; pulling slowly on the brass handle, he opened it. It was cold inside, and the smell of seawater and fish filled the air. It was dimly lit inside, his attention immediately drawn to the rows of tanks inset into the walls on either side. He stood under the beautiful brick arched roof in the centre and turned to look at the myriad of fish. They appeared agitated, swimming fast from one end to the other, back and forth; some hit the glass head-on, trying to escape. Something had spooked them; they were in flight mode, petrified – animal instinct to flee, sensing something wrong, something evil.

FIFTY-SEVEN

Rawlings bent down; the roof was not that high from the ground as he crawled into the cave to see if Elsbeth was alive; getting alongside her, he turned her over. He moved towards her, his head down, putting his right ear to her nostrils. He listened for any sign of life. She was breathing rhythmically and deeply as if in a deep sleep. He noticed something else on her lips: a sweet smell. He had smelt it before in a hospital. It was chloroform, which was administered to patients undergoing surgery, but it also had a darker side. It could be a way to sedate people against their will. Knowing the correct dosage was crucial: too much, and the patient could die; too little, and they would feel every incision made. It would require medical knowledge to dispense the drug to ensure the exact amount. But he also knew it from somewhere else, much closer to home, at The Dead House and its Coroner, Cripps.

Rawlings admitted to himself that Cripps was as corrupt as he was, he didn't deny that, but this was on a whole different level. If Cripps was involved in helping someone mutilate women and responsible for Elsbeth being here, where was he? After Jack Robertson's suicide, it all started to make sense. The organs they had found at Robertson's place must have been planted, and Cripps must have been the one to do it; he dealt in black market parts. He felt stupid for not seeing it sooner. He knew Cripps was a gutless weasel but never figured on him getting involved in anything like this. Cripps must be working with the real killer, had been all along, but why? That was something he looked forward to asking him. But for now, he had to get Elsbeth out of this place and to safety. Cripps would be back soon and would not be alone.

Getting her out of the cave would be one thing, but having to help her through the corridors and rooms which were poorly lit was another. He moved Elsbeth carefully, a bit at a time, the sand on the floor clinging to her coat and hair as her bonnet came away, falling to the side. He got her out, putting his arms around her; he lifted her free of the cave and into the music room next door. The door to the room was the only way in and out; there were no windows; the walls were clad in light oak panelling, with several chairs arced in a small circle for the musicians to sit on. He lay her carefully down and knelt next to her. He had little knowledge of how to bring someone around from chloroform, but gently moved her head from side to side, trying to provoke a response; at first, there was little reaction. Then.

'What, what are you doing? No... No. He brought me here. I... I can't feel my legs. There are two...' Elsbeth's words were slurred and disjointed.

'Elsbeth, it's me, Rawlings.' He kept his voice to a whisper. 'You've been drugged; you're in the aquarium just over from the pier. Do you remember how you got here?' Elsbeth shook her head. 'I know it was Cripps, and I know he's the one helping the real killer. We need to get out of here; we're too exposed. I'm going to have to help you?'

'Just run, save yourself; he's coming, Rawlings, Cripps is coming...He'll kill you.'

Rawlings ignored her. 'Elsbeth, I'm going to have to lift you; we don't have much time. Do you know where Amelia Stanton is? Have you seen her? Do they have her here somewhere?'

'She…she's dead,' Elsbeth screamed, using all her strength. 'Cripps took her for *him*. Then, left her alone with that monster in that terrible place under the pier to do what he wanted to her.'

'I know about that place, Elsbeth, we found it. We saw your bloody handprint on the wall. Abberline knew it was a message from you; he knew you had to be close. But there was no sign of Amelia. You say she's dead?'

'Abberline, where is he…tell him there are two of them, tell him Cripps knows who the killer is. Calls him The Ripper; they are…' Her words slowed, but she fought back to get her message across.

'Cripps was waiting for me when I got there. The Ripper wanted me to see what he had done to Amelia and had left Cripps to clear up. Cripps took pleasure in telling me he had dumped Amelia's body into the sea. It was a trap.' Elsbeth reached up, clinging onto his jacket collar. 'I saw her… I know you don't believe me, but I saw Amelia where she was being held in a vision when I visited her home. Then, at the police station, I had… I had seen a message on a wall where Mary was killed… I had to go. I had to try and find Amelia. Cripps drugged me, brought me here to be delivered to that lunatic. Please listen; we have to get out now. We gotta go *now*… Please.'

Rawlings didn't know what to think about her psychic visions. He had always thought they were a trick, but she seemed so convinced. But one thing was real: they were both in danger.

'Is this maniac, this Ripper here in the aquarium with Cripps?'

'I…I don't know. I didn't see him. Cripps said they used a tunnel to get me from the pier so nobody would see us. He said there are many tunnels, and the Ripper knows about them…uses them to get about. He said he's going to take me somewhere special, a place where no one would think to look, where the Ripper is waiting for me.'

Rawlings could see she was becoming more distressed. 'Elsbeth, I know you've been through a lot but try to stay calm.'

'That monster cut Amelia to pieces, strapped her to a chair, and took her liver out, and left it in my home,' she cried, tears falling down her face. 'I couldn't… I couldn't save her; she was already dead.' She choked a little, trying to get the words out, remembering what she had seen. Her head drooped to her chest; she was becoming incoherent.

'Abberline… be sure to tell him. *Everything.*'

Rawlings looked around for anything to use as a weapon; he would feel better if he could find something to protect himself with, but there was nothing to hand. Abberline had not found them; they had agreed thirty minutes before they split at the pier; it had now been at least forty, and there was no sign of him. Rawlings hoped they would meet him somewhere as they made their way out. He bent down, put his arm around Elsbeth, and lifted her. Sweat poured down from his brow and face onto his shirt collar, staining it. He was feeling something he hadn't in a very long time. He was afraid. They left the music room, making their way down the corridor.

Rawlings had to stop then. He wasn't the fittest, so he needed to catch his breath for a minute and sat Elsbeth on a visitor's chair in the corridor. Breathing heavily, his chest felt tight. He promised himself he would lose some weight after this was all over. 'Come on, Elsbeth, please try, just a bit for me, will you.' His voice was desperate and anxious.

Elsbeth fluttered her eyelids, trying to focus. He could see she was attempting to fight off the effects but was still very drowsy. A loud bang rang out from where they had been in the music room. It made Rawlings jump. A thousand thoughts raced through his mind, none of them good. But one thing was definite, they had to carry on and get out of this place.

'For God's sake, Elsbeth, we have to go, we need to keep moving,' he tried to appeal to her once more. Her head flopped over to one side. She called his name loudly. 'Rawlings… You don't understand the Ripper… he's evil incarnate. He will kill us all; he won't stop. Ever. You must… Stop him.'

'Shhhh,' Rawlings held his finger to his lips. 'Whisper, as sound travels in this place. Lean on me, we need to get out of this corridor. It will take us to the central hall, and then it's just one last push to the exit. Can you do that for me, Elsbeth? Can you help me?'

Rawlings managed to get to the next set of doors. 'Elsbeth, we're just outside the central hall. I'm going to have to leave you here for a moment. Just lean back into the corner and don't try to move while I go and check it first. Don't worry, you're going to be free of this place soon. I need to make sure it's clear. It's going to be fine; don't make a sound. I'll be as quick as I can, I promise.'

Elsbeth didn't look convinced as she grabbed his arm. 'No… No, don't, go…'

But before she could say anything else, Rawlings had moved into the hall. Besides the light from the enormous tank holding the squid, the room was dark. The black eyes of the beast looked directly at him. He got down on all fours to stay as hidden as possible making his way around the outside of the enclosure. Giant tentacles slowly tracked him, reaching out, pressing against the sides, feeling for a weakness in the glass. Rawlings wiped the dripping sweat from his face; as he crawled further around, he could feel his heart beating, pounding like a steam hammer, thump, thump, thump.

Then came the scream.

FIFTY-EIGHT

Rawlings scrambled back to his feet and dashed back through the doors to where he had left Elsbeth. She was pointing back down the corridor towards the doors to the waterfall exhibition.

'He's here... He's right here. I heard footsteps coming towards me.'

Rawlings helped her up from the darkened corner. 'Where, Elsbeth?' He looked back down the corridor to the doors of the waterfall they had just come through. The light was terrible, but he couldn't see anyone. Sound seemed to bend in different ways; the acoustics of the building made it deceptive, so he didn't know how near or far away the footsteps had come from.

It must be Cripps. He's found her missing from the cave. He must be thinking she's come round from the sedative and crawled out by herself. But he's going to be coming after her, Rawlings thoughts raced.

Elsbeth's words were still muffled; the pain, the panic on her face, was real. 'Don't let him take me, please.'

'Don't worry. We're getting out of here together, I promise.' Rawlings despised Cripps and knew he was capable of anything, but he had Elsbeth to consider. He was unarmed, and

Cripps most likely was, so they had no choice but to escape and try and find Abberline. Elsbeth was still suffering from the after-effects of being drugged, but he had to hope that she had enough strength to make the final dash. He returned to what he knew best, being a policeman and his training. There was no room for error. If he faltered, it would be the end of them both.

'Elsbeth, we need to get through these doors. I've checked the room, and it's clear; we're really close now, just a few more yards, that's all, and we're free, understand? Take a deep breath, hold onto me; we're not going to stop. I'll help you. We will go on the count of three.'

Elsbeth centred herself, glancing back down the corridor once more to make sure Cripps wasn't coming. She had to put her life in the hands of a misogynist, a person whom up until now she had no time for. But there seemed to be another side to Detective Rawlings, one she would not have believed existed before this night. She thought for a while as they prepared to move; maybe she had misjudged him. Possibly, they had misjudged each other.

Rawlings held onto her. 'Ready? On the count of three, we go.'

'One, two… Three.'

FIFTY-NINE

Abberline slowly walked past the last of the displays, reaching the doors into the central hall. He pushed one side gently, opening it just a crack, slowly put one foot into the room and then paused. He knew from experience that it was more prudent to take a cautious approach; the large tank in the middle of the room hummed its contents restless. He got closer, not having ever seen such a sight. The thing glided to the back of the tank, retreating into the gloom of the water, hiding, waiting. Abberline stepped around the outside of the installation, wary of what it contained.

Abberline pushed the doors to the next part of the exhibition, but something was blocking them from fully opening. He slid his body through the gap, noticing a strong metallic smell he knew only too well. It was the scent of blood. It was dark, so he couldn't be sure what the obstruction was until he got closer. His heart sank as his worst fears came true. It was the outline of a body crumpled behind the doors and the likely prospect of who it was, sickened him. He should have done more. *He should have protected her.* As he slowly knelt to see if there were any signs of life, a faint and strained voice spoke to him.

'I tried to help; I did what I could… I'm sorry.'

Abberline took hold of their hand, realising in that instant who it was.

'It's ok, it's alright, you need to rest. I'll get some help. You're going to make it. You're going to be alright. Do you hear me, Rawlings? I want you to keep your hand pressed hard against the wound to stop the flow of blood while I find something to bandage it up with.'

'No, it's too late. It was Cripps; he's been working with this maniac…calls him The Ripper. All this time, sir… right under our noses. Cripps set Jack Robertson up to take the fall.'

'Cripps?' Abberline said, shocked at the revelation.

'Yeah, I should have seen it. He's a slimy bastard, a villain; I know what he's capable of. I… I had dealings with him, and I ain't proud of that, but he's got his fingers in some bad stuff; he sells body parts to those that pay for such things.'

Abberline was not surprised by what he was hearing. 'Just try and rest, Rawlings.'

'I'm sorry I… I have to tell you something else. I must make me peace before…, before it's too late.'

'You're not going to die, Rawlings. I'm going to get you out of here, do you hear me?'

'That's nice of you to say, sir, but I'm a goner, I know that… I have to tell you.'

'Rawlings, it's okay. I know about Seamus Keane. I know what he was like: I thought you might be working on the side for him and that he was blackmailing you. I guessed as much.'

'I didn't mean it to go on for so long; you know I needed the money. You've seen my home, kids and wife and all. I wanted out, but he wouldn't let me go. Keane said if I stopped helping him, he would kill my family. I had no choice. I had to kill him. If this gets out… my family will be turfed out of the house, they'll have nothing, have nowhere to go.'

'Rawlings. I'm not going to tell anyone; I promise I'll make sure your wife and children are looked after. Anyway, as I've already said, you're going to live, so stop all this talk of dying.'

Rawlings looked relieved but pale as the blood drained out of his body. Abberline knew it didn't look good; he was losing him.

'He cut me deep, sliced me stomach open, don't... He has Elsbeth. I couldn't stop him, came out of nowhere.'

'It's too late for me; get after him; save her if you can.'

'Don't talk. Try and conserve your energy.' Abberline moved Rawlings's hand away to inspect the damage. It was a large gaping gash right across his abdomen, his intestine hanging out. He had already lost too much blood; he could see Rawlings was having difficulty breathing and was slipping away from him fast. He was dying, and Abberline had to find out some details before it was too late.

'Did Cripps say anything, where he was taking her? Anything you can recall will help.'

'I... don't remember much. We... were set to go through the doors, to get to the entrance, then from nowhere, I felt this pain in my gut. The next thing I know, I'm on the deck with me guts on show. Elsbeth,' he paused, 'she said something about tunnels leading from the pier to this place. That's how he got her here. There are others leading to the sewer system, maybe from here... I don't know. The Ripper knows them well. They run all over the town. That's how he gets about unnoticed.

'I heard her trying to fight Cripps off, but... couldn't help her. Sorry I let you down. There's something else. Amelia Stanton... She's dead. Cripps took her for this Ripper. It was her liver in Elsbeth's house. The Ripper cut it out and left her body, or what was left of it, tied to a chair in that room under the pier for Elsbeth to find. But it was all a trap. Cripps took Elsbeth and got rid of Amelia Stanton's body in the sea. That's why we didn't find it.'

'Try to remember. Was there anything... anything at all Cripps said about where he might be taking Elsbeth?'

Rawlings squeezed Abberline's hand tightly, letting out a loud cry of pain. 'I heard Cripps saying he was taking her to somewhere not far, where they would not be disturbed. That's all, sorry.'

Rawlings let out another huge cry of agony. 'Oh God… please stop this.'

'It's alright, Rawlings. Relax. I'm going to get you some help.'

'No… Please don't leave; stay here. I don't want to die alone.'

Abberline did what he was asked and waited by his side.

'Cripps. I'm sure he wasn't alone when he stabbed me and took Elsbeth. I'm certain there was someone else there. I couldn't see them, but I felt them looking, watching me, from the shadows.'

'The Ripper?' Abberline guessed as Rawlings looked at him, nodding his head.

'It's so cold… why am I so cold?' Rawlings, shivering, let out his last breath a few moments later; his pain was gone; death had taken him.

SIXTY

Abberline had no option but to leave the body of Rawlings at the aquarium; he knew what he needed to do. Time was running out, and he didn't have the luxury of looking for another tunnel that might be in the aquarium. If it was there, it was most likely hidden and known to only a few; he decided to return to what he always used. Logic and facts. He left the building and ran back up the stairs, crossing over the road to The Old Steine. It was late, but a few cabs were still waiting for the odd fare. He hurriedly climbed aboard and instructed the driver to take him to Brighton Police Station. When they arrived, Abberline quickly alighted, seeing a young constable manning the front desk.

'With me now,' Abberline barked at the young man. The officer immediately dropped everything and quickly followed him into the office.

'Look, there is no easy way of saying this as I don't have the time. Detective Rawlings is dead, I need you to get hold of some officers, get them down to the aquarium, seal it off and secure the building, don't let anyone in or out unless I expressly tell you, do you understand?'

'Yes, sir.' The young officer looked visibly shaken by the news. 'Dead, sir? Did you say Detective Rawlings is dead!' he repeated, still not quite believing what he had just been told.

'Yes, he died in the line of duty. Leave it to me to inform his wife and keep this quiet. I don't want the press getting hold of this.'

'Of course, sir. I'll make sure no one mentions it.'

Abberline rummaged through the drawers of Rawling's old desk until he found what he was looking for at the back of one of the drawers wrapped in some cloth. It was an Enfield revolver, 476 calibre; it had six a cylinder feed with a range of twenty-five yards, which would prove to be more than sufficient for the task at hand. He found some bullets in the next drawer and loaded the revolver, taking some additional ammunition. The young officer looked on with a worried expression as Abberline placed the gun and bullets into his coat pocket.

'You get off now. I need to think for a minute.' The constable did as he was told and left to secure additional officers as instructed.

Abberline was on his own as he pondered the events that had just unfolded, still coming to terms with them himself. He didn't much like Rawlings or approve of his methods. He was corrupt, had some business going on with Cripps, and was responsible for the death of Seamus Keane. But when it mattered, he had come through and tried to save Elsbeth, which went some way for Abberline to forgive his sins. In return, he would keep his promise and make sure his wife and children were looked after.

Now, he had to try to establish where Cripps had taken Elsbeth. He kept thinking back to what Rawlings had said to him. He racked his brain, trying to recall the details; then it came to him. Elsbeth had been moved to the aquarium from under the pier via a tunnel, and there were miles of tunnels under the streets of Brighton that made up the sewer system. The Ripper knew about them and was using the network to move about and stay undetected in this subterranean maze.

Abberline turned around and went over to a large map of Brighton pinned to a wall in the office.

He scoured it, looking at every detail, searching for something that gave him a clue. His attention was drawn to a part of Brighton called Kemptown. Very close to the aquarium, there was a small building with the words "Ventilator" beside it. Abberline knew from his interest in engineering that this structure was used to give access down to the sewer and main storm outlet. If the sewers became overloaded, usually after heavy rainfall, it would direct the overflow out into the sea instead of backing up into the streets and people's homes and businesses. Four main outlets serviced the forty-four miles of pipes in the town; this small building gave access down to one of them and was the closest.

Of course. That must be it, very near to the aquarium and somewhere where they will not be disturbed. He patted his coat pocket to ensure the gun and spare bullets were there and quickly left the office.

SIXTY-ONE

Abberline hit the roof of the cab with his fist just short of the ventilator building so nobody would see or hear his arrival, keeping the element of surprise on his side. Black skies hung heavy over the sea like marble, the weather was unrelenting, a bad omen, he thought. It had rained all day and continued into the evening; everything was cold and soaked through. He knew the sewer system would be under pressure, creaking at the seams, and Elsbeth was somewhere within. Avoiding the glare from the streetlamps, he approached the building from the opposite side of the road, the horizontal rain slowing him, pushing him back.

The building was a small, rectangular structure painted white with a slate roof and basic casement windows along one side, with a plain wooden entrance in the centre. It was one of four in the town where maintenance workmen could shelter from the elements, store their tools and gain access to the sewers and pumps below via a ladder. Sometimes, a workman might sleep over if additional work took them through the night, so a table, lamp and makeshift bed were provided. It was also the only way down into the system and Abberline had little choice but to enter, if he wanted to find Elsbeth. There seemed to be no one inside as he approached, but the thought crossed his mind that Cripps could be waiting for him.

He put his hand inside his coat pocket and took out the gun, holding it tight before moving closer. The handle to the door was stiff, but it was obvious it had been forced; the frame was damaged, and the wood split. It was a sign that he was in the right place as he stepped inside, looking around, weighing up the risk, but the place was empty. He breathed a sigh of relief.

It was a large room. The wall across the back section had another doorway and a sign above it stating: "Danger – Access to Outlet." On the right side of the room was a desk under the windows, with an oil lamp in the middle and a basic wooden chair tucked under it. On the opposite side to the left-hand corner was a single metal framed bed with a mattress and pillow, both dirty and yellowed with age. He placed the gun down on the table for a moment, took the lamp, and set a match to it, turning the flame down to a low setting, and went over to the other door where he could get access down to the sewers. He climbed down a flight of metal steps until he arrived at a wooden landing, finding a ladder to the side that went through a hatch and seemed to go on forever, eaten by the dark. Reluctantly, he had to put his gun back in his coat. He knew he couldn't carry the lamp and hold onto the ladder at the same time as he descended.

Slowly, one rung at a time, his palms clammy. Looking back up, the landing was getting smaller the deeper he went. The smell of decay and stagnant water hit him like a punch from a heavyweight, his ears ringing, nearing the end the ladder started to vibrate. A torrent of water thundered below him, shaking the foundations. Reaching the bottom solid red brick walls were on either side of him; holding the lamp high to see the way ahead, he gradually moved forward. A high square-shaped tunnel lay before him, big enough for a train to pass through. Thick wooden joists set into the sides spanned across the width at regular intervals. In the middle, wooden scaffolding planks ran over the joists for workers to walk on to check the condition of the tunnel and to help clear any blockages. Under this, tons of water tore past at an alarming rate from drains carrying the overflow, combined with raw sewage on its journey out to the sea. One side had a narrow path with a number of arched storerooms inset. Abberline made his way across the planks and onto the walkway.

The first of the archways had an iron gate fastened with a large chain. Inside, he could see several buckets, wheelbarrows, pickaxes, and other tools piled in the middle. He stepped past another three recesses, all containing much the same. The last one, he found the gate open, the chain hanging loose, and the padlock on the floor; just to the side was a cloth. He picked it up but didn't need to examine it for long; the sweet smell of chloroform was powerful enough and confirmation Elsbeth had been taken this way. A narrow egg-shaped passage about head height lay ahead. It was dark, humid, and eerily quiet. He took out the revolver once more, cocked the hammer, and with the other hand held the lamp high.

SIXTY-TWO

Elsbeth felt her shoulder and arms burning as she swung suspended from the ceiling by a thick linked chain that was secured over a hook. Her hands were tied together almost in prayer position, but there was no God here, just the stench of oil and stagnant water. A gag bound tight around her mouth made it impossible to scream, to shout, it was all part of what was yet to come. To see the implements of torture, to feel the pain, her skin punctured, cut, stabbed but unable to let anyone hear her, was part of the punishment. She was entombed underground in the lair of the beast within the walls of a prison and at the mercy of a sadistic, deranged maniac who had no empathy, remorse or any intention of letting her go. Her breathing was harsh, rasping, sweat drenching her hair and seeping through her clothes. Then she recognised a voice and the smell of amber.

'Now now, missy let's clean you up a bit shall we, want you looking your best, don't we?' Cripps squealed in pleasure as he watched Elsbeth twist and turn on the chain tearing the skin on her wrists. She grunted as he used a dirty cloth to roughly wipe her face. *Just give me one chance, one moment, Cripps. Just one lack of judgment and I'll…* Elsbeth thought.

'Shhhh now, no point, missy, making a noise now, no one

is coming for you, nobody knows about this place you're all on your own and you're going to die on your own.'

She felt her eyes fill with absolute fear as Cripps leaned in close. She turned her head away from him, retching. His breathing deep, he moved his hands over her body slithering closer to her and pushing himself against her. 'Now let's see if you're clean *everywhere*, shall we.' He bent slightly, taking hold of the hem of her dress, pulling it up to her waist, then letting it fall back down, grinning at her and letting her know he could do whatever he wanted.

Elsbeth felt sick and angry; she swung her body back and forth, pushing with her toes that barely touched the ground, using her weight to try and loosen her hands but the chain just cut into her more.

'Hmmm, you're mine after he's done with you.' He laughed and squealed at the prospect. '

'What ya think, missy? Not so high and mighty now are we, eh?'

'Leave us,' a voice, low and steady, controlled, spoke from behind.

There was a silence then Elsbeth watched Cripps shuffle to one side of her.

'Yes… yes of course. I was just preparing her for you. I'll go and check we haven't been followed. That Inspector Abberline, he's persistent; he won't give up.'

'*Get out!*' The voice commanded.

Cripps quickly stepped aside and made good his exit, not even looking back at Elsbeth. She felt a heavy, suffocating energy in the room that she had felt before, when it all began in her home, the night of the séance. Where she and her guests had all witnessed the dead spirit of Mary Quinn. At the bakery where Rosie Meeks had been torn apart, as well as beside the body of Amelia Stanton. There was an intimacy of evil, she could feel it, but there was something else underlying this moment that concerned her more. There was a connection between herself and the person standing behind her. She had felt this for some time and now it had become a reality, like a shadow revealing its secret, the journey of a nightmare that she had been chosen to follow, to hold hands with death, to walk beside it on a path to an unknown destination. It felt as if the air had been sucked out of her lungs as he got closer, touching, playing with her hair, then the feeling of leather on her skin, his gloves brushing over the nape of her neck.

'At last, Elsbeth, here we are, and you in such a predicament. So beautiful, and you have the gift of seeing the dead, seeing my work.' His voice was educated, calm, and soft, considered in the way he delivered each word, as if he had rehearsed them a thousand times. Not the ravings of a madman as she expected. A madman that lay hidden for now. Elsbeth turned her head, trying to see his face.

'Don't do that, Elsbeth. I will only reveal myself to you if *I* decide. Is that clear?'

'Why don't you show yourself to me, let me see what a monster looks like.'

'Ah, Elsbeth, so strong, so righteous. We share a commonality, we are bonded by death, you and I, by that dark empty *timeless* moment. The decay of bone and flesh, that veil between life and the rotting corpses we become. One day we will be joined together in a marriage of the dead. But that will have to wait, ma chère, as I have work to do, I must grow into the person I am destined to become.'

'Why don't you just get on with it? What's stopping you? All this effort of Cripps bringing me here, what else for other than to kill me? That's what I'm here for, right?' Elsbeth, angry, knew she was taking a huge risk provoking him this way. He could easily snatch her life at any moment.

'Hmm, that would be too easy. It would be like simply crushing a butterfly in my hand. No, I have other things in store for you. Your demise will be slow, and you will suffer; you will be one of my greatest achievements, the great Elsbeth Hargreaves, laid bare for all to see, naked, stripped of dignity and skin down to the bone, down to that tormented soul of yours. For you are tormented, aren't you, Elsbeth? You are not the only one with a gift to see. But you already know that don't you?' He smiled.

She sensed him move and then appear in front of her. Tall, lean, and cloaked. A white expressionless mask made from clay covered the top half of his face with just openings to see and breathe through, disguising the darkness behind it. He said nothing, just moved closer as Elsbeth looked into the two slots where his eyes glared out. They were jet black, cold, without any sense of life or feeling behind them; they were dead. She felt the fury and the hatred emanating from them; here standing before her was a man devoid of all human feelings, his soul ripped out and discarded like the women he hunted and killed, an empty abyss filled with nothing other than evil.

Cripps rushed back into the room, his breathing rapid. 'We need to get you out. Someone's coming. I've heard movement; I don't know how many. It must be that bloody Abberline; he's worked out where we have her. I'll take care of her, then I'll take care of any others.'

'No, she's mine. Leave her, I will come back and deal with her.' The Ripper firmly instructed. Then with that, the door to the room was slammed shut and locked, leaving Elsbeth alone.

SIXTY-THREE

Abberline touched the sides of the tunnel; the brick felt new and clean, not gnarled with age and damage. Small metal plates were affixed, stating the distance in feet. It all made sense to him now, the wheelbarrows and pickaxes at the beginning; this was an additional sewer outlet, a fresh excavation. He went on, making sure each step he took was made with caution as the inky blackness wrapped itself around him. Hollowed-out sections in the walls of the tunnel created blind spots, providing the perfect place for an attack to come from as he gripped the revolver tighter. He knew that both Cripps and the maniac responsible for the grisly killings were in here somewhere, paused, waiting like coiled snakes. But then, so was Elsbeth. Faint noises from further up fractured the silence. Waves of conversations, the volume low then high as if it was moving, getting closer than fading away. The tunnel reached an intersection with only two ways, left or right; instinct told him to fork left. He questioned whether it was his inner guidance, as Elsbeth would have said, but he didn't know. He guessed he would find out soon enough.

The route came with a reek of human waste and worsened with every step; the voices, now high-pitched shrieks, mixed with the sound of the water, made it hard to distinguish between what was real and what was not. His long shadow stretched out into the void he felt as if he was becoming squeezed into a tight space; his chest tightened, his skin perspired. Rats scurried past through his legs over his shoes, common in sewers, but these were huge, feasting off the raw untreated detritus, they had become mutations, screeching as they went. He leaned back into one of the recesses in the wall for a moment, waiting until they had passed. A few steps further, he came out into an inspection area that was bigger, wider, and higher. He felt relieved.

Abberline was still listening; the voices had stopped, but he knew they could have come from anywhere, in any part of the system. Sound travelled for miles in this subterranean world. He started to doubt himself. Was his mind playing tricks on him. Maybe if he had chosen to go down the right-hand side instead of the left, that would have been better, he might have found Elsbeth by now. *Had he made a mistake? Was he too late? Was he going to die like Rawlings, alone in this maze of underground tunnels?* He was about to return the way he had come when he stepped onto a large metal drain cover with the words "Flow Control Pumps". This was his last attempt. If this came to nothing, he would have no option but to turn back. As he lifted the hatch, a faint cry came from below. This time, the voice was close. It was right beneath him.

'Help, please help me.'

Abberline wasted no time getting down a short ladder as quickly as possible. 'Keep talking, don't stop, it will guide me to you.' He knew immediately it was Elsbeth.

There were enormous bits of machinery on solid brick blocks, with a number of huge pipes coming out along the sides of the walls and the roof, one of the largest labelled "Release Valve." The area was cramped, making getting around difficult, but he followed the voice. Eventually, he came across a solid steel door secured with a slide bolt and padlock.

'Can you hear me? It's Abberline. I'm going to get you out.'

'I'm here, hurry.'

'Hang on, Elsbeth; I'm trying to find something to break the lock off the door.'

'Please hurry. I'm scared, they will be back soon; please hurry.'

Abberline searched the floor with the lamp, looking for anything to break his way in. It was littered with all sorts of metal objects and broken pipes. He picked up a length of pipe, jamming it between the slide bolt and padlock. He pressed all his weight down, trying to break it. Sweat saturated his shirt as he exerted all his effort. The pipe bent, then fractured, snapping away.

'*Please…*, just get me out!' Elsbeth sounded more and more panicked.

Abberline didn't reply, instead focusing on finding another solution. Under the release valve was a giant iron wheel that said, "*turn this way to open Flood Gate*", to the side was a big heavy-duty spanner. He took the spanner, placing it in the same position as before, he applied all his weight. Pulling and grunting, he put one of his feet up against the door for more leverage; then, without warning, the padlock snapped in two, the force throwing him back onto the ground. Quickly getting up, he fed the chain through the slide bolt and prised the door open. He stood at the opening of the room, frozen by what he saw.

SIXTY-FOUR

Elsbeth was hanging by her wrists which had been bound together, off a chain from a hook in the ceiling. Like a carcass in a butcher's shop. He put the lamp on the ground and rushed over to her, putting his arms around her waist. He lifted her body upwards, letting her bound hands slip over the hook, then placing her carefully on the floor. The room was filthy, cold, and stank. There was nothing else in it besides an old can lying in the corner.

Abberline kneeled. 'You're going to be alright now? It's over. Can you move? Are you able to walk, we don't have long. Remember you said to me that they'll be back soon? How long have they been away, Elsbeth?'

'I don't know. Cripps brought me here, tied me up like a piece of meat then he, the one Cripps called The Ripper came. The one who has been haunting me all this time, he spoke to me. Listen, Abberline, we must stop him. We have to kill him. There's no other way. He won't stop, he's insane. I have never felt so much hate, so much anger, he is consumed by it. Please tell me you understand me?'

Abberline had not seen her like this before. She was petrified. Abberline picked Elsbeth up by the arm to make sure she could stand and started to untie the restraints.

'I'm sorry, Abberline, I should have waited for you at the police station. I was foolhardy, I just felt I had to follow my gut instinct. What I saw at the cafe I told you about, well, I also experienced another vision while at the police station. I just didn't think there was any time to lose. I just had to act; I had to go. I was going to get word to you, that was the plan, but it was a trap: Amelia Stanton was dead, strapped to a chair, cut to pieces by the Ripper, and Cripps was waiting for me.'

'Elsbeth, there's something else I need to tell you. Rawlings is dead. Cripps killed him.'

Elsbeth looked visibly shaken by the news, shaking off the last straps that had bound her. 'He tried to get me out of there... He tried to save me.'

A loud thud came from outside the room. Both Abberline and Elsbeth stared at each other.

'They're back,' Elsbeth said.

Then, there was another sound that sent fear through Abberline, he had heard it before at the beginning of the tunnel. Water. He ran over to the door and looked out into the inspection area. A large outlet pipe had water gushing out of it at an alarming rate, tons spilling out and flooding the room. He waded over to the pipe to see if there was a way to stop it. The large wheel to the outlet pipe had been deliberately turned, sabotaged, and broken. There was no way of stopping the flow. He returned to Elsbeth.

'We need to get out, or we're going to drown.' Freezing, filthy water rushed around their feet and up to their waists in no time.

'How do we get out?' Elsbeth screamed over the noise.

'There is a hatch; come on, follow me.'

The water was rising at an alarming rate. It would only be minutes before the entire room was submerged. Abberline took Elsbeth's hand and guided them out of the room and around the machinery towards the ladder. He handed the lamp to Elsbeth as he stepped onto the first rung and made his way up to the hatch. The water was now up to her chest and rising. Abberline told her to get onto the ladder and start climbing towards him. She had reached about halfway when she looked down at the swirling torrent already touching her feet.

'Abberline, hurry, it's rising fast. I can't… hold on much longer.'

Abberline desperately pushed the hatch, banging it with his fist and then his shoulder, but it wouldn't budge. 'I… I can't move it; it's wedged shut.'

'We're going to die any second if you don't get that open,' Elsbeth shouted, clinging on one rung away from him.

'Turn your head away and hold the lamp as high as possible so I can see.'

'What did you say?'

'I said turn your head away. I've got an idea, hold the lamp up,' Abberline shouted.

Elsbeth put her right arm through the ladder to secure herself from being swept away by the water, now halfway up her back; she held the lamp as high as she could.

Abberline frantically searched for his revolver, took it out, placed it up against the hatch where the lock would be on the other side, cocked the hammer back, and pulled the trigger. Nothing, it didn't fire.

'Abberline!' Elsbeth yelled in desperation.

Abberline broke open the gun and took a bullet out of the chamber, his hands shaking so much he nearly dropped it. He rubbed the bullet on his coat to get it dry, then placed it back in the chamber, closed the gun and fired. This time, it worked. Orange and yellow sparks rained over them. He pushed the hatch open with his shoulder and pulled Elsbeth out by her hand onto the concrete floor just as the water rose to the top. Abberline kicked it shut to stop it from coming up any further.

'That won't hold it; we need to move fast now.' As soon as he said it, water surged through the sides.

SIXTY-FIVE

Elsbeth followed Abberline out of the inspection chamber and down the narrow tunnel heading towards the way out. Abberline, still holding the lamp, its usefulness dwindling as the light flickered one last time and then expired, leaving them in near-total darkness halfway through the tunnel. Elsbeth stopped and whispered. 'I can't see a thing. Do you have any matches left?'

'No, they're all soaking wet, about as much use as this lamp.' Which he dropped on the floor.

'Stay close and use your hand against the side of the wall as a guide. It's a straight run there, but we need to be fast. That water is already on its way through and won't stop until it gets to the main outlet into the sea, and we're right in its path.'

'What about them, Cripps and The Ripper? They could be anywhere. Cripps had me chained up down here, and to be honest, they both know this place better than us.'

Abberline pressed on; he was aware there were countless spots they could be waiting for them, but he had no other option but to push ahead. Abberline turned round.

'I'm hoping they think we drowned back there; that might just give us the time to get out of here. Once we get through this section, there is an intersection we need to go straight on, and then the system opened up into a much wider tunnel. It's a climb up the ladder, and we are then inside a building on the surface, then out onto the streets. We get there, and we're safe. I've put several officers at the aquarium who'll be there for hours. Once we leave this ventilator building, we can try to get there on foot if you can; it's not far. Or, if we're lucky, flag a cab down.'

Elsbeth was tired of being scared, cold, and wet; her layers of clothing clung to her skin, making it heavy and uncomfortable. She just wanted to get out, get dry and warm, and be back in her own home. But she was stuck underground, and no one other than Abberline knew where she was. They felt their way along until a loud rumble under them shook the ground like the first stirrings of an earthquake.

'What was that?' Elsbeth asked.

Abberline stopped. 'Water, tons of it; we don't have long.'

'How long?'

Abberline looked back at Elsbeth. 'None, run.' Just as he had said the words, hundreds and hundreds of rats sensing imminent death scurried past, biting each other to get ahead, to survive.

'Keep going, keep moving. Don't stop,' Abberline shouted back. 'Don't let go of my hand.'

Water rushed past Elsbeth's ankles, rising fast; Abberline saw the walkway and the scaffold boards ahead. More importantly, he could see the ladder to take them up and out of danger. Elsbeth felt her grip slipping, her ankle twisted and giving way. She fell, crashing down onto the stone floor. 'Abberline,' she screamed out in pain.

Abberline looked back and saw Elsbeth behind, trying to get to her feet, her arms stretched out for help as a massive swirling wave of black water gathered speed, rising behind her, its jaws open, ready to devour anything in its path. With seconds to spare, he rushed back; picking her up over his shoulder, he bolted back as fast as he could, launching himself onto the ladder, holding on for all his life as the loud noise of the tons of water swept by, stripping the scaffold boards and metal rails as it went, snapping them like twigs.

'Hang on,' Abberline called out, pushing, clawing his way up one rung at a time, his feet slipping on the metal. He had two more steps to go, and then, with one last surge, he made it through. They both lay exhausted in the dark on the wooden floor of the ventilation building; made it with only seconds to spare, they were safe. Elsbeth in pain from her ankle, lay back, catching her breath.

Abberline breathed deeply and turned his head over to look towards Elsbeth. 'Do you think you can walk further if you lean on me? If not, we can try to get a ride outside.' He looked towards the windows. 'It'll be dawn in an hour or so, and cabs will be making their way to the railway station for early fares. If we can get to the aquarium, I'll get one of the officers to take you to the hospital to get that ankle of yours looked at.'

'Be careful, Inspector, or people will start thinking you care,' Elsbeth said with a smile, while wincing again at her injury.

Abberline laughed and picked himself up, offering her a hand up.

'What of Cripps and The Ripper?'

Abberline thought for a minute while walking over to an oil lamp on the table, lighting it with some matches that sat next to it, and taking it with him. 'Hopefully drowned.'

'Why would Cripps have used such a high-risk strategy of flooding the entire system like that?' Elsbeth asked, hobbling on one foot towards a single bed in one corner to rest her ankle.

Abberline went over to check out of the window to see if the police officers were still milling around the aquarium, which was close by. 'Well, it's there to flush out the main sewers if they get blocked and they are unable to remove larger objects by hand. The pressure from the amount of water pushed through is enough to clear anything out, including us. Or that's at least what he must have thought. As you say, it was a high risk, and Cripps probably thought they had enough time to escape, but we only just made it ourselves, and that was probably by more luck than judgment.'

'Your boss will be pleased?'

Abberline thought about Monro and his dislike for him. 'No, I doubt that, but I'm certain he will take the credit for it.'

Elsbeth pushed herself up from the bed; a shooting pain was still there. She wasn't going to let it beat her, and she was damned if it would stop her from walking out of this place. She slowly put her left foot forward first, then her damaged right, moving gradually towards the centre of the room.

'Look, Abberline, see, I'm fine–'

Abberline looked back to see Elsbeth in the centre of the room, but his expression quickly turned. A figure had rolled out from under the single bed in the corner of the room, standing behind her in the semi-darkness, his face obscured, but his intention was not. In one hand, a flash of steel; he pulled hard at Elsbeth's hair, putting the knife, its razor-sharp edge, to her throat.

'Don't even breathe, or I'll slice her pretty little head off,' the man said.

Elsbeth recognised the voice immediately. It was Cripps.

'I thought you had drowned along with that madman,' Abberline said.

Cripps laughed like a hyena. 'No, not as clever as you thought, are you, Inspector.' His grip tightened on Elsbeth as she wiggled to get free.

Abberline moved towards him, trying to get an advantage.

'Ah, I told you not to move, didn't I? Last chance, one more step, and we're going to see what her insides look like spilt out all over the floor like Rawlings… Mm.' He pushed Elsbeth forward towards the light of the window. '

'You didn't have to kill Rawlings,' Abberline shouted angrily.

'No, but I wanted to feel what it was like; I wanted to see that look in his eyes when he realised, he was going to die; it's… it's so empowering. He was pathetic, begged, cried, and told me he had a wife and kids. But that made it all the more enjoyable. In that one moment, I was God, and I had the power to take his life whether he liked it or not. It was exhilarating… and made me feel complete. I was taught by the master, you see.'

'Where is your master now? The sick coward that attacks and kills innocent vulnerable women?' Elsbeth asked, still trying to get free.

Cripps pulled her closer, forcing her head around to face his while watching Abberline. 'I can smell your fear. You have no idea whom you are dealing with.'

He laughed again, pushing the knife harder into the skin of Elsbeth's neck.

SIXTY-SIX

Abberline didn't want to agitate Cripps any further, so he kept him talking. 'So, it was you who put Jack Robertson in the frame for the murder of Mary Quinn and Rosie Meeks, then? You planted the evidence for us to find?'

'Robertson was stupid; he knew Rosie Meeks, and with some imagination, he could be seen to have also killed Mary Quinn. We needed a distraction, someone to take the blame and someone to join the dots. And for a while, you did exactly that. I didn't realise that Robertson had a wife in Leeds who would prove to be a credible alibi for him. But I understand he's taken his own life anyway, so it turned out well enough. He was going to hang anyway; Scotland Yard would have seen to that.'

'What about the jars of human parts we found at his lodgings at Brighton Station and the knife?' Elsbeth asked, still in his iron grip.

'The parts were taken by my master during his work, for his personal use, shall we say. But we needed to throw you off the scent, so I borrowed them to set that fool Robertson up. I knew you would return them when you found them and brought them to me to identify.' He grinned at Abberline.

Abberline saw Elsbeth was finding it hard to stand on the

injured ankle; her body slumped; he continued questioning him and then remembered the gun in his coat pocket. He prayed that the other bullets left in the chamber had had time to dry out.

'But why take Amelia Stanton? Why go to all that trouble of following her and abducting her, keeping her hidden, only to then mutilating her body like the others? Why, Cripps?'

'She should have kept her mouth shut and not made those comments in the press. She had already dug her own grave. But turned out she would be very useful in the end, as it brought Elsbeth along to try and save her. By then, of course, the Stanton woman was already dead, *he* had cut her up like fish bait but saved a nice bit of liver for missy here.' Cripps pulled Elsbeth up, moving the knife from her throat to her upper back.

'But you still haven't answered my question. Why do this?' Abberline interrogated him further.

'It's not why, but *for whom*. I have a very lucrative sideline, there are people, Inspector, who will pay a pretty sum and have an appetite for unusual things, human things. The stranger, the more desired, and the more they pay. My relationship with a certain person proved to be beneficial to both parties. He had heard of my auctions and sales of these collectables, and we saw a way we could combine our skills, shall we say. He gets to continue his work, whilst I assist the police in my duties, I can inform *him* of any investigations, and in return, I get parts that I can sell at a good profit, such as the two women he killed at the start. These unfortunates had become well known in the press, so the organs he had removed had become prized among collectors and commanded a healthy price. You see, we both get what the other needs. The more famous he becomes, the more the demand goes up for any parts associated with his work, and the more people will pay to have them. It's human nature, a simple case of supply and demand. And let's face it, who's going to miss some local prostitutes, eh?'

'You make me sick to my stomach, Cripps.' Elsbeth yelled. 'Rosie Meeks was *not a prostitute*, she was a working mother who will be missed by her son, who gets to grow up alone.'

'I don't know or care why he chose her; maybe he was experimenting or just saw an opportunity and took her. But in doing so, he diverted your attention and found a likely scapegoat in Jack Robertson, and that made it all worth it. As for her son, who is now all alone in the world, maybe he can make some coin on the back of her story.' Cripps laughed again.

Elsbeth struggled hard to kick his legs and bite his arm, she was so filled with hate for this disgusting man.

'Easy now, we are a fighter, aren't we? Now, missy, be careful, or maybe my knife will slip, taking out one of your kidneys. Now that would fetch a handsome price and fun to do.' He licked his lips, smirking at Abberline.

Abberline had heard enough. 'Fun, you say. I can't wait to see your neck stretched at the gallows for what you have done. You have no remorse, no conscience, you protect and let a lunatic loose on the streets to brutally murder and rip three innocent women into bits. What sick, evil mind could do such a thing?'

'Oh no, you misunderstand. I am an admirer. You remember back during one of your visits to the mortuary; I was playing with you, teasing you when I said the wounds inflicted on the first two victims showed a real skill. I enjoy the dead; they say little but give so much pleasure to one who knows how to get the best out of them.'

Abberline was raging with anger; he knew hanging was too good for both of them.

'So where is this Ripper, your teacher, your master, this one you look up to so much? Why isn't he here to finish the job himself? Where is he, Cripps!' Abberline shouted at him.

'He is in the shadows, in unlit alleyways, in your house…

In dark corners when you hear a creak on the floorboards or a noise in the middle of the night. He's in your worst nightmares. I'll tell you, Inspector, what you and missy can't see is you stand at the precipice of greatness. You are witnessing the birth of someone who will become the stuff of legend. His name will be whispered on cold nights when it's dark, and the wind howls outside. You are both a part of that, whether you like it or not.' Cripps pressed the knife more firmly into Elsbeth's back.

Bang! Thud. A loud sound came from where Abberline and Elsbeth had come through the hatch into the room. Someone else was coming up the ladder, fast.

Elsbeth took a massive gamble and propelled herself back onto the knife. It slid through her dress and partway into her back; she felt the warm flow of blood almost immediately. It caught Cripps entirely off guard; he staggered back as Elsbeth pushed herself forward off the blade, moving away from him as best as she could.

Abberline, without thinking, threw the oil lamp he was holding at Cripps; it smashed onto his body, the hot oil soaking his jacket, the flame igniting it. Within seconds, he was engulfed by a human torch, screaming in agony. He ran at Elsbeth, his hands welded to the skin of his face. At the same time, someone rushed from the shadows towards Abberline, the blade of a serrated knife glinting in his gloved hand, held high, ready to strike.

Abberline instinctively took the gun from his coat pocket and fired two shots without thinking, first at Cripps to save Elsbeth, who was just inches away from her, then quickly turning, he fired again twice at point-blank range at The Ripper. Seconds from death, Abberline shifted sideways to avoid him but felt an acute pain as he was pushed violently back, losing his footing and crashing to the floor. The knife had missed his torso by centimetres but had sliced through his arm.

The Ripper paused at the window for a split second and looked back, not at the burning body of Cripps, or at Abberline, but at Elsbeth. His black, lifeless eyes stared at her from behind the mask; she felt them searing into her; she connection, and then came the message, words forming in her mind as clearly as if they had been written.

This is just the beginning.

The glass smashed as he fell through the window. Abberline got to his feet and rushed over to finish the job, but there was no body to be found. The Ripper had vanished.

SIXTY-SEVEN

A few weeks later, after Abberline had been discharged from the hospital, he was able to call around to see Elsbeth at her home. He got down from the cab slowly, still in pain from his injury, and knocked at the door. She answered it, smiling and welcoming him in. Abberline noticed a man in a robe sat at the kitchen table, drinking some coffee. Abberline smiled at Elsbeth. 'Some recovery of your own, I see.'

'Well, we all heal in our own ways, Inspector. He's not a permanent fixture; he's just here to remind me what it's like to feel again.' She smiled back at Abberline as they entered her front room, closing the doors behind her for some privacy.

'So how are you, Inspector? I hope recovered. I must say I have missed working together.'

'I am better, thank you, and thank you for the flowers. It was most kind of you. I've been at home for the past few days back in London. My wife's been looking after me. But I wanted to come down, I had to go and see Rawlings' wife just to make sure she and her kids had been looked after. I gave him my word before he died. I told Scotland Yard that he tried to protect you and paid for it with his life. You and I know he was far from a saint, and he killed Seamus Keane; not that the thug was any great loss to society, but Rawlings is gone now, and there was no point in ruining his family's life by making that known. They will struggle enough without him.'

'That's very honourable of you, Inspector, but I'm sure you found it hard as it must have gone against your principles, and we all know how you like to follow things precisely.'

'Yes, well, I'm not saying I agree with it or find it easy, but maybe I've learnt something. Maybe things aren't just black and white. I also had to go and see Joseph Stanton, and that was difficult.'

'I still think of them, Amelia, Mary Quinn and Rosie Meeks. I feel I failed them all somehow; I feel it was my fault. Their spirits will not rest; they will be stuck, unable to move on, until their killer is caught and pays for his crimes. I... I blame myself for that.'

'Elsbeth, if there's one thing I have learned in this job, it is that you must not live with guilt; you are not responsible. Amelia Stanton took it upon herself to publicly shame the killer, and that made her a target. There was nothing you could have done; she was dead from then on. It was just a matter of time. As for the other two, again, there was nothing anyone could have done to save them. I don't pretend to understand the gift you have or agree with it, but I've come to accept it and know that you are a genuine and truthful person.'

'That almost seems like a compliment, Inspector.' Elsbeth smiled. 'And what of Joseph Stanton? I suppose he was as cold and obnoxious as ever?'

'No, he was changed in many ways, seemed calmer, almost reserved. He had resigned from his position and wanted just to be at home with his children. He didn't say much, he thanked me, thanked us both for trying, especially you.'

'That's good to know, makes me feel a little better. When do you go back to work, to London, Inspector?'

'Well, I'm not sure, I have a meeting with Monro in London soon and we will see what he has in store for me then. He's not pleased with The Ripper getting away and I know that they want the whole affair to just go away and be forgotten about. Not good for *police morale* apparently. But somebody's head is going to roll, the commissioner expects it, but you can be sure it won't be Monro's. With Cripps now dead, and being an informer right under our noses, it doesn't look good.'

'I wonder where The Ripper is now, what he will do next.'

Elsbeth walked him out of the room and to the front door. 'Thank you for saving me, Cripps would have…' Elsbeth looked tearful as she recalled that time.

'It's ok, Elsbeth, you don't have to say anything, Cripps got what he deserved.'

'And The Ripper? What of him?'

Abberline thought for a while, looking confused. 'I shot him. I know I did; hit him at least twice in the chest, but then, when I looked, he had gone. It's almost as if the bullets went right through him. I can tell you wherever he is, I, for one, will not give up looking for him; we owe that much to the women he's killed.'

Elsbeth looked concerned, remembering back to that moment. 'I didn't tell you this, but he looked back at me before he went out that window. I saw what he was thinking. It was like he was writing the words in my mind to see.'

'What did he say?'

'"This is just the beginning." He's not going to stop, Abberline; he's hungry for more. I can feel it.'

Abberline nodded silently in agreement, knowing she was right. Elsbeth opened the front door of her home to a busy street with people and cabs going about their business as she watched him leave. Closing it, she leaned with her back to it, looking down at her visitor, who was waving impatiently for her to join him. She knew, even if Abberline didn't, they would meet again. She smiled to herself, walked back down the hall to the kitchen, and closed the door.

EPILOGUE

A YEAR LATER, WHITECHAPEL, 1884

It was what Londoners called a *Black Summer*. The sun had been replaced by heavy rain, flooding, and high winds across most of the capital. Monro and Commissioner Sir Charles Warren at Scotland Yard had covered up the Brighton murders, presenting Abberline as the fall guy and making sure the press and all those involved stayed silent. They put their careers and reputations first. Abberline was quickly reassigned to desk duty at a small insignificant police station in the suburbs, while Elsbeth had gone back to holding her private readings and séance evenings.

The Ripper stood upon London Bridge looking out across the Thames towards Whitechapel. Its narrow streets, the poverty, and the disease-stricken inhabitants made it a perfect hunting ground. Like a fledgling bird learning to fly for the first time he had made mistakes in Brighton but now he was ready, his path was clear. He watched people passing by, the fine and educated women chatting, glancing an eye and a smile over his way. They had no idea what he was capable of or what he could do to them, no idea how close they were to death.

His attention went back to the view of the city, the waterways, and the prostitutes walking along the side of the river looking for trade. He would be back one day to fulfil his destiny and for them to meet theirs. But for now, he had to stay safe and concealed. Taking out a newspaper, he read the personal and obituary columns. He smiled as an article caught his attention. A doctor had recently passed, and his wife was holding an open wake at their country estate. It was to celebrate her late husband's life and give those who knew him a chance to pay their respects. He folded the paper up, placing it in his pocket. *Perfect.*

He pulled his coat collar up against the weather, picked up his doctor's case, and walked back towards the train station. He would reemerge once more, rising from this bad seed, a fallen angel, to spread his dark wings across this land. This was a new chapter, a new beginning. His excitement grew, his pace quickened, and Hell followed him.

Acknowledgements

I want to express my heartfelt gratitude to the following individuals for their invaluable help and support in bringing this novel to life.

Sara Starbuck

Sarah has been such an inspiration during the editing and shaping of this book. Her professionalism and experience have been invaluable, and I thank you for all you have contributed.

www.sarastarbuck.co.uk

Ruth Lunn - UK Book Publishing

Thank you for all your help proofreading the manuscript, insightful comments, and experience.

www.ukbookpublishing.com

Jane Dixon-Smith - Book Cover Design and Formatting

Thank you, Jane, for your incredible cover design and formatting. Your patience and ability to know what I wanted when I didn't were genius. Simply the best!

www.jdsmith-design.co.uk

Laura Hasson

I would like to thank my editor and proofreader, Laura Hasson. Your guidance and unwavering support during the refinement process of this novel has been fantastic. Thank you for embracing this story with such passion, for immersing yourself in Elsbeth's spiritual ability, and for channelling Abberline's meticulous attention to detail (especially with those rogue commas!). Even Jack, our complex villain, benefited from your dedication. Thank you for believing in this journey with me.

laura.freelanceediting@gmail.com

Kevin Wilsher - Brighton & Hove Regency Society

Thank you, Kevin, for your help, assistance, and kind permission for the images.

www.regencysociety.org

Rachel Clark Chief Executive - West Pier Society

Rachel, thank you for the information and assistance you gave me while researching this book.

www.westpier.co.uk

Debi my wife, without whom this book would never have got off the starting block. Thank you for all your patience, belief, and unwavering support.

Made in United States
Cleveland, OH
05 March 2025